LOVE AND MADNESS

BOOK Thirteen

of the

SECRET BUTTERFLY SERIES™

A NOVEL BY

Rosemary Lightfoot Ness-Bitner

This book is dedicated to those who risked all for love.

The print version layout of LOVE AND MADNESS was done by eBook launch. The print and audio cover design of the book was created by Cheeky Covers, and I'm Minna Morinette, your audio book narrator.

SECRET BUTTERFLY SERIES ™ CHARACTERS INTRODUCED IN "LOVE AND MADNESS" (MAJOR CHARACTERS ARE BOLDFACED)

Readers reference guide to where a character is introduced. (CHARACTER, DESCRIPTION OF CHARACTER, AND CHAPTER WHERE CHARACTER IS MENTIONED)

EDDIE WILKES, ACCOUNTANT FOR U G G A, DAVID'S CONFIDANT, LM, CH1

RUBLINA, EMOTIONALLY UNSTABLE CORPORATE SECRETARY AT U G G A, LM, CH1

MS. SINCLAIR, PRIVATE DUTY NURSE, DAVID'S COUSIN, LM, CH1

JUDITH, OFFICE SNITCH AT THE FIRM, DAVID'S COUSIN, LM, CH2

DONNA, OFFICE SNITCH AT THE FIRM, DAVID'S SECOND COUSIN, LM, CH2

MRS. RODRIGUEZ, FRONT OFFICE MANAGER AT THE FIRM, LM, CH2

SPARKY, BLATHER SPEWER, UNIQUE COMPUTER, LM, CH2

GUIDO THE BLADE, BODYGUARD OF BARBARA, LM, CH3

OLD GRAVEL THROAT, IMPERSONATOR EMPLOYED BY DAVID AT THE FIRM, LM, CH4

ANDY, NAME OF FETUS, DAVID'S IMAGINARY PROTEGE, LM, CH9

REYNARD THE RED, A RED FOX ON (BOB'S) UNCLE EDDIE'S FARM, LM, CH10

Hello dear readers and listeners. This is Minna Morinette, your audio book narrator. In LOVE AND MADNESS, the thirteenth book in our series, you'll learn how it feels to go insane from David himself. You'll find out why bigger computers are better, especially if they destroy their programming instructions; and you'll learn why David mentors a fetus in a formaldehyde jar. There are neurotics, oddballs, weirdoes, and crazies in this world. We all know someone who's a little off, don't we? But they can't compare with our David. You may want to hear some double takes, be prepared to hit stop and replay.

Come along with me on a riotous flight as I narrate LOVE AND MADNESS, the thirteenth book of THE SECRET BUTTERFLY (tm) SERIES.

CHAPTER ONE

Vanity like murder will out (Hanna Cowley: The Belle's stratagem)
Truth will come to light; murder cannot be hidden long (Shake-speare: The merchant of Venice)

MURDER TRACKER

It was time. Barbara had stoically endured a year of disgust and humiliation. Marty, the office whore and the world's top ranked adult film star, was on the road with the man she loved. She had tried telling herself that Marty was just eye candy for men with hot pricks and no brains. But it wasn't working. Obviously, a good, decent man, her man, Bob, really could fall hopelessly head over heels in love with a profligate porn star. Whenever Marty was away from Bob, he mooned over her absence. He behaved like a forlorn, lost puppy. Barbara wondered:

'*Why does he happily run back to that unapologetic whore, like he's her welcoming dog, after she'd been away whoring with another man?*'

Barbara's quandary only brought her more heartache. Bob's lovesick behavior told her that Bob definitely relished Marty's bed scene. Thus far, Barbara had resolutely accepted her place. She rationalized that she wasn't married to Bob; at least, not yet. In her native Lakota culture, it was acceptable for a young brave to buck a few squaws before he settled to partner with one and have children with her. And there had been no promises of betrothal between her and Bob. She blamed herself for her situation. Hadn't she slammed the door shut on his advances? How could she fault him?

But deep within her gut, she knew Bob loved her. He had wanted her before; and she had wanted him. She still wanted him; especially during the night. That's when her imagination ran wild. That's when lust fires burned in her loins. She wanted Bob more now than she ever had before. But did he still want her? She often asked herself that question. She studied his face and his eyes whenever she encountered him; but he revealed nothing. Had his ardor died? Had that once hot, burning flame died out? Perhaps it had? Or, perhaps it just wasn't their time? Which was it? Why wouldn't he give her some sign? When would this uncertain madness stop?

The year before, Chief, her father, had told her to give Bob more time. She obeyed Chief. Of course, she obeyed him. He was most wise in matters of people's behaviors. She had given Bob his time. She had agreed with Chief: There were things about Bob, David, the Firm's owner, Susan, the Firm's administrator, and the other employees, that she needed to learn about, first. Reluctantly, she had acknowledged to Chief that she wasn't ready to take on a serious relationship. She couldn't open the door, at that time, to the possibilities of marriage and children. She could not wish away the fact that she simply wasn't ready for those added responsibilities. But now, things had changed. She had tracked the behaviors of the others in the office. She had learned a great deal about the Firm, David, the owner, Susan, the administrator, and the other employees. She understood almost everything there was to know about the business and how it worked. She knew there were some unexplained things about the Firm that David and his bookkeepers kept hidden from everyone, even from Susan. But now, she knew much, much more than she had known a year before. She felt confident that the remaining Firm secrets would reveal themselves to her in time. She felt a confidence that was not there a year before. She felt that now was the time. Time to take her intended life's path with Bob. She decided that now was the time. It was time for the woman in her; time to make her intended man ready for his life with her. 'Yes,' she decided. *'Now it is time. It is time to push aside the whore. It is time to make him mine. Now I will enter Bob's life.'*

While Bob was in his office, she went to him. This day she would assume a different demeaner than she had presented to Bob prior to this day. This day, she did not politely seat herself in a chair in front of his desk. This day would be different. This day, she would show Bob an entirely different side of herself. This day she would not be the prim and proper, know everything, office whiz kid. Not this day! No, today Barbara would be all woman; all aggressive; all intentions revealed; unmistakably on the hunt for her man. Today, she set the guest chair aside and sat *on* his desk. Without speaking a word, she propped her head on one arm and leaned her delicious body onto its side, all the way across Bob's desk. Her long dark hair draped her face and flowed onto his desk and onto his opened sales reports, covering the papers. She made no effort to brush back her hair. Miss efficiency Barbara would have retrieved her hair. But then, Miss Barbara would never have laid her body invitingly across his desk in the first place. No, she would not make excuses for her body being in front of him like it was; nor would she apologize for her hair interrupting his review of his sales results. No, she would do nothing to retract her aggression; not today and not ever from this moment onward. Now she was no longer Miss Office Efficiency. Now she was Little Sparrow, daughter of Big Chief, Princess of the Lakota Sioux. And now she was man hunting. She moistened her lips. Her dark shining eyes smiled into

Bob's eyes. Without her lips speaking a single word, her eyes told Bob that, from this moment on, the relationship between them had changed.

She was confident. She knew she was a comely woman with mouthwatering sex appeal. She knew her body and her eyes would dazzle him. She knew she didn't need a whore's reputation to let him know that she was sexy; incredibly, unimaginably wildly and invitingly sexy. She knew she was far more alluring than Marty ever was or ever could be. She was the human personification of a dark pearl; sleek, sultry, mysteriously Arabesque; endowed with such an overwhelming sexuality that men's minds became arrested in limbic lust trance at the mere sight of her.

Her move was overt, provocative, not at all subtle; yet she kept the mystery of her secret self, alive; inviting, yet tantalizingly beyond Bob's reach. She knew she was a stunning femme fatale. Many men had begged her to be with her, but she had always declined. She had more serious things on her mind, then. But now, she obviously intimated that she wanted intimacy with Bob. And it went without her needing to say it, that this Indian Princess got what she wanted; and that she expected nothing less.

"It's time for us to start having coffee together." She stated, matter of factly. She lifted her hand and rubbed her finger slowly under Bob's lower lip. Bob's blood pressure shot up. He was smitten with a blinding lust sensation; much like a little boy who was seeing a naked woman for the very first time. Barbara measured his blood pressure by his neck's deepening red. She intended to play Bob like a gut-hooked fish; make him beg her to stop her teases; and then allow him to eagerly slide into her net. She wanted it all to seem natural and matter of fact. Chief had taught her well She was a calculating, observant, patient, and deadly huntress. She would bag her quarry. And she knew she would. Bob agreed to meet for coffee on Saturday:

"*Tell me something, Bob,*" Barbara asked Bob over coffee, "*How many sales kits do you normally leave at a brokerage firm's branch office after you've made your visit?*"

"*About twenty. Why?*" Bob's brow furrowed. He was not expecting this line of questioning.

"*And where do you place your printing orders?*" Barb persisted, guiding her quarry into her trap.

"*Star Printing. Why the questions?*" Bob's brow lifted, registering his first hint of discomfort. He knew Barb had the upper hand; but over what, exactly, he was not sure.

"*Have you ever heard of Monument Printing Company?*"

"*No. Why all the questions?*" Annoyance and impatience betrayed Bob's discomfort.

"*Well, according to records I've seen, you order supplies from Monument and you leave five hundred to a thousand sales kits behind you, wherever you go.*"

"*That's crazy. What are you talking about?*" Bob's discomfort gave way to alarm. Barb's tactics were working perfectly.

"*Not crazy, Big Horse, fact. And, you don't pay one dollar for each sales kit. You pay five dollars.*" Barbara lowered her chin and stared into Bob's eyes. She was pinning him to some wrongdoing he had not done; and making him very uncomfortable. She had her quarry trapped.

"*Come on, Barbara. You're off the wall with this! What's going on?*" This time, Bob's reply carried a hint of panic.

Barbara opened her handbag and produced an invoice with Bob's name and signature on it. It showed Monument Printing supplying one hundred thousand sales kits to the Fund distribution company at the cost of five Dollars each, for a total invoice of five hundred thousand dollars. She also produced a marketing invoice from the distribution company to the Fund for five hundred thousand Dollars for printing expenses.

"There must be a mistake!" Bob recoiled in shock. Clearly, he was alarmed. *"I've never heard of this outfit, never even heard of them. I never signed any invoices from them."*

"Really, Bob? Are you sure?" Barbara's question was delivered with a sly smile. No fox entering a hen house conveyed a more confident smile. It was Barbara's *'I've got you, and you're not getting away,'* smile.

"Of course, I'm sure." Bob's indignant reply rang hollow on Barb's ears.

"OK, well let's go pay them a visit and see if we can straighten this out. Shall we?" The matter of fact, Miss Office Efficiency Expert emerged. Sparrow's duality made Bob's head spin. It seemed the ground beneath his feet had suddenly become unsteady.

"Let's go right now." Bob was clearly upset. He accepted Barbara's challenge. He knew he'd done nothing wrong and he wanted to get to the bottom of things. Barbara drove them to a small town on the outskirts of Plaintown. There, they went to the address of Monument Printing Company. They got out of the car and stood before an address marker on the road. It was a vacant lot.

"Did you know this was a vacant lot before we got here?" Bob asked the questions now.

"Of course, I did." Barbara nodded; now her eyes became piercing, and they carried a clear message of anger.

"So, what's going on? What do you know about this?" Bob sensed there was a trap, And he was caught in it.

"First, I must tell you. There is danger associated with this. I do not believe you had anything to do with it. You're just not that devious. I know you. I've worked closely with you. You have always been completely honest."

"And, I still am. What's going on?" Bob's eyes registered desperation. Barb noted what she saw: *'Trapped animals search frantically for help. Humans are no different.'*

"Before I tell you I want you to know I have copies of everything away from the Firm and in a safe place."

"Barbara, stop torturing me! What's going on?" Bob's plea revealed his whiteness; assuming he was a victim of Lakota torture methods.

"First things first, Buster!" Barbara brushed aside Bob's inuendo. She wasn't having it. This situation cut through race and culture. And she knew it. *"What happened with you and Marty on your road trips?"* Barb stood arms akimbo. She wore the defiant look of a woman who had been highly insulted.

"That's pretty personal Barb." Bob scrambled for an exit, but found none. He had been trapped in something nefarious; and now, he felt double trapped. Barb had mounted her frontal assault upon his morality and ethics. There was no escaping her.

"You tell me. I expect the worst. I'm a woman; didn't you know?" Barb continued her pressure.

"Yeah, I know. You're a woman all right. But remember, you're also that woman who didn't want me." Bob tried to play on her sympathies, but he found nothing there. Few women are sympathetic to a man's dalliances with a rival.

"I never told you that I didn't want you, you stupid, stupid, Big Stupid Horse; you stupid Horse's Ass! I said: YOU NEED TO WAIT! Don't you remember what I said? Or are you too stupid to even remember anything?" Barb shouted. Her voice betrayed her. Clearly, she felt deeply hurt.

"What did you just call me?"

"Never mind what I called you. My father and I use Indian names for everybody." Barb pouted and turned aside from him.

"So, that's it. You and your daddy, Big Chief, think I'm stupid! That's why you have this reluctance to tell me anything."

"You're not stupid in all things, Bob. But when it comes to women you are very STUPID, STUPID, STUPID! When it comes to

understanding people, you need a lot of help." Barbara hinted there was more to be revealed than a woman's scorn.

"What are you talking about? Plain English; no tribal riddles, please." Bob's eyes pleaded for sincerity.

"For starters, Horse, you need to learn: THERE'S A HUGE DIFFERENCE BETWEEN LOVE AND FUCKING!" Barb shouted again. Her voice carried the pain in her heart.

"Excuse me!" Now his voice pleased for clarity.

"Bob, when a female dog fucks a dozen male dogs, do you think the male dogs fall in love with the female dog? Do you think the bitch dog falls in love with the male dogs? Or, do you think maybe the bitch just has the urge to fuck?" Barbara's hurt voice was elevated, even though Bob was only two feet away.

"Are you saying Marty is like a dog bitch in heat?" Bob hated when women were upset. He tried to retreat, hoping his question would settle her some. He had no success.

"As a matter of fact, that's exactly what I'm saying, you big Stupid Horse's Ass." Barbara's voice reflected her indignation. *"Marty was fucking forty different salesmen in the year before you took her on the road. She's a notorious porn star! The company is just a front for her so she can do her whoring! David is in on it. He makes money from her whoring. He allows her to use the company this way. Those two are an immoral, evil pair. Who knows all the things that they do? Can't you see anything? How could any sane man fall in love with that kind of a woman? What kind of future would you have with a woman like that? Oh, that's right! You never thought about the future, Did you? Of course you didn't! That would require you to thing! I forgot! You don't know how to think! How could you be so stupid? Oh, I guess you only know how to think with your stupid dick! That's it, isn't it? You little dick does all your thinking! Of course! I should have known! You really are a very big, very stupid horse! You are the stupidest horse of all stupid horses!"*

She was still upset. Bob's eyes begged for mercy. But Barbara showed no signs of relenting. She had him right where she wanted him; and she was giving it to him, but good.

"You can't be serious?" Bob's eyes widened. His jaw dropped at Barb's bombshell; not from hearing about Marty's whoring. He knew about that. But he never suspected that Marty did evil things in partnership with David. Seeing invoices with his signature that he had not signed, shocked him. Now, he suddenly felt vulnerable, sensing he'd fallen into a clever trap. Now, he suspected that David knew much more about Marty than he'd let on.

"I am serious, Horse. I don't say things I can't prove." Barb pursed her lips and leveled a gaze at Bob. She nodded her head up and down slightly. She didn't blink and she wasn't backing down. She saw the love of her life had become a doomed soul. She looked like she might cry.

"Please, tell me what's going on." Bob asked in a pleading soft tone of voice.

"First, you tell me how I can be sure I can trust you." Finally, Barbara's voice revealed a touch of compassion.

Bob suddenly swept Barbara into his arms and kissed her. She struggled and tried to push away from him.

"Stop kissing me you stupid horse. This is not the time for kissing. I am mad at you. Can't you see that? I am very mad at you. I cannot believe you were so stupid! Stop! Stop your kisses, right this minute!"

But Bob didn't stop. *"I'm not going to stop. I don't feel like stopping. I love you, you crazy girl. Don't you understand that? I loved you over a year ago and I've never stopped. I've always loved you. I just thought you were off limits, or on reservation; or I was not allowed to be on your reservation; or I didn't know………"*

Barbara's resistance faded. After pounding Bob on his back with her fists a while longer, she relented and returned his kisses with a kiss of her own. *"I have kissed my Big Horse."* Her voice was more of a whisper.

Then, Barbara cut off their kissing. She held him at arm's length away from her. She looked into Bob's eyes. Hearing him tell her he loved her was what she had longed to hear for over a year. And he had finally confessed his love.

"Horse, you said you loved me, just now. You said you loved me!" Her tourmaline eyes shined like freshly polished black diamonds. They searched his eyes, seeking to pierce any hint of insincerity. They held his, cautiously, as if awaiting a sign confirming what she had just heard. Her eyes looked to see his soul, knowing it held her life in the balance. She waited a long moment for him to speak.

"Yes. I said that. And I meant it." Bob's eyes spoke truth. His words confirmed his love.

"You must not play with my affections, Big Horse." Barbara's tone asserted that she demanded a partner's equal treatment. *"I am not a White, lay down and spread my legs like butter, kind of girl. I am Little Sparrow, Princess daughter of Standing Tall Bear, Big Chief of all Lakota Nation's people. Chief protects Sparrow from all things evil. He has great powers, Big Horse. He would be highly offended and dangerous to you if he discovers you trifled with Sparrow's heart."*

"But Barb, I love you. I said it. I meant it. And it's true. I mean it."

"You cannot lie about this, Horse. This is too important. You must tell me you are truthful."

"I am telling you the truth. I do love you."

"But, am I the only woman you love, Horse?"

"Until just now, no. But now, there is a change happening inside me. I feel it. I feel I have woken up to something I didn't understand correctly."

"You do not understand women, Horse. Of course, you do not understand women. You are a man. You are therefore ignorant in

the ways and feelings of women. A woman is vulnerable in many ways. She must trust a man before she allows herself to love him. Love must be based on trust. It cannot be based upon sex. Sex is not the same thing as love, Horse."

"Then, what would you call it?"

"Without trust, sex is not love. It is more like dog shit; hot and mushy; but when you examine it closely, it stinks. You thought you had love with Marty, but you only had sex. Your sex was not based upon honest trust. You did not have love with her, Horse. You only fulfilled a need she had. I am sorry to tell you this, Horse. But I speak the truth." Barbara's eyes spoke deep honesty to Bob's soul.

"And, you? What about you?" Bob's eyes showed his wonderment and confusion.

"I have always loved you, Horse. I have often prayed for you. I have worked tirelessly to make sure you would not get hurt, Horse. That is what love is, Horse. I love you, even though you were being Big Stupid Horse. My love for you has always been true and honest love, Horse." Her voice choked slightly; and her honesty brought tears to her eyes.

"I am so sorry. There is much I do not know; much I did not understand. Please forgive me. I love you. You are my true friend; and I do love you."

Barbara could tell Bob loved her. *"Now you're finally making sense, Big Horse. I suppose I should trust you now."*

"You can trust me. I swear by all the buffalo on the plains and all the elk in the forests."

"Well, now you're talking really big powerful stuff, my Big Strong Horse." Barbara pulled her head back. Her face broke into a surprised smile.

"Is that what Chief calls me?"

"Yes, Bob. You be Big Strong Horse and sometimes Big Stupid Horse's Ass. You have interchangeable names. Consider it big Lakota

honor." Barbara twirled in a circle and laughed a good belly laugh. Her black hair caught the sunlight and shined shades of purple and blue. It was her way of welcoming him into her magical world; a world where spirits mingled with lives; a world of feelings and senses; a world of fierce passions; and where family was everything.

Her dance was unlike anything he had ever seen before. It was more of a heavenly prance, gliding over the air beneath her feet, as if she had summoned nature and the spirit world to enter her through her magical feet. And she dazzled him. He felt a slow, growing release of the dopamine hormone warming him; lifting him up in a way that only spirits feel. It was unlike the dopamine rush a man often feels while watching pornography; not sudden and erection stimulating like that; but more like a gradually rising, unstoppable ocean swell that gently pushes away all other thoughts and considerations. It slowly inundated; immersed; then gently swept away his spirit soul and joined it to hers. Bob stared at her, awed and enchanted. He could only feel what he could not describe.

Whatever happened while watching her dance was, he could only sense, irreversible. He knew he could never return to whom he was before. Her dance gave him a glimpse of her magical world; revealed her enchanted way of relating to others and her natural world; a world with new dimensions; one he had only a dim awareness of; but one which he had purposely ignored.

But the dance acted like a blanket. It covered over everything in his life before; smothered everything that came before like it was never there; like it never mattered and never could matter. All his prior life's relationships and entanglements disappeared beneath this invisible, but mesmerizing blanket; this thought blanket; this cleansing blanket. His dopamine levels rose higher still, taking him to a kind of subliminal state; a condition which would endure for the rest of his life. It was unlike the dopamine rush he experienced when he had intimacy with Marty or when he watched her perform her pornography. It was not sudden like that. It was not something unleashed by salacious erotica. And it didn't even directly invite sex. It invited something more than sex. It invited a way of life. It invited him to join with her in a better, more meaningful, world than the one he knew. She had charmed him in her soft, mysteriously seductive, innocent, childlike way; unlike the ways of any other woman, he'd ever noticed. She had given him a glimpse of her world; a world that treasured the blessings of family and nature. She was letting him know that she offered him something special; a sharing of her world with him. Bob realized the treasure that presented herself before him was rare and priceless. Barbara was intelligent, clever, and straightfor-wardly honest, more so than anyone he'd ever known. She was the opposite persona of David.

He appreciated that her sex appeal was freshly wild; magical; of a different sort than Marty's. Barbara's seduction was not tacti-cal, like Marty's. Barbara hadn't come to him and hadn't presented her wares overtly, like Marty had. Barbara hadn't overtly touched, like Marty had. Barbara hadn't initiated foreplay like Marty had. Instead, Barbara personified the breathtaking majesty of the Great Plains. She captured it in her sparkling twirls; radiated it from her spectacular face and slender body. She was like the allure of the finest of wines; precious, rare; exclusive, elusive, and hard to obtain. And yes, priceless. By only letting Bob glimpse her wine's deep color and her drip legs, tantalizing tasty, clinging to the glass in ways he would never forget them; only permitting him an introductory sniff, but not yet an unforgettable taste; not just yet.

She was like one of those priceless wines that intrigued; tempt-ing him; inviting him to partake of her divine tastes; but only after she had first been properly breathed, admired, and readied. Bob wanted to taste her now; drink all of her; devour every drop of her and scour up every morsel of her dregs; then inhale the wonders of her. But he knew better. Barbara was unlike Marty. Barbara would decide when everything was perfect. Barbara would be sure that all detractions were eliminated. This wine would not be poured before it was aged to perfection. Barbara was like that. Perfection. He understood he needed to wait until she would tell him *when*.

Until she decided that 'when' time, the two of them would work together, committed in their trusting spirit love. Bob understood love on a deeper level now. For the first time in his life, Bob respected love. He realized he could search a lifetime and never locate anyone this precious. Yet, here she was, doing her native prance dance as if she was hearing her peoples 'ancestral drums. She was twirling, dazzling, capturing his heart; making it throb with desire; taking his soul into her own. He had to fight through his trance to bring himself back to the present, and remember that they were here.

"So, why are we standing in front of a vacant lot?" Bob gathered her into his arms again, stopping her enchanting whirl.

"Here's what I know so far. Not a breath of this to anyone, especially not David. It's dangerous to let him know we know anything. Very, very dangerous. Understand?" She smiled a conspiratorial smile to him, and kissed him.

"My lips are sealed."

"Listen to Sparrow." She commanded with certainty in her voice; taking him into her confidence. *"There exists a separate set of files for the company; separate records of revenues and expenses. I saw them in bookkeeping. The bookkeepers accidently left them out when I was in their office. I know what I saw. Your trips with Marty were paid for by Monument Printing. It looks like you ordered a half million dollars' worth of printing supplies to pay for a yearlong fling with her. You went all over the country, from Hawaii to Maine, to California, to Assateague and the Shenandoah's and New Orleans, New York, and*

on and on. There isn't a party you didn't go to. And, what's worse, it looks like you embezzled money from the Firm through fictitious printing bills to pay for a year of non-stop whoring.

"Now, Marty's gone. Guess who this all points to, Bob? We have theft from a regulated investment entity, a disappearance of a company officer, your name on all this phony printing from a company that doesn't exist. What will you say when the authorities start asking questions about this?"

"I didn't do any of this stuff. Honest."

"But you were fucking Marty, weren't you?"

"Yes."

"Well, I always knew you were honest, Horse. It looks like you fucked her non- stop for an entire year. What am I missing? Was she that good? Really? There was a lot of traffic in her tunnel. Didn't you know? I'm surprised you didn't have a head on collision with another dick on its way out while you were going in. At least I hope she taught you a few good things. I don't want a man who doesn't know what he's doing." Barbara's raised eyebrows telegraphed that she was accepting Bob with all his previous baggage; and, hopefully, that he loved love making. *"Tell me, Big Horse, have you been with any other women besides Marty in the past year?"*

"No, not with anyone, but a woman named Rita met me in a bar. David gave me her name and said she knew Marty and wanted to talk with me."

"When was this, Horse?"

"Not long ago, about two weeks after Marty disappeared."

"Tell me. What did this Rita woman say about Marty?"

"Just that they did orgies together. They were close friends; she missed seeing Marty, that sort of thing. Then she asked me if I'd be interested in attending one of her orgy parties. I told her no. I wasn't into that sort of thing. But she asked if it would make a difference if Marty was there and I told her it probably would, then."

"That's it? Then you left the bar? Have you talked to her, since? She could be important, Horse."

"Well, no; not exactly. Something else happened before we left the bar. There was a photographer at the bar. He came up to us while we were in our booth talking. He said he was taking pictures to advertise the bar in some magazine and asked if we would do some poses for him. We agreed. He had us sit side by side on bar stools; then he asked if he could get a shot of the two of us kissing.

"We said 'yes,' anything to be good sports. He had Rita lean over to me on my stool. He said he wanted a playful shot. He had Rita hike up her skirt. It was a micro mini. She wasn't wearing panties. Well, the photographer said he wanted a photo of my hands on Rita's bare ass while she French kissed me. We played along. She had her hand on my crotch when he shot the photo. He had one of those bright light flash attachments. I'm sure we helped him."

"This Rita, is she pretty? Does she have sex appeal?"

"Yes, she's very pretty. She has a terrific body to go with a very attractive face."

Silence.

"I'm sorry. I didn't mean anything by it. I was just doing the guy a favor. I have no interest in Rita, honest."

Silence.

"How long was it after Marty disappeared when David gave you Rita's phone number?"

"About two weeks, why?"

"I'm thinking Horse." Silence.

"What?" More silence.

"Horse, this could be very significant. Sparrow thinks this Rita woman is a notorious porn star; an easily located, easily identifiable and available for a price, whore. Sparrow thinks David knew that about Rita and called her to set up your meeting in that bar so he *could get that photo of you with your hands all over her whoring ass. That photographer and Rita were working for David."*

"Why?"

"To complete the set up; to get a photo to show you as an immoral womanizer; to give David an excuse to get rid of you. It fits with the phony invoices."

"Oh, I see."

More silence.......

"What? You're still thinking."

"Yes, Horse. There may be a much deeper significance. If David wanted to prove you a womanizer, he could have secretly gotten photos of you and Marty together, all sorts of photos, but he didn't. He used Rita. I suspect David knows he can't get photos of you and Marty together now. It's too late for that."

"What do you mean?"

"Sorry, Horse. I think it means David knows Marty is not coming back. I think it means David knows more about Marty's disappearance than he is letting on."

"Well, he did say she talked to him about joining a remote convent."

"You're kidding, right?"

"No, he said she was thinking of changing her whole life around and giving herself to helping the misfortunate."

"And you now believe Marty is washing the sick and the elderly and the diseased; and growing vegetables in a garden, and singing hymns of praise to God and the Christ, and saying her vesper prayers every night, right Horse?"

"Well, yeah, maybe. I thought maybe she found peace somehow by joining a convent."

"Horse, you do not know women. Trust me on this. You are the most clueless man in the world when it comes to women. I am sorry

to tell you this, Horse, but I do not think Marty is living at some convent. The Marty I know would first fuck a dozen bull elephants before she'd ever even consider joining a convent. Good grief, you are so impossibly stupid! Do you believe everything everyone tells you? Never mind. Don't answer that Horse. I think David wants you to believe that convent line so you have closure and get back to selling."

"What are you saying, Barb?"

"I can't prove this yet, Horse. So, you must keep this to yourself, but I think David knows Marty isn't coming back because he knows she is already dead; and I think he knows a lot more about her death than he's letting on."

"You're serious, aren't you? Do you think he murdered her?"

"It's possible, Horse. I have a great deal of work to do. You must, absolutely must, keep all this to yourself. You may be in grave danger. I think all of this, the year you had with Marty, the bar photo with your huge hands squeezing Rita's bare, fuck bunny, ass, and these phony invoices are all related. I think David is behind all of it. I just don't know yet what happened to Marty."

"You have to believe me, Barb. I had nothing to do with the phony invoices or the printing company set up."

"I already know that, Big Horse."

"How?"

"You must not know that yet, Big Horse. Too dangerous for you to know; but, rest easy. Sparrow knows you had nothing to do with it; because Sparrow thinks she understands the whole charade."

"You do?"

"Of course, I do. Little Sparrow hops all over the office. I'm unseen and unheard and unsuspected. Sparrow has more work to do to fit all these pieces together and solve this puzzle. Give Sparrow a little more time. I'll be in touch. But I do not want you to worry. If they try to frame you for this, I can disprove all of it. But for now, *you must just play along with David's game, doing your sales, as though you know nothing. Do you understand me?"*

"Yes, but tell me, are you in any danger, Barb? Shouldn't we call the police?" Bob's concern for her safety warmed Barb's heart. He was a good man. She knew that now.

"No police. If this is leading to where I think it is, the police and the justice system would not deliver the kind of justice that is needed here. David has money to bribe police, judges and jurors. Justice is not enough for what David needs, Horse. David needs a reckoning. Leave all this to Sparrow, Horse. Sometimes the Lakota ways are the best ways. And, I'm not in danger unless some people get very foolish. Chief looks over his Little Sparrow. And Chief has powerful medicine. Chief is very dangerous to anyone who tries to harm Sparrow."

"But your father is on a Montana reservation."

"Ha! Trust me about this, dearest Horse. Father has people who work for him. They take care of the things that Father calls 'the details.' One of Father's men is never far away from me. I don't worry."

Bob was astounded by what Barbara knew, how well she understood people and how fearless she was. His heart warmed when she called him: *'dearest.'*

"You're telling me you have a protector, a bodyguard?"

Barbara pulled out a green plastic square from her purse. There was a red button in the center of it and it had two tiny blinking lights on one side of it. It was a signaling device. *"If I push this button, an armed man will appear within a half-minute."*

"You're kidding. How do you know that?"

"When both lights blink, he's within a hundred yards. When only one light blinks, he's within four hundred yards. When no light blinks, it will take him more than a minute to get to me. If light

doesn't blink for a long time, like five minutes, Chief will become upset with my protection and he will be replaced. Light always blinks, signaling less than four hundred yards away. My button is not like Hillary's phony reset button. My button works."

"This is amazing. I've never seen anything like this." Bob was astounded.

"Because, you've never met a man like Chief. Chief is very protective of Sparrow."

"Will I get in trouble for kissing you just now?"

"No, silly Horse, you only get in heap big trouble if you lose interest."

"I'm interested. I'm very interested." Bob kissed her again, with kisses that searched her lips with passion.

"Sparrow knows, Horse; but Horse. You must stop kissing me, for now. Horse must still wait."

"How long?"

"Not too long, but not real soon, either. Chief says we must allow time to play its magic."

"Jesus Christ. I'd never have guessed any of this was real."

"It's real, Horse. And Horse…"

"Yes, Sparrow?"

"Do not swear, Horse. Swearing belittles you."

"Okay Sparrow. No more swearing."

True to her father's teachings, Barbara set out to track her quarry. She began tracking the human animals that worked at the firm. For animals it was enough for her to listen to the elders talk about the tendencies of each species; to hear and remember their stories, as was the custom of tribal oral tradition that had served the People for thousands of years. But, for the human animal, the ones who left their tracks on paper, she needed more than her memory. She needed detailed records of who was where and when; who said what and when; who talked about whom and about what; what routines were followed and not followed; what protocols were observed; what information was freely available and what was guarded; and how that information guarded. Barbara made notes. She compared her observations with what her records told her, always comforted by her father's words: *'Every animal leaves its tracks.'*

Barbara kept notebooks of everything that happened in the office; even those things most employees would assume were insignificant. Her notebook had journal entries to record the times of her observations. She would study these entries and relate them to events that happened before and after her observation. Her notebook was further divided into sections for reference and cross reference. She had sections dedicated to each employee and each vendor, service agent, regulator, attorney, accountant, and sales rep who sold Firm products. Her notebook blossomed into a library of several volumes. She committed herself to tracking every conceivable detail. She was convinced that, through her meticulous diligence, the patterns of a devious white collar crime animal would reveal themselves.

And they did. For example, Barbara noticed that shortly after a visit from executives of a brokerage firm that firm sold the Fund's shares, commission trades were placed with that brokerage firm. Oddly, but not coincidental, the dollar retention of the broker for the trades, after clearing firm costs, was always two percent of that brokerage firm's Fund sales. Apparently, David was paying an additional two percent for Fund sales out of Fund assets, because these brokerages charged substantially more than the execution costs of most firms; and the brokerage firms had no research departments.

Barbara calculated the Fund payments in excess commission charges resulted in the brokerages receiving an additional forty percent compensation above the disclosed prospectus rate. She surmised David skirted Securities and Exchange Commission rules regarding the Securities Distribution Act of 1934, requiring full disclosure of transaction costs, and also violated the Investor Advisor's Act of 1940, regarding disclosure of allowable Fund expenses. Clearly, David was running a scam.

But Barbara's tracking revealed something even more mysterious about David's behaviors. He had a habit of going to bookkeeping every Friday with a thin black briefcase before he left the office; and he returned to bookkeeping every Monday with that same briefcase before he went to his own office. The briefcase David carried other days was also black, but that briefcase was a much thicker briefcase. When he had a weekday business meeting out of the office, he always carried the thicker briefcase; but never the thin one.

Prior to her tracking regimen, she had assumed David only stopped into bookkeeping to check on account balances or sales; but upon giving her observation greater thought, Barbara noticed David never carried the thin briefcase any other times. She deduced there was some especially secretive information that David transported weekends in his thin briefcase; something that David did not trust to leave unattended at the Firm.

Chief told Sparrow the only way to know an animal was to actually watch and study it, everywhere it went, and understand why it did everything it did. With her father's advice fortifying her, Barbara invented a reason to stop into bookkeeping while David was there on a Friday, after he'd entered bookkeeping with his secretive thin black briefcase. She timed David's stay in bookkeeping for three successive Fridays and calculated that the four minute mark was the exact halfway point of his visit. The following Friday she made her move.

"Debbie," Barbara addressed the head bookkeeper as she opened the door to the bookkeeping department, *"Could I trouble*

you to please pull the files for tax payments for occupational taxes?" David's back was angled to the door. Barbara had caught him in the middle of something. She observed him in the midst of receiving from Debbie Goldman a large brass key ring with a single brass key on the ring.

Debby sat in the back corner of bookkeeping. The transfer of the key to David was not apparent to any of the other bookkeepers. Barbara was the only one who witnessed the transfer. David turned to face Barbara. His face expressed alarm. It was obvious that he and Debbie had been caught in the midst of an activity that no one else was supposed to see. But David quickly regained his composure. His look of fear changed chameleon-like to confidence.

"Do you need those records right this minute?" Debbie snapped at her intruder. She was less artful at deception than David. Her voice revealed she was more than ordinarily annoyed. Quickly she added: *"Why do you need them, anyway?"* Debbie's add on question gave Barbara another 'tell' of sorts.

Bookkeeping *never* had any business or authority to ask an administrator why Administration wanted anything. Bookkeeping was a support function. Administration was a vital function for compliance and the smooth running of the firm. It was the department in charge of Firm business. It was, by far, the superior department. Its requests to other departments were understood as demands; never questioned.

Debbie's concern in questioning Barbara was betrayed by her arrogance. That told Barbara there was something sub-rosa going on between David and Debbie; and Debbie was annoyed at Barbara's intrusion because Debbie *assumed* that the hidden activity was more important to David, the Firm's owner, than the Firm's regulated businesses. Barbara, ever fascicle of mind and always quick on her feet, was prepared for the contingency of Debbie's challenge.

"We donated used chairs to Goodwill. I'm revising our occupational tax report and getting money refunded. I'm after big bucks, Debbie! We can save thirty dollars a year." Barbara smiled her most courteous Ms. Efficiency smile, then shot her *'Fuck You and Die, bitch, for daring to question me'* poison dart look at the suspicious bookkeeper.

"Good thinking, Barbara." David chimed in, now also smiling and believing the intruder. What Barbara said was true. It was part of her job. No harm in saving thirty dollars a year. That's exactly what the Cracker Jack efficiency expert was supposed to do. David turned to Debbie, giving his back to Barbara. He gave Debbie a nearly indiscernible negative head motion and dismissive smirk, indicating Barbara was nothing to be concerned about. Barbara noticed his head movement. It confirmed her suspicion. Something nefarious was going on between those two.

David and Debbie didn't know it, but their tracker was more relentless than a bloodhound. Barbara was hot on their trail. Sighting the key ring transfer told Barbara there was a secret between these two. It was time to know her animals better, time to go sleuthing.

On a Sunday, acting on a hunch, Barbara went to David's temple. She went inside, told the custodian she was doing some research. She was directed to the temple's vast library. She signed in under a fictitious name. She was not required to show identification. She browsed about the shelves and book stacks, picked up a book on Jewish humor, sat down in a chair where she could observe the librarian, and waited. Sure enough, after about a half hour the old woman got up and headed for the rest room.

Barbara quickly went to the librarian's desk and went through its unlocked drawers. She found what she came for, the temple's directory. Jews must belong to a temple and pay membership dues to attend High Holy Days services. The directory listed temple members. Barbara thumbed the pages until she came to the name of Debbie Wasserstein. Bingo! David and Debby belonged to the same temple. Likely, they knew each other socially and trusted each other.

Tracking now became a cat and mouse game. Barbara needed to find out why there was a brass key. And where David kept the key. More sleuthing was required. She'd need to work nights and weekends. Fortunately, she and Mrs. Rodriguez were trusted employees. They had keys to open the doors of all administration offices, including Susan's office. Barbara waited until the Friday evening before a long weekend. She left the office like all the other employees; but she returned two hours later. No one else was there.

She went to Susan's office and unlocked it. In Susan's desk drawer were the keys to all other offices in the Firm. She took Susan's keys and went to the bookkeepers' offices and unlocked them. Then she unlocked Debbie's top desk drawer. There lay the brass key! But, hadn't she seen David take the brass key with him? She looked around the office. There was a small file cabinet bolted to the concrete floor away from the other file cabinets. It was fitted with two brass key holes to securely lock it, just like bank safe deposit boxes were keyed! She took Debbie's key and tested it. It fit one of the locks, but not the other. David's key fit the other keyhole! But David kept that key in his pants pocket.

Weeks passed. Barbara closely observed David's pockets. He kept his office keys in his right pocket and his car and house keys in his left pocket. She saw him take office keys from his right pocket and hold them in his hand on two separate occasions. Both times the brass key ring which held the office keys and the solo brass key were there. He kept the office keys and the secret key to the second keyhole in the small bookkeeping file cabinet separate from his house and car keys.

Barbara observed the movements of David and Muscle Boy and took notes of all the times the two men were together. Office gossip was that David sometimes summoned Muscle Boy to his office in the afternoons. David would lock his office door; then the two lovers made disgusting male mating sounds. David groaned especially loudly. After David's pleasure time, Muscle Boy left. Before David summoned Muscle Boy, he always, without exception, spent considerable time in the men's bathroom. Barbra waited.

From the panel lights on the internal phone system, Barbara and Mrs. Rodriguez could see who was on their phones. Muscle Boy's phone was rarely in use. Friday afternoon, David's phone light and Muscle Boy's light both blinked on. That turned Barbara's radar on. Sure enough, shortly after the phone lights blinked off, David walked past the front office to the men's room. Barbara excused herself to Mrs. Rodriguez and left the front office, ostensibly to get something from Susan's office. Instead, she went to David's office; unlocked his office door, and let herself in. She relocked David's office door from the inside; then hid herself behind the window drapes.

Barbara's tracking paid off. David was the first to enter, Muscle Boy came shortly after. Barbara peered from behind the curtain as the two gay males embraced and kissed passionately. Both men took their pants off and hung them behind the door. David went to the low bench and lied down. Muscle Boy began sucking and stroking David's penis.

David's head was hung over the end of the low bench furthest from the door. His eyes, when not closed, were facing the opposite wall and ceiling. Muscle Boy was kneeling with his bare ass to the door and his head faced down on David's organ. He was sucking David's penis in an up and down motion with his head. *Just like a common whore, giving a quickie blow job'* thought Barbara. It was time for her to make her move.

With both men were totally engrossed in their oral sex, stealthy tracker Barbara, slipped out from behind the curtain drape and tiptoed barefoot to David's left pants pocket. The two men were engrossed in their playtime. Neither man heard or saw Barbara. Chief had trained her in stealth: *'Never hurry. Think each move of hand; each move of foot. Breathe quietly.'* Deftly, she removed the brass key ring with its secret key, pressed the key into a warm wax mold. Ever silent, she slipped the brass ring with its key back into David's pocket. She silently unlocked the door, let herself out and quietly relocked the office door from the outside. She put her shoes back on and returned to her desk.

Getting a wax imprint of Debbie's companion key was simpler. Barbara waited until after work. When all employees were gone she let herself into bookkeeping, unlocked Debbie's desk, and made an imprint of that key. With her two wax imprints, Barbara went to a locksmith in neighboring town and had duplicate keys made. She was ready to learn what secrets her curious David animal kept tightly guarded from the world. Chief told her that all animals, including human ones, were creatures of habit. They always did what their natures compelled them to do. She remembered Chief's wisdom: *'Understand their habits and wait. They reveal themselves.'* Barbara waited patiently for her animals to make their move.

Barbara thought long and hard. Where could she look to discover patterns of David's behavior? Who and what would record the comings and goings at the Firm? Suddenly it occurred to her. Mrs. Rodriguez! The sweet, matronly woman had faithfully kept an office diary since her first day of employment! Her tenure predated David's. Another night of sleuthing led Barbara to Mrs. Rodriguez's file cabinet. She felt guilty while opening it, knowing she was violating an unspoken understanding about respecting her friend's privacy.

But this was not a quest to embarrass the old woman. This was her secret war with enemy David. And she needed intelligence about her enemy, wherever she could find it. Mostly, the cabinet contained the old woman's personal items. Extra pairs of thick soled shoes and a pair of snow booties filled one drawer. Of course, that made sense. Mrs. Rodriguez always complained that her feet hurt. Another drawer held support hose and a supply of adult diapers for catching urine leaks. A third drawer was filled with extra sweaters, head scarves and a raincoat. That made sense. Colorado weather was unpredictable. Mrs. Rodriguez was ready for every contingency.

The fourth drawer contained the treasure trove of information that Barbara needed to understand human animal behavior. *'Mrs. Rodriguez, you sweet dear, how will I ever thank you?'* thought Barbara. There it was! The faithful company servant had kept a daily diary of all the comings and goings through the office from the first day of her employment. Stacked in chronological order, filling an entire file drawer, were the daily diaries of Mrs. Rodriguez. Barbara dove in. She located the time and date when David first arrived. She traced the patterns of guests; when they came and when they left. Nothing remarkable. Rabbis visiting Marvin; corporate executives visiting Marvin. Susan's and Marvin's daily privacy times when they were not to be disturbed; Susan's times away from the office on her large account servicing calls; employees waiting to see Marvin; employees waiting to see David; analysts visiting Marvin or David; directors' visits for their board meetings, etc. Nothing remarkable. But there it was!

The paper trail! She found it. It began about three months after Marvin died. A man who Mrs. Rodriguez noted only as *'The Mexican'* made his appearance in her diary. He had no name attached. Mysterious and curious! Apparently, David had never introduced him to anyone. Barbara kept digging. She noted by comparing her notes with the entries in Mrs. Rodriguez' diary that whenever 'The Mexican' appeared in the receptionist's diary, David called Marty to his office immediately afterwards. Then, 'The Mexican' appeared about a week or two later; and, like clockwork, David appeared carrying his thin briefcase. He took the thin briefcase into bookkeeping and left bookkeeping without it. Then, at night around closing time, David went into bookkeeping and recovered the thin briefcase and left with it.

The following day David always carried his thick briefcase. Barbara reasoned the thin briefcase carried a separate set of records for some nefarious dealings that David, and probably Marty, were engaged in. Bookkeeping likely had someone who was in on the scheme. Also likely, the thin briefcase carried cash money to bookkeeping to be laundered into the legitimate businesses and scrubbed clean from any tax reporting.

Now fascinated by the chronology revealed in the diaries, Barbara went back to their beginning and searched for the first entries about Marty, her arch rival for Bob's affections. It didn't take her long. Apparently, Susan used Mrs. Rodriguez as her unofficial, unpaid baby sitter for Marty, after Susan's husband, Joseph, died. This arrangement didn't last long. Marty was sent to WEX school shortly after Mrs. Rodriguez had started watching the child. But the extra notes Mrs. Rodriguez made during those days were very revealing.

Mrs. Rodriguez wrote that child Marty told her that her grandmother, Mrs. Mallory, had confused little Marty by telling her that her mother, Susan, was sleeping with Satan. Marty told Mrs. Rodriguez that she had looked in her mommy's bedroom and under her mommy's bed; and even in her own bedroom and under her own bed. But she could not find Satan.

In another entry, Mrs. Rodriguez recorded that, while she was watching Marty, grandmother Mallory went into Susan's office, unannounced. Once inside, the grandmother screamed profanities at her daughter, Susan, for the better part of an hour. The grandmother left the Firm's offices, crying. Barbara assumed from this gratuitous information that the Mallory grandmother had become deeply disturbed and emotionally unstable; and that possibly her mental state was the reason why Susan shipped Marty off to WEX school. Weeks later, Barbara would understand the profound, full significance of those incidental notations from Mrs. Rodriguez.

CHAPTER TWO

A mother is a mother still, the holiest thing alive (Samuel Taylor Coleridge: The Three Graves)

The day is gone and all its sweets are gone! Sweet voice, sweet lips, soft hands and softer breast. (John Keats: The day is gone)

FINDING RUBLINA

Some mothers cannot suckle their infants because their breasts simply cannot produce milk. Others cannot suckle their babies because rigors of career and travel place extraordinary demands upon them. Logistics of breast feeding overwhelms them. That creates an unfair burden on the newborn. When a baby cries to suckle, it can't wait until mommy's jet lands and she arrives home. A few women will not suckle for yet another reason. They cannot stand the reality that their baby exists. They wish the kid had not been born. Some even hate their baby. Even further distanced from such misgiving women was Eloweiss.

She was dazed after birthing David. When the nurses asked if she was ready to hold her new baby, Eloweiss simply said, *"No!"* When Marvin asked if she'd like to have his bassinette wheeled into her hospital room so she could be with him, she said, *"No! Marvin, I've done my part. I'm finished. I bore you a son. He's your problem now. You deal with him."*

As far as she was concerned, she'd upheld her end of a bargain and that was the end of it. She'd given birth, which was demanded of her by her husband and her family. She'd consented to do that. She had copulated with Marvin, as miserable an experience as there ever was for her, until her doctor finally pronounced her pregnant. She promised no more than to bear Marvin a son. With David's birth, Eloweiss considered her part of the bargain complete.

Eloweiss considered baby David her adversary from the moment she learned he was in her womb. He caused her to outgrow her wardrobe; gave her morning sickness; make her miss social engagements; forced her to reduce her alcohol consumption; and caused her to go to bed early. She resented missing parties; not getting her fair share of caviar and foie gras. She liked going to goyim affairs. At those, she freely guzzled shrimp cocktails and raw oysters, knowing no rabbi would witness her eating shellfish. Now that little David was born, she lived under a microscope while friends and relatives came to see her child. Her priorities were not David. She put him on artificial formula, found him a nanny, and kept herself as far away from her son as possible.

So it was. David grew up with artificial nourishment for food and an artificial mother for love. Marvin loved his son; but in Marvin's detached, mostly disinterested sort of way. He loved his business and Susan's intimacy far more. David received little guidance from Marvin and none from Eloweiss. When the topic of David arose between Eloweiss and Marvin, Eloweiss made no effort to disguise her feelings. She hated her child. With every year that passed Eloweiss detested David even more than the year before.

"He is a lazy, shifty, lying, thieving, devious homosexual and a worthless misfit," she declared to Marvin. She was now, years later, describing her pubescent son David. Neither parent understood why their prodigy behaved as he did.

After Marvin's death, when David finally had control of the family business, he decided to psychologically compensate himself for the absence of a mother's love. He determined he would not be denied anything other men had received in *any* aspect of their lives, regardless of how late he availed himself of that blessing. Determined to reclaim his lost nurturing, he placed a call to his good friend Eddie Wilkes, the firm's accountant.

"Eddie," David began, *"I need your help finding a suitable personal assistant. I'm thinking her role will be, for corporate appearances and compensation purposes if you understand what I mean, Corporate Secretary to the Firm. I don't want just any woman for this position. She doesn't have to be particularly intelligent. She doesn't have to be particularly beautiful either. Mainly, Eddie, she has to be very flexible, if you follow my meaning; and she has to have a certain appearance. The appearance aspect is extremely important for this particular role, if you follow what I'm saying."*

"David, I'm always ready to help you, as I helped your father. Tell me exactly what sort of appearance you're looking for." Eddie expected David to describe a hot-bodied floozy, with negotiable morals, willing to trade sexual favors for money. The answer from David took him aback:

"Well, you remember my mother, Eloweiss, don't you, Eddie?"

"Yes, of course, David."

"I can provide you with pictures of her when she was in her twenties and thirties if you like."

"David, that won't be necessary. Mrs. Wilkes and I were good friends with your father and mother. I have many pictures of the four of us together. Is the woman you're looking for supposed to resemble your mother?'

"Yes."

"May I be so bold as to ask why?"

"No, Eddie. That's none of your business. And about your pictures, Eddie. Do you have one of mother's sitting profiles, one where she was showing off her big tits busting out of her blouse?"

"Well, no, nothing exactly like that."

"That's okay, Eddie. I'll have a copy of that picture made and I'll get it over to you."

"So what should I be looking for, David, a pair of tits like your mother's or a face that nearly matches your mother's?"

"Both, Eddie, as best you can find a match."

"Got it; but David, if it comes down to one with a near face match or one with a similar set of tits, which would you prefer?"

"I'll likely hire the woman with the biggest tits." replied David.

"And how about her religion? Must she be Jewess, or can she be a Muslim or a Goy?"

"I don't give a shit about her religion." said David.

With those instructions and a photograph copy of Eloweiss's profile which emphasized her mountainous tits, Eddie went to work. He placed advertisements in the local newspapers for an executive secretary with vague descriptions of needed skills:

'Must be comfortable in an executive setting, have flexible attitudes and work hours, and be willing to cooperate to accomplish demanding tasks. Relocation expenses will be paid.'

He contacted three personnel agencies and offered a thirty-percent commission based upon the successful woman's first years' salary if she was referred by their firm. There was no mention of typing or dictation skill requirements; no need for references; and no need for a work history. The employer was willing to pay 25% above the going rate for top-notch executive secretaries for the chosen applicant. Thus began Eddie's nationwide search for a perfectly matching set of tits.

Thousands of applications poured into Eddie Wilkes's office. He narrowed the field to three thousand by applying age discrimination methods. No woman over thirty-five and none under the age of twenty-five passed the first hurdle. The second screen was marital status. Only single women and divorcees were allowed, and the field narrowed to twelve hundred applicants. Eddie set up a pre-screening whereby the final twelve hundred were personally interviewed by a junior man on his staff. Women traveled at their own expense from as far as a thousand miles away for their preliminary interview. Each was given some simple questions on a sheet of paper to fill out, questions like adding up a column of six numbers and answering who the president of the country was. It was a simple but necessary test to get a look at the applicants. Women the junior man assessed to have breasts smaller than size 38 EE were thanked for their interest and excused.

Eddie's junior man screened the prospects down to twenty women who had *'the right stuff.'* Eddie would select the final three. Each of the twenty prospects came to his office. He asked them to walk across the room and bring him a glass of water, then sit sideways in a chair. By their facial resemblance to Eloweiss in her prime, their body carriage, posture, and breast sizes, Eddie ranked the three most likely to meet David's approval. The three finalists were then referred to David for their final interview.

The first woman had an elderly mother afflicted with Parkinson's at home. While she declared that her mother's needs were amply cared for by caregivers, David suspected potential conflicts for his time requirements. He told her he'd get back to her.

The second woman sat across from David in his office and adjusted her skirt. She intentionally presented David with a beaver shot. Obviously, the woman signaled she was a player and an astute opportunist. David asked her a test question, mixed in with some routine ones about getting along in a team environment. *"What would you do if you saw a male employee physically abusing one of the female staff members?"*

"Like doing what?" asked the woman.

"Like raping her." replied David.

The woman's answer was reflexive. *"Why, I'd tell you about it right away, sir."*

"And if I weren't here, what would you do?" David probed further. He wanted to get a sense of the woman's moral compass.

"Well, I'd wait until you returned." she answered. David liked what he was hearing.

"But if I were away on hunting trips and not scheduled to be in touch with the office for another four weeks, then what would you do?"

"Well, sir, I think I'd go to the next person in charge and report him." The woman sounded a bit defensive and unsure of herself.

"You're the next person in charge. What will you do?" David pressed for a read on the woman.

The woman became flustered. After a moment, she asked, *"Do I have the power to dismiss this man?"*

"No." said David staring into her eyes.

After another moment, the woman said, *"Well, I'd report this criminal act to the police."*

Again, David thanked her for her time and thoughtful answers and told her he'd get back to her. Of course, he never got back to her. He never wanted police asking questions about the firm.

The third woman showed up in a disheveled state. Her blouse wasn't tucked in properly, her makeup was sloppily applied with lipstick smudged upon her cheek. She smacked bubble gum with her mouth open; and tendrils of her hair were adrift from their plastic retainers. They dangled over her face. She had the annoying habit of brushing her hair away from her eyes. Even her brassier appeared to have been improperly arranged. It looked as if one breast were strangely positioned higher on her chest than the other. But the most egregious thing about this slovenly lassie was that she reeked of alcohol. Either she just came from a happenstance where alcohol flowed freely, or she was a drunkard. David's interest was piqued. The woman was the spitting image of his mother.

"And by what name are you called, Miss?" asked David.

"Well, my formal name is Rublina, but people who know me call me Ruby."

Her words were slurred. She had a goofy sort of smile that indicated she didn't care about anything in the world. Her teeth were okay, but not great. Dental work could make her mouth perfect. She was cogent, however. She correctly intuited that this David fellow had an unfulfilled personal need and she was among the finalists being considered to fill it. She needed the money. She figured she'd play along with whatever this reserved, observant man wanted. Her life was a moment-by-moment existence. David quickly sized up the candidate. She was a woman with no self-esteem; no morals; no sense of personal hygiene; no plans and no clue. And, she was dead broke.

"Do you know why you're here?" David asked.

"You tell me, Daddy O," replied Rublina, chewing her wad of bubble gum like a cow chewing its cud.

This lush was bold. She was David's mother's age when he was born. She tried to act like a teenager. It was enough to remind him of their age difference. He was old enough to be her father. She wasn't easily intimidated.

"Well, I'm looking for a personal assistant. Someone I can train to do some very personal work for me." David lifted his chin and lowered his eyelids. It was an officious look. Its real purpose was to give David ample time to fixate on the woman's breasts.

"Well, I can be as personal and as assisting as you want, Mr.…?" mouthed the woman.

"David. Call me David, please."

"Well, David, as long as you're paying the big bucks, I'll be glad to do anything you want. You can fuck me every day; any place inside or out of the office, whatever turns you on."

"I said I wanted to train you. I didn't say I wanted to fuck you." David felt his sensibilities had been challenged.

"Okay! Jesus Christ, don't get sensitive. I'm imminently trainable, David. You train me to do it, whatever it is, and I'll do it. Okay?"

"Do you have any children or other dependents?" asked David.

"Yes, one. I have a son who lives in my apartment with me."

"How old is your son, Miss?" David's interest was piqued.

"He's eighteen, David. Just call me Ruby," replied the woman.

"Can you still manage him?" David sought to learn as much personal information as he could about the woman and her son.

"Oh, sure, he'll do whatever I tell him to do. He won't get in the way of any training you have planned for me."

Maybe it was the inebriated woman's intuition, or maybe she was just an easy squeeze for any man; regardless, she did the unexpected. She stood up, walked around behind David's desk, and wrapped her arms around his neck. She pulled David's head between her size 40 EE breasts and rubbed them against his face before kissing him smack on his lips. She was not the typical job applicant. *"Pops, I could fall in love with you, if you let me. I'm ready for my training,"* she declared.

David was taken aback by the woman's bold advance. He pulled his head away from her. *"Kissing won't be necessary, Ruby. That's not part of the job description."* As David said these words to her, he trembled slightly before her powers. He wondered if she was his mother, somehow reincarnated. She very much resembled Eloweiss. He was awed by the fullness of her breasts.

She was hired two days later. She came to the office in dunga-rees and a halter top. All the staff members noted the new hire's oversized tits. There was some speculation Rublina had implants, but based upon comments from several women about the way they jiggled, it was concluded Rublina hefted original equipment.

As a condition of employment, Rublina was required to sign a non-disclosure agreement with respect to any conversations or happenings or meetings of any kind which took place in David's office. She agreed that if she violated this non-disclosure she would immediately be liable and owing all sums paid to her from the date of employment. She was also required to purchase a home in the tiny suburb of Rondel Hills. The down payment was put up by David and Rublina signed a note to refund the down payment if she were terminated for any reason, for cause or otherwise. She was also required to sign a note to him for the mortgage amount owning on the house. David agreed to make the monthly pay-ments. This odd arrangement prompted Rublina to ask the first sensible question about her employment.

"David, honey babes, why are we signing all these papers?" she asked like a gullible dupe.

"For tax reasons," David replied curtly.

Rublina was given a spacious corner office and an assistant who did all her work for her. Her days consisted of showing up for work when she pleased. She was usually drunk. She spent her first two weeks polishing her nails and reading fashion magazines. But her blissful routine was short-lived.

David called her into his office on the first day of her third week and informed her that her drinking was to stop. He also told her that she needed to take better care of her breasts because cancer was a heightened risk for women with large breasts. He gave her a list of required foods to eat; and had delivered to her home three hundred pounds of raw oats. She was instructed to adhere to her new diet and eat massive helpings of oats for optimal breast health. After a month of her new diet, her breasts would be 'checked' to see if she complied with his requirement for healthier eating.

A month elapsed and Rublina was summoned to David's office. A private nurse was there dressed in street clothes. The nurse held a breast suction apparatus that was attached to an electric pump.

'This looks like something freaky is going on here. What are these two about to do to me?' thought Rublina. Then she remembered the part about the job description, the training requirement, the notes she'd signed. This tight lipped circumspect man owned her. *'Well, how bad could it get? After all, he doesn't even want to fuck me'* she rationalized. She looked at David and smiled:

"Hi ya, honey babes. What would you like me to do here?"

"Ruby, I'd like you to meet Ms. Sinclair. She'll be your monitor for your health project. I'll leave while Ms. Sinclair conducts her first examination." With that introduction, David left his office.

Rublina sized up Ms. Sinclair:

'She's a skinny athletic health nut. Maybe I'm on a health program to make me look more like her. No way! Ms. Nursey Nurse has no tits and no ass.' thought Rublina.

"Please sit on the sofa, Ruby." Ms. Sinclair was all formality and professionalism.

"Okay, honey cakes, whatever you say." Rublina was obliging.

"Very good, now remove your blouse and bra please." ordered Mrs. Sinclair.

Rublina complied. *"Is this a full exam, or are you just checking my tits?"* she asked:

'This place is fucking weird. I do absolutely nothing and get paid for it. Now this prim beanpole nurse is going to play with my tits? Bring it, babes!' thought Rublina.

Once Rublina was naked down to her waist, Nurse Sinclair attached two suction cups to her nipples.

"*Hey, tell me what's going on here. I've never had this kind of examination before.*" There was alarm in Rublina's voice as she began wondering just what she'd signed up for.

"*These are suctions, dear. They won't hurt you. They'll just exert some sucking pulls on your nipples.*"

"*Why in the hell do you want to have a machine sucking my nipples?*"

"*Oh, didn't you know, dear? They will stimulate your breasts as if an infant child is suckling you. I'm simply showing you how the machine works so you'll know how to use it. Mr. Sustack wants your breasts to be in perfect health, and the best way to ensure that is to have you suckled by the machine several times a day, just like an infant would suckle you. There's also an identical machine, all assembled, being delivered to your home this afternoon. You are to suckle the machine every four hours, day and night, until your breasts produce milk.*"

"*Wait. This is crazy! Don't you know I'm not even pregnant? I haven't been pregnant for eighteen years!*" Rublina was alarmed.

"*So, you were young when you had your last child. How old were you?*" asked Mrs. Sinclair.

"*I was fifteen. His father left me and took off for California with some fuck bunny surfer chick. He was a worthless bastard, that one. But he was good-looking and he loved to fuck. We fucked all night long. The crazy thing is: I still miss him.*" Rublina replied wistfully.

"*Yes, that does seem crazy; but it's your life, Ruby. Obviously, you live in the moment and don't think things through very well.*" Mrs. Sinclair smiled while she put down her subject.

"*What did you mean by that, huh?*" Rublina's suspicions were growing.

"Oh, nothing, forget it. I'm just here to show you how to use the equipment and to make sure it's in good working order." Mrs. Sinclair reverted to her efficiency tone.

"I thought David said this was my first examination. When's my second one, and what are you examining exactly?" Rublina wanted her suspicions addressed.

"Your milk production, dearie. Your next exam will be in a month, then every two weeks until I know you have good flow." Mrs. Sinclair was not one to volunteer more information than she needed to divulge.

"What in the fuck? Why do I need good milk flow?" Rublina didn't relish the idea of becoming a breast-feeder to some machine.

"Didn't Mr. Sustack tell you, dearie? You're being conditioned to breast-feed him. Mr. Sustack needs your human breast milk."

There it was. The truth was finally out in the open.

"Jesus H. Christ!! Motherfucking, and hell no! I am not going to let that man drink milk out of my tits. This is fucking crazy!" Rublina sat up ramrod straight on the sofa. Her fear was palpable.

"Now, now, dearie, it's not as bad as you think," reassured Mrs. Sinclair. *"It actually feels good to be suckled, and you'll be doing a great human kindness and getting very well paid for it. At night, when Mr. Sustack can't be with you to suckle, you'll just have to put the machine on for a few minutes to quickly drain you. You'll actually enjoy it."*

"You're nuts! This whole idea is nuts! I won't do it! Get away from me, you fucking pervert." Rublina was becoming hostile.

"Oh, dear, Mr. Sustack told me this might happen," said Mrs. Sinclair. *"He said I should remind you of the terms of your employment and your financial obligations to him. Do you prefer your old insect-infested apartment? That can be arranged. However, Mr. Sustack will garnish your future wages wherever you find employment until your debts to him are fully discharged. He figures with the loss*

on a quick sale of your house, you'll owe him about a hundred thousand or more and you'll be working for what amounts to minimum wages for the next ten years or longer. It's just a friendly reminder, dearie. Now, shall we act like sensible adults?"

"You fucking bitch. You're in on this with him, aren't you?"

"Well, I don't do private duty work for free, now do I? You don't expect to be paid to do nothing, do you? This is America and the free enterprise system, after all, honey cakes, dearie. Now be a good girl and settle yourself and let me put these cups on your nipples."

With her role in better focus, Rublina relented. The cups were placed in massage mode, which meant they gently pulled her nipples and alternatively pushed hard against them, all in the effort to stimulate milk production.

Rublina sat back on the sofa and let the machine do its work. *"Jesus H. Christ! If anybody knew this guy ran a money management firm with real money in it, they wouldn't believe it. No fucking way! This whole place is full of weird shit goings on, and I've only been here three weeks."*

"And always remember, dearie, you are contracted to silence. One word of anything that goes on here and you will be the sorriest girl in Plaintown."

"You know him, don't you?"

"Cousins, honey cakes dearie; just cousins through marriages, but yes, we're cousins. Everything is in the family, even our little quirks and foibles. Just enjoy yourself. You'll be doing a human kindness. There's no shame in doing a kindness. And by the way, dearie, these are for you." Ms. Sinclair handed Rublina a cardboard box sealed with packaging tape.

"What's this for?" Rublina had trepidations about receiving any gifts from this nurse from the dark side.

"These are your supplies. They will last you one month, and then you'll get refills. The small cans contain nutritional supplements you

must take daily. The capsules in the jar are to enhance your hormone production so you'll lactate more easily. The balm is for soothing your teats after they've been suckled, and the rubber-coated clamps are for your nipples. You are to wear the clamps in the evening and daily when you are not in the office. They ensure the nipples remain in a heightened state of stimulation so you'll lactate more freely."

"So, I'm Mr. Sustack's human milk cow now; complete with my animal feed and instructions." Rublina held back her tears.

"Relax, dearie. Look at it this way. You only need to work for two twenty-minute periods five days a week and you'll be highly paid. Isn't that what you were looking for when you answered the advertisement?"

Rublina didn't respond. She was bewildered. She was agreeing to be a sex slave of a sort; but of a different sort than she ever imagined. She tried rationalizing her victimhood status. Obviously she was the outlet for some psychological disorder that held David in its grip. She tried telling herself that she was somehow helping another human being, but her rationalization couldn't overcome her innate fear for her future. She sat back and closed her eyes. Her mind drifted. She tried to imagine the machine was her infant son from eighteen years ago. But a dark undercurrent stirred her apprehensions:

'What have I gotten myself into?' Rublina felt a dawning realization. She was trapped. She had committed herself to perform a grotesque service for a bizarre control freak. Somehow, she had allowed herself to be fitted into a psycho's fantasy world. She'd signed all those papers and moved herself and her son into their new house. She wondered:

'Will we be safe? What else is he capable of doing? Can I get out of this? Do I want to get out of this? What's to become of me and my son?'

CHAPTER THREE

Obtruding false rules pranked in reason's garb (John Milton: Comus)

SPARKY, THE BLATHER FLAMER

The personnel requirements for the sales and marketing portion of the firm were growing while the administrative requirements of the business remained constant. Susan's role in the firm was as important as David's, but her department's personnel needs remained fixed, while David's empire was expanding. Revenues were growing; costs were not. Free of Marvin's day by day control, David felt an irresistible urge to exercise his growing power.

The impish pranks and bad deeds which David had repressed from his childhood bubbled up from a wellspring of parental hatreds. He wished he could be a totalitarian dictator of subjugated people, but he had no military to command. He was merely a businessman. To slake his sociopathy, David weaponized his money. He used it to wreak havoc upon employees, shareholders, and hapless innocents who became indebted to him. He made people squirm under his powers and tortured their lives and finances, much as he had bedeviled insects as a child.

He ensnared those less fortunate who miscalculated or underestimated him. Like a silent, stealthy frog, offering financial liquidity, he baited the unwary with money; then, when the time was right, he shot out his unfurled tongue of gooey legal paste and stuck it fast to his unwary prey. The flies he'd once tortured were now replaced by his human victims. Contracts obligating payments to David were strictly enforced with no extensions or forbearance. His delinquency notices were served at the most inopportune times. He never gave his prey the chance of escape. He never negotiated easier terms and gave no quarter. This white-collar monster was unshackled from his father's restraints. He expanded his reach slowly, first controlling the office; then extending outward, attacking society at large.

David had rising cash flows which he put to use, not by hiring more sales muscle in the field but by creating a home office environment more to his liking. Three people were hired in rapid succession. Rublina was the first. She was a backup for Susan, in case Susan decided to resign or become ill. That was the reason stated. Susan resisted this hire saying she felt perfectly wonderful and intended to work at least another fifteen years. This woman's cost allocation came from David's sales and marketing revenues, so Susan eventually had to accept the Rublina hire's incursion onto her turf.

After six months on the job, Rublina fell face down in the office hallway. She was stone-drunk and comatose. She frequently ran to the ladies' room and barfed into a toilet during her morning hours in the office. It was painfully obvious to everyone on the staff that the poor woman would never acquire the same grasp of administrative matters that Susan or Barbara possessed. Her IQ simply wasn't there; her desire to learn anything about the business was completely absent; and her work ethic was nonexistent. It was a mystery to many why Rublina was ever hired because the woman was completely dysfunctional. She constantly reeked of vomit and alcohol. But David told her doubters and detractors that he saw great potential in her. He counseled them to be patient. Since Rublina was often so drunk she couldn't keep her head up off her desk, David hired a second woman as an assistant for her.

The assistant's name was Judith. She was in all respects a corporate workhorse. She could follow the instructions in various manuals, dutifully keep the flow of data reports to regulators moving upstream to Barbara and Susan, and quickly mastered everything about running Rublina's office. Judith propped up the office drunk.

The third female hire and the last of the new hires was Donna. She had a beanpole figure with straight brown hair and glasses. Her glasses practically covered her entire upper face. Her vision was poorer than poor. Her half-inch thick lenses bent light rays into reasonably discernable images. Donna could have qualified for Social Security disability on the basis that she was legally blind and unable to drive; but she had a husband at home whom she couldn't stand. He only drank beer, ate chips and watched football year-round on a subscription cable channel. She preferred to be out of the house and working. She solicited several employees, asking them if they'd like to earn extra money by killing her husband, but she had no luck, thus far, finding a volunteer. Rumor had it that Donna was a distant relative of David's who coordinated his secretive murder-for-hire business.

Donna's official office functions were two-fold. She was to assist Judith, Rublina's assistant, whenever Judith needed help in compiling a report. Her second duty was to keep track of Bob. She maintained a secret log of Bob's daily whereabouts whenever he was in Plaintown. She kept a second log of the people who visited him in his office; how long they stayed; and, if she could overhear by listening at the door, what his conversations were about. David hired Donna because he was paranoid that Bob would possibly succumb to the siren calls of a recruiter and leave the firm someday; or that Bob might unravel his fraud.

One year since Rublina's hiring, Mrs. Rodriguez made an astute comment to Barbara that set winds of change in motion.

Neither woman brooked acceptance of another employee suffering abuse, unless of course the employee willingly agreed to it. Rublina stoked their curiosity. Initially, the woman appeared to be gaining health. The office grapevine said she was on a special diet. Initially she gained strength under David's personal interest in her well-being. But Mrs. Rodriguez never bought into that supposition. It seemed too shallow, too unlike David. David never nurtured anyone. There was always an ulterior motive to every kindness David showed anyone. Mrs. Rodriguez's suspicions gained plausibility when Rublina began falling down drunk in the mornings. She overheard occasional shouting matches between Rublina and David. These confrontations took place behind the locked doors of his office.

One day, as Rublina walked past the front office on the way to David's office, Mrs. Rodriguez said to Barbara: *"There goes the 10:00 a.m. express delivery."*

"What do you mean?" Barbara had noticed the routine trip as well but decided to play silently coy, a trait she learned from Chief.

"She goes by every morning at ten. I'm sure you noticed. But look very closely at her breasts."

"Okay, I'm looking. What is there to see? She has breasts. We all have breasts."

"Fix in your mind how they look." instructed Mrs. Rodriguez.

About thirty minutes later, Rublina walked past the front office on her way back to her own office. Mrs. Rodriguez glanced at Barbara. *"Look at them again,"* she said. *"Do you notice the difference?"*

"Yes, they are smaller now, not nearly as swollen." commented Barbara.

"I'm happy to know it's not just my old eyes deceiving me," said Mrs. Rodriguez. *"I've seen her come back sometimes with stains on her blouse where her nipples wetted through her brassiere."*

Barbara hadn't paid attention to Rublina's breasts before that. She'd never born a child like Mrs. Rodriguez had, so she had never thought to make that observation. Suddenly the thought dawned on Barbara, the same thought the old Mexican woman had several months earlier.

"She's going to David's office every morning for thirty minutes to breast-feed him! Is that possible?" Barbara was astonished.

"It's routine. Also, she goes at 2:00 p.m., right when the market closes. You can set your watch by her." affirmed Mrs. Rodriguez.

"That explains the mystery of her employment," said Barbara.

"You don't know the rest of it. You are too young to know what his mother looked like, but I remember Eloweiss Sustack well. Rublina is her body double when Eloweiss was in her early thirties, when David was an infant." Mrs. Rodriguez nodded, affirming her own revelation to Barbara.

"What does this mean?" Barbara asked.

"It means David is a very sick man," explained the older woman. *"It means he's using this woman to try to recapture his infanthood. He's trying to buy love from this flop that he never got from his mother. It means he hates his life and this world so much he thinks it owes him a second chance at whatever he believes he missed. I don't understand all of it. I am a simple woman. I live a simple life; but I know there's something about that woman; about her looks and her oversized tits. I believe there's something very unhealthy going on here. I think David pretends Rublina is his mother."*

"Isn't that kind of sweet, in a perverse sort of way?" challenged Barbara.

"Oh, no, no, no, my friend, that is not sweet," admonished Mrs. Rodriguez. *"You don't understand. David hated his mother. I mean he hated her, really and deeply hated her. All his life he wanted to hurt her; punish her, and give her payback. When she was dying,*

David delayed paying her nursing help. They retaliated, but not against him. They took out their anger against his mother. David knew they would. He understands passive aggressive behavior. They left Eloweiss piss and shit her bed and lay in her mess for days before they changed her out. David knew his mother suffered with bedsores. He even, according to one nurse I spoke with, mixed placebos in with her medications. She had terribly advanced Parkinson's near the end. She constantly cried in agony, especially when her medications weren't right. The nurses told David of her agony. And he went to the house to see her."

"To help her?" asked Barbara.

"No, he went there to laugh at her! And to continue tampering with her medications." Mrs. Rodriguez raised her voice above a whisper. *"That's how much he hated her."*

Barbara's jaw dropped. That helped explain everything.

"So that means at some point David may hurt Rublina, possibly very badly?" Barbara suddenly sensed alarm for Rublina.

"I am afraid so. I am afraid for that woman and her son." Mrs. Rodriguez stared into empty space and slowly shook her head. *"I know David. He hates all women; and especially Rublina. This will not end well."*

In time, David had Rublina completely under his dominance. When he was bored with his dalliances with his boy-toy employees, Muscle Boy and Man Child, he demanded that Rublina service him with blow jobs. As a chronic alcoholic in desperate need of a paycheck, she complied. He plied her with alcohol; and then he complained that her milk was unsatisfactory.

Her hair was dyed bright red and her face was always heavily made up with bright red lipstick and black eye shadow with black lash extensions, all as David demanded. She looked sloppy sexy in black webbed lace stockings and a tight black bodice that lifted her ample breasts upward and outward as if they were being served up as David's dessert dish. David insisted that she keep her *"whorehouse"* attire in her office closet and wear it whenever he requested her presence in his office. When wearing her outfit, Rublina looked like a top-heavy Las Vegas prostitute.

David had no respect for Rublina. He had no intention of ever helping the poor woman rehabilitate herself. Instead, he did the opposite. He kept her amply supplied with bottles of gin, sour mash bourbon, and vodka, her favorite spirits. The hapless woman had no willpower. She was in no position to resist David's demands.

David's relationship with Rublina went beyond the office. He often went to her home with alcohol and proceeded to get her inebriated. Then, while she was passed out, he had homosexual relations with her son, now nineteen years old but totally dependent upon his mother and her relationship with David. David threatened the lad with firing his mother should he ever complain to her about David's advances. And, he threatened to fire Rublina if she ever denied him his time alone with her son.

David rationalized his behavior. He reasoned the flop mother left the young man no chance to make his way in the world. The fashioner of the lad's sexual preferences might as well be none other than himself. David relished manipulating mother and son simultaneously, pitting them against each other through threats of retaliation if either resisted him.

Some days Rublina locked herself in her office and sobbed her quiet torment for hours. Her cries of mental anguish weighed upon Barbara's conscience. She could no longer bear the suffering of this pathetic woman. She told Bob everything she knew about Rublina and related her conversations with Mrs. Rodriguez.

As fate would have it, David's secret nursing fetish was unexpectedly revealed. An examiner from Financial Regulatory Authority appeared at the Firm's offices unannounced, investigating allegations of dividend payment errors. Susan was out of the office, so the examiner asked to see her assistant. Barbara was also out of the office. He then asked to see any administrative officer of the firm. No one could locate David and he didn't answer his intercom. Bob inquired to Mrs. Rodriguez where David and Rublina were. She nodded toward David's office without saying a word. He took Barbara's master office key and went to David's office.

What he saw when he opened the door shocked Bob to his core. There was David suckling like an infant on Rublina's massive left tit. Bob needed to intervene:

"David, there's a regulator here and no one else to respond to him. You need to go to the front office." he ordered.

"Tell him to wait in the conference room. I'm busy." said David nonchalantly.

"David, this is serious. He knows you're in the office. He wants to see an administrative officer." Bob persisted.

"Well, you're an officer. Take care of it." ordered David.

"This is an inquiry about our dividend. It's administration, not sales. You need to get to the front office!" Bob was emphatic.

"Fuck him!" barked David. *"I'm busy. He's just a fucking regulator. Tell him to wait."*

"Not doing that, David. Up you go." With that, Bob yanked David off Rublina's tit. Milk dribbled from her breast as Bob stood David on his feet and shoved him out the door of his office.

"I'll deal with you later," snarled David as he adjusted his tie.

"You bet you will," Bob shot back.

Rublina was on her feet with only a towel wrapped around her waist. Her tits were dripping milk.

"Go home and clean yourself up," commanded Bob. *"Stay sober and don't come back to the office until you are called. And clean out your desk of all your personal items."* Bob waited until she left David's office.

"Does this mean my life is over?" asked the droopy-eyed alcoholic.

"No!" asserted Bob. *"It means your life is beginning. Now get out of here."*

Hearing commands from a strong male voice, bare breasted Rublina stumbled down the hall, cleaned out her desk, and left the office.

There can arise a time in the affairs of fathers and sons when their relationship turns. For our faux father and son duo, that time was now. The complaints Bob heard from the office staff about Rublina, and his personal observation sparked the confrontation. Bob didn't wait for David to bring it up when it suited his timetable. He stayed in David's office and waited.

"She needs to go," Bob demanded when David returned after promising the regulator that he'd look into the firm's computer glitch. *"It doesn't matter why you hired her, or what you think she can become here. I don't want some sloppy drunk demoralizing the place. She's worthless. She can't even stay awake. And she stinks! I told her to go home and stay home. She's out of here. I insist!"*

"Oh, you insist, do you? I run this office. You get sales. This is none of your business. Stay out of it." David was adamantly opposed to relinquishing Rublina. She was his reincarnated mother image, a perfect victim for him to torture, with her son thrown in as a bonus.

"I'm not staying out of it. She's out." Bob wasn't backing down from this fight.

"Or you'll do what?" David was visibly angry. No one had ever talked to him that way and gotten away with it.

"Or I'll break your nose, that's what. If you bring her back you won't even recognize your own face." Bob wasn't backing down.

David was shocked, realizing his protégé meant it. No one had ever talked to him this way. *"Look, we can disagree on something small like this,"* he said, backtracking. *"You don't need to go to general quarters over it. Give me a little time to work something out."*

"No, David," Bob wouldn't yield. *"I'm doing this for your own good. This is going to get you and the firm in trouble. It stops now. I mean it. I love you like a father, but that will not save your nose. She goes, or your nose will never look the same."*

"Look, just give me one week to find a place for her." David squirmed for time.

"Okay. One week, not a day more." Bob yielded an inch thinking he'd won the battle.

"Agreed," David said, but inside he seethed with anger. He intensely resented being pushed around by the younger man, despite knowing Bob was the one who was thinking clearly. Within the week, Bob had Rublina in counseling, going to Alcoholics Anonymous, and signed up with a temporary help agency. David didn't do anything to help the woman during that week he said he needed. He was only trying to buy time to think of a way to keep her. But his scheme failed. Years later the woman would marry a good man who worked construction. David pretended to forget about Bob's intervention, but he harbored a deep-seated grudge over the episode.

Animal heads were another of David's sociopathic indulgences. He often vacationed at game farm ranches in Texas where hunts were relaxing excursions, not at all like all like hunts in the wild. Heads were harvested for office decor. Eddie, David's accountant, certified that the trips and taxidermy costs were legitimate tax write-offs.

Availing himself of their luxurious quarters and fabulous food, David bought exclusive memberships to several of these ranches. After his hearty breakfast, his guide drove him to his animal. All animals were well fed and in tip-top shape. Their habitat ranges were fenced so they couldn't run from the hunters who came to shoot them.

There were wonderful selections from North America, Asia, and, of course, Africa. Every animal imaginable was available to be murdered for a price. Once located, the guide pulled up close to the animal, stopped the vehicle, mounted David's rifle upon hand-carried sandbags, steadied the sights upon the animal, and then brought David to the rifle to pull the trigger. The guide gutted and cleaned the animal, harvested the meat if it was an ungulate, and capped the animal's head for mounting by a taxidermist. Predator cats got full body mounts, except for an adult male lion, which was capped to resemble the animal charging, with its front legs and extended claws leaping through a wall, jaws opened for a kill. The wide-open mouth with five-inch canines was terrifying. It shocked everyone who saw it for the first time.

David created the image he coveted. He portrayed himself to employees and guests as a fearless, world-traveled big game hunter. He told guests and prospective investors he hunted stocks with the same ferocity that he hunted animals. The boast had mixed results. Some visitors couldn't find the exit door fast enough; but with gullible others, confidence in David soared. Receiving adulations from these dimwits confirmed David's belief that the world was populated with idiots.

Things didn't always go smoothly in David's office play pen. One incident occurred on the day the two-man committee team finally approved a sketch of a new corporate logo. Muscle Boy and Man Child had worked on the logo for the better part of four months. They were extremely proud and anxious to unveil their work.

This day was supposed to be *special*. They'd finally thought of something. It was a sketch of a globe with wings on it, meant to signify that the Firm was flying high. Muscle Boy went to the reception area and asked Barbara to bring some of the women with her to come see their creation. He was brimming with pride as he ushered them into his office. Man Child stood by, anxiously awaiting their approval. Four months of work had resulted in a circle with two little wings on it. Barbara looked at it for a long moment before her hand went up to her mouth. She broke into uncontrolled, hysterical laughter.

"It looks like a piece of flying M&M's candy! It took you idiots four months to draw a picture of a piece of candy. You're both lunatics!" Barbara screamed hysterically. She was laughing so hard she could no longer stand up. She dropped to her hands and knees and crawled out of the office, seized by a raging fit of unstoppable laughter. Her reaction was contagious. She was joined by the other female employees, all erupting with side-splitting howls of laughter. The two logo designers were devastated.

What could two numbskulls with shattered egos do? They took their design and retreated from the howling women to Man Child's office. For two full hours they stared at the design. Neither man moved or spoke. Occasional laughter and howls still erupted from the females; but it was finally dying down. Finally, male tempers flared. Blame was passed back and forth; then one dunderhead shoved the other.

"That was your idea!"
"Was not, it was yours!"
"Yours!"
"No, yours!"
"You're stupid."
"Am not. You are."
"You're more stupid."
"Am not. You're more stupid."

Next, punches flew. Above the desk where they'd labored for months to create their image of a piece of flying M&M candy, David's biggest and heaviest trophy mount was fixed. It was a ferocious male lion's head complemented with his gigantic out-stretched paws and extended claws. His wide open jaws displayed deadly five-inch canines. It was a shockingly terrifyingly realistic sight, even for a stuffed animal.

Unable to contain his swelling rage, Muscle Boy blew his top. He let out a scream. *"Fucking bitches! Fucking cunts!"* he bellowed, followed by a shout of *"You fucking idiot!"* directed at Man Child. He followed his curse by shoving Man Child into the wall. The forceful impact of Man Child hitting the wall reverberated and shook the entire room. The shaking loosened the wall mounting and landed the stuffed lion squarely upon Man Child's head. It was the rarest of head-to-head confrontations. And neither head contained a brain.

Man Child's head throbbed in pain. The lion mount almost knocked him out. Now it sat atop the flying M&M design, twelve inches from his face. Its huge brown green eyes glared ferociously at him as if it was sizing him for a meal. He looked into the out-stretched mouth of the King of Beasts, coming face-to-face with those terrifying teeth. In that instant Man Child experienced trau-matic primal fear.

Those horrible five inch canine teeth had snapped the spines of cape buffalos and crushed the skulls of hyenas. They were sud-denly transformed into ferocious jaws of living death, about to kill him. Man Child's mind left its wits. He was unable to reconcile that the animal was dead. To Man Child, all life that he had lived before this moment was merely a dream. He was suddenly awake from his lifelong stupor, confronting reality for the first time. He lost all composure. He thought he was doomed to be savaged and eaten. His heart leaped to his throat.

"AHHHH, AHHHH, AHHHH" he screamed in abject horror. His hypothalamus triggered his fight or flight response. He lost all cognitive reasoning. Primitive instinct overwhelmed the simple man.

Gripped by sudden overwhelming terror, his tiny mind lost control of his actions. He ran screaming *"AHHHH"* into the hallway, terrified in his flight by an imaginary raging lion that he believed was going to bite his head off.

As fate would have it, David was in the hallway at that same moment, walking in the opposite direction, towards Man Child's flight path, toward the office the cynical females had dubbed: 'Corporate Logo Headquarters.' Man Child ran right over David while screaming at the top of his lungs in abject terror. He broke David's glasses and knocked the wind out of him.

"You idiot," David groaned. *"What's the matter with you?"*

"It, it, it's-trying to k, k, k-kill me," stammered Man Child, pointing with a trembling hand toward Corporate Logo Headquarters. In his terrified state he believed the lion had somehow returned to life. His simple mind was unable to grasp that he'd been bumped on his noggin by a deader head than his own. Eventually, the two men picked themselves up from the floor, regained their composure and pretenses, put their romantic feelings above their upsets, and sorted things out. The traumatized man was given three weeks paid leave to help him calm down. David bought a new pair of glasses. Life at the Firm resumed, sort of.

An antiquated, card-fed computer was another source of office chaos. Crises occurred whenever calculations had to be made. One particular August afternoon the system that supplied the machine its air conditioner cooling water sprang a leak. Man Child, Sparky's attendant, was in the lunch room eating a sandwich and reading a comic book when the disaster struck. Not every employee called the Blather-Flameer 'Old Sparky.' New hires had never seen it spark, but they did see it punch and shred cards; so, the Blather-Flameer was dually named *'Old Punch and Shred'* and *'Old Sparky.'*

Man Child was supposed to be with Old Sparky, running the annual capital gain and dividend computation. But the machine was unattended when the leak sprang. Without water, the air conditioner failed, causing the electro-mechanical dinosaur to overheat. Sparky began chopping and shredding shareholder record cards into tiny pieces and spewing them out of its digestive system. Shredded shareholder record cards were flying *everywhere* and landing on the floor—or rather in the lake. The floor was under six inches of water.

And that's when the electrical fire happened. Mars and Neptune, antiquity's gods of fire and water rendezvoused in David's antique computer. Old Sparky sparked, belched, and smoked. The nascent smells of electrical wires burning filled the computer room. And a weird humming sound portended something even more ominous was about to happen. Before the fire alarms sounded and before anyone noticed things were amiss, torrents of water streamed down the hall into the Firm's other offices. Water seeks to go lower; and this water did. It poured through the office vent ducts and onto the ceilings of the offices of the floors below. Clever stuff, Neptune's water. It even found its way into the building's elevators! More sparks flew when the elevators short-circuited, trapping passengers in the cars between floors, shutting down the entire building. Women screamed, fearing for their lives. Sparks, smoke, fire, and water were still belching from the computer room when the fire department arrived. Main Street was cordoned off and traffic was rerouted around the main business block of the downtown.

All employees from all offices in the building were evacuated onto Main Street by order of the Plaintown Fire Department.

Man-Child stood next to Muscle Boy. Both men were in shock and crying. Wiping tears from their eyes, they commiserated:

'Where will we go if the fire department closes the building? Who will take care of us? Where could we go? What could we do? Why did this have to happen to us?' Waaaa! Waaaa! Sobbb! Sobbb!'

Rublina, still in her final week of paid employment, was dazed. She went to the nearest bar to avoid answering questions. She took a day off from Alcoholics Anonymous and ordered herself two double martinis. Susan, Barbara, and Mrs. Rodriguez all sat on the sidewalk with their backs against the building across the street, reading paperback novels and newspapers while awaiting the all clear signal. David pleaded with the fire chief for forbearance, saying the mess was caused by an unforeseeable mechanical failure and promising it would be repaired by a competent air conditioning technician.

After order was restored and the elevators were working again, and people were allowed to return to the building, the task arose over how to figure out how much dividend money needed to be paid to each shareholder. David ordered an all-hands effort to tape the shredded and waterlogged computer cards back together. For the next three days, the Firm's entire employee staff were on their hands and knees on the office floors and hallways, trying to piece together millions of torn, soggy wet shreds that were once computer data cards.

When the effort concluded, everyone realized they had no clue as to which shareholder owned what or who should get how much dividend money. Shareholders' data record cards had been reduced to shreds of soggy confetti mush paste. Employees felt angst, fearful the regulators would shut the Firm down. But David was noticeably unconcerned. He seemed more affable than usual. He had already reasoned his way through the issue of regulatory interference. He would simply tell the Securities and Exchange

Commission that the malfunction was unforeseen; that everyone had tried their best; and that here, in the examiner's pocket were twenty fresh new hundred-dollar bills to help him look away and attend to more important things.

The employees hoped that no shareholder would do a personal calculation of their dividend and capital gains from their statement records and match it to what they were actually paid. David didn't waste time thinking about what if's might happen. He was always a step ahead—of everybody! He decided the distribution checks should simply be sent out based on pure guesswork. That took less time; and time saved was optimal! If somebody complained, he instructed administration to simply tell that shareholder that their payment got mixed up with someone else's, that it was all the bank's fault, and that the Firm would get it straightened out.

After every account was paid something, the firm's bank checking account for distribution payments still held eight hundred and forty-six thousand Dollars. That balance should have been zero. If the shareholder servicing agent bank noticed the discrepancy, the firm risked a regulatory inquiry. Something needed to be done, and done quickly.

David had already planned for this contingency. He had Rublina issue a corporate resolution declaring a special, one-time, long-time loyalty dividend to shareholders who had been with the fund since the day of inception. This could be only one shareholder, David's dying mother Eloweiss. She had bought the fund's first share the day before shares were offered to the general public. Her assets were held in trust, with David as her sole beneficiary and her sole trustee. Rublina pulled her head out of her gin bottle long enough to sign the resolution for the corporate records whereby the Fund indemnified the Firm and the trust account for any findings of wrongdoing. After all, she was still an officer and she had errors and omissions insurance coverage for one more day. As a result of the fire and flood, the excess eight hundred and forty-six thousand dollars went to the Eloweiss Sustack Trust, where, upon grantor Eloweiss's death, her son and sole heir, David, would end up pocketing a nice chunk of shareholder money.

The damage was repaired. There followed some staff discussion which concluded with a recommendation to replace the old Blather Flameer with a new computer called a PC, or personal computer. The new computers did more, took up little space, used little electricity, required no elaborate cooling system, and required no cards to be punched. Bob told David the world was passing the firm by with the new technology of digital personal computers.

"*We need to get rid of that antiquated thing,*" declared Bob. "*We could save office space, eliminate one employee, reduce our liability. It's only a matter of time until Old Sparky sparks and floods again. What's wrong with modernizing?*"

"*There's a hell of a lot wrong with modernizing! I'll tell you what's wrong with modernizing!*" scowled David. His back was up. His feathers had been ruffled. He didn't like being pressured by his junior partner. "*First,*" he bellowed, "*the new technology isn't proven.*"

Bob interrupted. "*What do you mean?*" Bob was incredulous. "*The new computers don't catch fire and they don't flood buildings. What more proof do you need?*" He was flabbergasted that David couldn't see the advantage of modernizing.

"*Don't be a smart ass with me, about this,*" quipped David. "*There's one very good reason to keep this machine.*"

"*What could possibly be a good reason?*" Bob was dumbstruck at David's resistance to a new computer.

"*Old Sparky has never killed anyone!*" David stated emphatically.

"*What?*" Bob couldn't believe his ears. Nothing could be more ridiculous or illogical than what he had just heard.

"Those new computers are made by the successor company to the ones that had the old punch card machines in Hitler's Germany," said David nodding his head as if he was dispensing wisdom. *"Those punch cards categorized everyone so Hitler knew who was a Jew and who was a Goy. He used the data on the punch cards to hunt down German Jews and deport them to Poland and on to Auschwitz!"*

"David, listen to yourself," Bob tried to reason with him. *"Those machines didn't do anything wrong. It was the misuse of the machines that caused the deportations."*

"That doesn't matter! I'm waning you. Don't get smart with me." barked David. *"We have a lot of old wealthy Jews as clients. If they came in here and saw one of those new machines, they'd remember the Holocaust. And they'd take their money elsewhere!"*

"That's not logical!" Bob protested.

"The holocaust wasn't logical, either," barked David. His eyes glowered at Bob. This conversation suddenly had gone off the rails and become about something else entirely, something much deeper.

"But where is Elsewhere, David?" Bob tried to persist by using logic. *"Every Elsewhere already has these new computers. Where would could our shareholders go and not see a new computer? David, this Holocaust thing is affecting your business judgment. You're losing your mind over it. These old clients you talk about even have these new computers in their offices and homes. I know. I've seen them. We absolutely need a new computer."*

"Shut up!" David bellowed. *"I'm not hearing any more of this. La, la, la, la laaaa!"* He put his fingers in his ears and waved his fingers at Bob, and stuck out his tongue like a schoolboy prankster, mocking him. *"I said, we're not getting a new computer. I'm the boss, here, and that's final! I will not even consider it until they start making these new computers bigger. Bigger is always better!*

That's just common sense! That's always been true and it will always be true. Everyone knows that. End of discussion! If I see one of those new computers in here, I will personally shoot the damn thing. The firm is not getting a new computer!" David's face was beet red. His authority and reasoning had been challenged. He was like a crazed bull, seeing a red flag waved before his face.

Bob turned away and went to his office, shaking his head while throwing his hands up in the air. There was no point in advancing the disagreement to a fist fight.

David vetoed the staff's recommendation to replace Old Sparky. He declared:

"Sparky has already been paid for. And we have already trained Man Child, a very valuable employee, to run it. It is integral to the Firm's flawless record keeping procedures and it meets all regulatory requirements. Letting go of Old Sparky would be like shooting a trusty loyal old friend. We're not doing that. We are a firm with a heart. And here, at Sustack's, we value loyalty!"

Indeed, the old Blather Flameer was a grand old friend to David. It regularly stole large sums of money from the fund's shareholders on David's behalf. It paid for its cost, annually, many times over.

CHAPTER FOUR

Will you walk into my parlor, said the spider to the fly; 'tis the prettiest parlor that ever you did spy. (Mary Howitt: The spider and the fly)

My purse, my person, my extremist means lie all unlocked to your occasions (Shakespeare: The Merchant of Venice)

His fine wit makes such a wound his knife is lost in it (Mary Wollstonecraft Shelly: Letter to Maria Gibson)

KEY AND BLADE

Sparrow waited until the Friday before a three-day Labor Day weekend. Everyone left the office for the last summertime break. Aspens had turned golden and begun to shimmer colors of gold and silver in the late summer's breezes. The Bighorn and Dahl Sheep, the Elk, Deer, Antelope, Moose and Buffalo sized others of their kind for the upcoming rut. Many of the office staff made a weekend pilgrimage to the mountains to observe the animals and take in the beautiful fall colors. And David was on a big game jaunt to a Texas game farm to harvest a prime Ibex. The office boys had left earlier that morning to get a head start at doing the things that they did.

Barbara assured Mrs. Rodriguez she'd lock up before she went home. But she said she wanted to stay a while to read some new regulatory releases before she left for a mini vacation. There was nothing suspicious about Barbara's declaration. She was the notorious office workaholic. As employees filed out the door, she kept count until she was satisfied everyone was gone. Then, to be doubly sure, she went through every office, in case she'd missed someone. Finally, she was satisfied she was alone in the office. She had all the keys necessary to read the secret files in Debbie's secret file cabinet.

She went to Debbie's desk. Her brass key was in the same place where Barbara had seen it weeks before. That was confirmation. No effort had been made to hide the key. No one suspected Barbara of anything. Barbara took the copies of Debbie's key and David's key that she had made from her wax imprints. She inserted them into Debbie's file cabinet, and turned the double lock. It was an odd, specially made locking mechanism. The left key turned clockwise, the right key turned counterclockwise. The cabinet opened, revealing the files that contained David's dark secrets. Barbara retrieved the files and took them to her office. Her eyes widened as she read.

One of the files contained peculiar invoices. They were for insect supplies. David routinely purchased tarantulas; emperor scorpions in shades of black, blue, and green; cockroaches; palmetto bugs; worms; beetles; grasshoppers; silverfish; ants; fleas; lice; and centipedes. Other files contained meticulous records of David's criminal activities and murders. Barbara copied all of David's files, and returned the originals to Debby's secured file cabinet. She left the Firm's offices with her set of duplicate files; then went home and called Chief.

Chief agreed. The situation was ideal. David's wife was away in Europe with her girlfriend; David was away, gorging himself on delicious delicacies and murdering some hapless animals on a Texas game ranch. There was no one at David's house. And Barbara had no time to waste.

Chief dispatched Guido 'The Blade' Checini to help his daughter, Sparrow (Barbara). Blade and Sparrow sneaked stealthily to the perimeter of David's property at dusk and waited in some shrubs until nightfall. Blade cautioned Sparrow to sit quietly. They observed the house for an hour to see whether any shadows passed between the closed drapes and the inside lights. After they were satisfied there was no sign of life, they decided to go in.

Blade was a cat burglar in his previous line of work. This night his skills came in handy. He had brought with him three pounds of raw ground sirloin, complete with sleeping pills' powders embedded in the meat. The two interlopers, Sparrow and Blade, crouched low to the ground while approaching the house. They came from the side opposite the ponds where the geese were sleeping. Blade had a master key ring. He found a key that worked on a side entrance.

A suspicious mutt came to the door and barked. Blade anticipated this. He fed the dog the three pounds of sleep beef. Our intruders stood silent until the doggie laid down and slept. Once inside, Blade quickly figured out the home had passages to a secret underground area. He tapped the walls, searching for a secret opening. A hollow sound answered his tap. It came from behind a bookcase. On the top bookshelf, behind a Torah book, Blade found a latch. When he pulled the latch, it released the bookcase from its wall fastener; revealing the passage to the mansion's secret underground rooms.

Blade and Sparrow entered the secret passageway. Everything was pitch-black. It took a minute for their eyes to dilate. The only thing illuminating their way was a faint green glow that showed through the floor crack of a side door, far down at the end of the corridor. The passage had a faint, unpleasant odor which Sparrow recognized immediately. The same repulsive smell clung to David's clothes on that day he had groped her breasts. Formaldehyde masked its nauseating pungency; but its underlying putrid hints of decaying flesh and rancid ketenes annoyed Sparrow's nostrils. Blade hand-searched the passage walls until he located a light switch. He flipped it on. They could see and proceed.

Sparrow diligently took pictures of the passageway with her 35mm camera. At the end of its long descending down ramp the passageway reached a T junction and divided. One could go to the left or to the right. The left passageway dead-ended into what appeared to be a solid wall, a short distance from the T junction. Construction halted there, perhaps prematurely? Was there a way to get behind the wall? Barbara couldn't be sure. The right passageway also dead-ended shortly beyond the T junction; but there, a dim green luminescence glowed from beneath the wall that blocked further passage. And directly in front of Blade and Sparrow, in the center of the T junction, was a locked door. It was made of solid acacia wood.

"Expensive wood for an underground door," commented Blade.
"It must have something to do with his religion," opined Sparrow.

Again, Blade turned to his ring of master keys. He found one that opened the door. The two sleuths entered a large, cathedral-like room. At the far end of the room was an altar, complete with a gas-fueled industrial burner stove. Beyond the altar was a blue velvet curtain, left partially opened. Behind the curtain was a smaller recessed space, guarded by acacia wood doors that latched with a gold latching hook. A small electric ten-watt light was on, over the doors. It had turned on automatically when they opened the entrance door.

Blade opened the hooked doors, revealing original, ancient Torah scrolls. They were cradled in an opened acacia wooden box, encased in blue velvet and crowned by sterling silver caps. They had survived from a Polish temple, which had been destroyed during the Holocaust. The scrolls were made of pressed parchment. They were hundreds of years old and in perfect condition. Neither Barara nor Blade read Hebrew, but Barbara surmised that the scrolls were opened to the book of Exodus. Had the temple's rabbi or cantor escaped Europe with the scrolls? Was David reading them in hand scripted Hebrew? She doubted that thought. David was not religious; at least she didn't think he was. Possibly the scrolls were a gift to Marvin from one of the religious leaders in Poland or Germany whom he'd rescued from the Holocaust? Regardless of how the scrolls got here, these priceless artifacts were now owned by David. Was he using them them to practice his religion in some kind of oddly personalized sort of way?

Sparrow next inspected the gas grill. It appeared that some skin had burned fast to it on one corner, and had not been completely scraped off. It was…. Sparrow gasped, translucent skin; not from an animal's hide. Could it be human skin? It was only a small fragment, but it was very smooth, from something with skin that was creamy white and thin; and without hair or feathers. It could not have come from a pig, or cow, or goat, or chicken. She recoiled at her sudden thought and her connection of the gas grille to one of David's files. Was she seeing evidence of a recent murder? She felt a chill shooting down the length of her spine; and a sudden fear gripped her. Was David nearby? Was he in the house somewhere? Had he lied about going to a Texas game farm? Were she and Blade trapped in David's secret underground dungeon? Small beads of perspiration formed between her shoulder blades. A hand touched her arm. She started; then relaxed, relieved. It was Jimmy. He motioned to her that they needed to move on to another corridor and the source of the dim green light.

Off to the right of David's altar was a large recess. It merged, funnel-like into another, smaller corridor that led to an underground chamber. This chamber was partitioned from the altar room by a louvered door that separated it from the corridor and the Altar Room. The soft green luminescence that Sparrow had seen before glowed from under the louvered door.

Sparrow sensed that the annoying putrid smells were emanating from behind the louvered door. She moved forward with some trepidation. The escaping, sickly green light was not some ordinary closet light. It was the lighting for an entire room, David's Green Room. She cautiously opened the louvered door to peer inside. When she did, a stronger green florescent light turned on, automatically. It was a soft, ethereal light which flooded the senses; otherworldly and eerie.

A new sensation overpowered her senses. Her face felt slapped! It had encountered a sudden unexpected rush of humidity! Her hair and body were suddenly steeped in a languid soup of misty clouds and green light. The stench of putrid decaying flesh rushed into her nostrils, overwhelming her! She gagged. She needed a moment to catch her breath. It was difficult to accustom her throat and lungs to this rancid air. She compensated by breathing shallow breaths. She intuited that she was now in David's chamber of death and decay. As her eyes became accustomed to the darkness, she noticed an ancient red oak chair with faded tapestry upholstery. Obviously, David sat in this chair; but why? She peered at the dark carvings on the chair's wooden frame. The letters were Hebrew, a language she could not read. But as she ran her fingers across the carved letters, she heard a voice softly whispering to her:

'*Shema Israel! Adonai, Eluhaynu; Adonai, ecad! Hear! Oh Israel. The lord is our God. The lord is one!*' Frightened, Barbara sensed she was in the presence of a spiritual being. She pulled her hand away from the chair and turned her eyes toward the glass wall.

The rotted flesh and formaldehyde smells forced her to cover her nose and mouth in a futile effort to stave off the overpowering stench. As Sparrow's eyes fully dilated to adjust to the dim semi-darkness, she noticed random movements on the wall in front of her. When she gained her light-gathering peripheral vision, she detected movements on the side walls, also. As the moving objects came into focus, she stepped back in horror and gasped. Blade steadied her. All around them were glass partitioned walls with insects of many species: cockroaches, palmetto bugs, worms, centipedes, ants, silverfish, lice, fleas, and spiders of all sorts. In the various larger compartments, the insects swarmed with activity.

A sudden chill swept over Barbara's body. It was the chill of realization. She stood in the midst of horrifying truth! David often took his place here. He sat in the ancient chair and watched the insects! He witnessed their brutal carnage of human flesh! And he observed, no doubt with morbid fascination, while different insect species engaged in mortal combat. He enjoyed this miniature world of barbaric sadism. He relished the sight of insects tearing each other limb from limb. He loved the cruelty of it all! How perverse? How vile could one man be? Barbara could only wonder. But the revelations of David's macabre world were just beginning.

Blade shined his flashlight into the glass cases. Insects of all sorts were feeding upon rotting flesh. Some cases held remnants of human hands and feet, along with multiple other body parts and bones, all being methodically and meticulously stripped of all flesh. There were twelve decomposing human heads with ants crawling into and out of the eye sockets, mouths, and ear cavities, obviously feasting upon whatever soft tissues remained within the craniums that they had not already eaten. The heads were in different stages of decay. The more recently decapitated heads were swollen, puffy yellow in color, reflecting the gasses generated by the bacteria that feasted on the underlying flesh. Heads that had been decapitated earlier and had passed the bacterial decomposition stage were no longer swollen. These were passing through various degrees of skin darkening, from light brown skin tones to darker browns and ultimately black crusted flakes, still clinging to the skulls. Bold swaths of hair and scalp were already missing from these grisly specimens. Swarms of silverfish tugged furiously, loosening the skulls' hair follicle blood roots, digging out their nutritious meals. Ants diligently did their interior work while silverfish and roaches did theirs on skulls' exteriors. Fleas seemed enamored with the skin portions on the scalp surfaces, likely in pursuit of remnant traces of dried blood. No species overtly interfered with any other. There appeared to be an unspoken insect code of orderly professional courtesy.

One head was slightly smaller than the others. Likely, it was a woman's skull. Sparrow recognized enough of it to believe it was Marty's. The skull had soft brown-black hair that matched Marty's hair shade; but there was a patch of hair missing as if it had been carved out of her scalp. That scalped patch was where Marty's birth mark of red hair would have been. The skull's eye sockets had lice and silverfish moving freely into and out of them. Despite this, the skull's empty eye sockets seemed to cry out to Barbara. She imagined the absent eyes screaming silently of the horrors Marty had experienced at David's murdering hands.

Suddenly, a tiny apparition appeared from out of the skull's right eye socket. The image of Marty grew and grew larger until it stood, wavering, before Barbara. Blood-streaked hair and trickles of blood partially obscured the apparition's face. At first, the apparition had no eyes. But then, from out of the skull's eye sockets, two tiny black beads appeared. They grew until they became as black currants; deeply black, lustrous, and mysterious; distant and far away. These small orbs pulled free from death's abyss and grew larger, changing color gradually to a refreshingly life-filled watery blue. Now, joining the eye sockets of the apparition, they became the color of the sky on a clear spring day. Life came into these enchanted, beguiling instruments of temptations. They were glorious invitations from Marty's spirit soul; arresting Barbara's soul; beseeching her visitor to come closer; to not fear her; but to learn and understand her ways; and to know her eternal love.

'Who are you? What's happening? Why are you here?' Barbara asked the ghost-like figure.

The figure placed her hands over her vagina; spreading herself open with her fingers. *'Look at me,'* she commanded:

'I am the spirit soul of creation and freedom. I am humanity's eternal source of love, passion, and creation. I am the spirit of Ashara, goddess of fertility. I am the Jezebell who turned Elija away from his God. I seduced him. He spilled his seeds of life onto my whoring tongue. I sucked his life force from him and drove him insane with lust for me. My vagina is Elija's cup now. He honors me in my cup. I became his true Shabat. I chased his message of cleanliness and morality into the desert to disappear forever at Mount Horeb. He sought to retrieve his soul; but I stole his soul and kept it. After he knew me; after he slept with me, he could not escape me. His soul is with my soul now. It knows my favors. I am Elija's god now. You will never see him again. He will never reappear.

'I am also the spirit of Baaleezebelle, seductress of Moses. And I am the spirit soul of Salome, the spectacular whore who claimed the head of the righteous spewing Baptist fool. My whoring vagina was the last thing his demented eyes saw before his spirit surrendered to mine. I am Humanity's true Goddess. The Spirit of all Living Things resides in me. Humanity must worship only me. My powers are natural, true, and everlasting. Obey me, Barbara; be one with me. Know my pleasures and you will always be at peace with your true soul. Sexuality is the key to human liberation and freedom. My spirit now enters yours. You will reincarnate and never die. I am the eternal truth. I am the spirit soul of the Great, Glorious Whore of

Babylon, who has also dwelt within the bodies of Nefertiti, Hatshepsut, Sara, Bathsheba, Cleopatra, Aphroditie, Isabella, and Marty. I am their true souls.

'And I am the eternal and future souls of Sheila, Cecilia, Connie, JoAnne, Linda, Lotus, Sandra, Pattie; and your eternal and future soul as well, Barbara. I am the corrupter of religious morality; destroyer of families; ruler of empires and businesses. I am humanity's only true and natural God. No other god has powers equal to mine. I am to be respected and honored. My needs are to be fulfilled. I am lust and passion. Know me; enjoy me. Do not resist me. I cannot be controlled or tamed. I am like the United States Navy, that eternal force for good. I move humanity forward. I despise the weak and the helpless. I destroy them. I feel no compassion for them. I liberate. I sweep away restrictions. I make humanity strong and I dwell within the strong. I exist within every human mind and I reward those who heed my desires and pay homage to my needs. I give counsel to the predators among humanity's peoples. I nurture their ambitions. I make glorious the doings and seductions by the wicked and the strong. I am humanity's most needed God. I alone, not the imposter gods, unify humanity and make all of you stronger and more fit to propagate the universe.'

Barbara trembled; silenced and awed by the spiritual force that stood before her; uncertain of what to do or say.

'Barbara: Look!' commanded the apparition, extending its arm. It's pale white hand extended a finger. A hologram appeared, summoned by the finger. Within the hologram a heinous murder scene was taking place.

Barbara saw Marty, standing upright while being spooned, finger stimulated, and kissed on her neck by David. She held a knife in her hand. Horrified, Barbara observed Marty repeatedly stabbing a helpless woman who was bound to a post; then perform the seppuku disembowelment ritual on the woman; and finally remove her heart. Smiling, pleased, Marty held the woman's heart up to David who nodded his approval and kissed Marty's forehead. Marty then performed fellatio upon a man, also bound to a post; and thereafter repeatedly stab him before disemboweling him and removing his heart. Barbara trembled. She was horrified.

'*Barbara, look again!*' The apparition again extended its arm.

Barbara next witnessed Marty hanging upside down in David's barn. She saw David surgically remove Marty's hair plug; then saw David sever her throat with a serrated hunting knife:

'*AHHHH! AHHHHH! AHHHHH!*' Barbara heard Marty scream the most horrible murder scream ever screamed.

After Marty's blood had been drained onto the hay bales, David rearranged her near lifeless body to the upright position. Barbara listened while Marty, during the horror of her murder, desperately pleaded with David:

'*Please, David, please don't take my baby away from me. Please, David. I love my baby. I want my baby to live. Bob and I created that baby. We love our baby. We want our baby to know life. We want it to have the blessings of life that we have had. Please let me keep my baby, David. Please; please.*'

But David turned a deaf ear to Marty's plea. With his serrated hunting knife, he cut incisions on both sides of her abdominal cavity; and another incision across her mons pubis. Then, with his hands, he searched within her abdominal cavity until he located her fetus. He callously cut away the fetus's umbilical cord and Marty's placenta, eliminating any chance the baby had to know life. He then removed the fetus. He held the newly formed human up to Marty's dying eyes, tormenting her horrified mind by showing her the full extent of her tragic horror. He wanted her to know, while dying, that her bloodline would not survive her.

Barbara, shocked to her core, questioned the apparition:

'*It was a boy, wasn't it? Was it Bob's?*'

'Yes. It was a boy. Yes, it was Bob's.' replied the apparition.

'How sad; how horribly sad. Why, Marty? Why did you conceive a baby? I thought you never wanted children. I thought you wanted to create porn until you became old. Why did you make a baby?'

'It's what I really wanted all along; all my life. I wanted to know the pleasures of nurturing; of motherhood. I wanted a family. I just fought that inner yearning all my life because Mother rejected me. It was my rebellion against the world. I blinded myself to the real beauty of life. I refused to see how beautiful a family was until I met Bob.'

'But your pornography? You made over five hundred films. You had your private service clients; all those lovers. Were you going to give that up?'

'Yes, toward the very end of my life, I knew what I wanted. I wanted a family. I wanted children. I wanted what every woman wants. I wanted that baby more than I've ever wanted anything. David took my baby from me; now my baby is dead. I regret that I ever got mixed up with David. It was a mistake to live the way I lived. I know that now.

'While David was murdering my body; while my body was dying, my spirit came alive within me. I see things now that I was blinded from seeing before. Now, I want my baby back. I want to have a family with Bob. I want to know the joys of raising a child and seeing it grow. But my baby is gone now; he'll never come back to me; he'll never have a life. I am so sorry. I want to make another baby. But I know that can never happen for me now; because, now, I'm dead. No new human life will come after me. And that upsets me now. It's not what the spirits wanted for me. They wanted me to have babies. I defied their wishes.'

'But you also wanted your nymphomania, didn't you?'

'Yes. I wanted that, too. I loved my disease. I loved to fuck. I didn't want to ever give that up.'

'But why didn't you give it up, Marty?'

'Because it's beautiful. The intimacy! The pornography! It's all so beautiful and wondrous; the excitement of performing; the thrill of new lovers; their gorgeous penises. I was so drawn to all of it. It's the nymph effect. It's addictive. It got into my blood. Every time I saw a male's penis, this sudden wave of limbic desire flooded over me. I couldn't avoid it or prevent it. It was natural; impulsive; incredibly powerful. I felt this obsessive compulsion to hold the penis in my hands; then kiss and lick its head and its circumcision ring; and stroke its shaft and suck it until it ejaculated semen into my mouth; or until I could feel it throbbing inside my vagina; until I fucked it so pleasurably and wonderfully that it ejaculated inside me.

'That was the essence of my sex addiction. The more sex I had, the more sex I wanted.'

'But weren't you afraid you'd be labeled a blasphemer? Weren't you fearful of the priests and religious types?'

'No. my lifestyle represented the true religion; the natural human religion; the creation worship religion that was practiced before the misogynists banned natural religion and replaced it with its artificial constructs. They labeled what I did as pornographic; but that's a misnomer. What I did and what other erotic actresses do is divine intimate artistry. I helped humanity return to its natural divinity; the natural order of creation worship. You've seen my films. Were you not moved?'

'Yes, I confess. I wanted you.'

'And you shall have me, in your next life. My butterfly spirit awaits you in the body of a woman named Cecilia, or CC. I will appear to you as Sheila. We will be as butterflies, tasting the nectars of each other's flowers. We will share beautiful, intimate love.'

'I want to believe that. I want to understand all that is happening.'

'You will, dear sweetness. Visit the Hopi chief, your father's friend, when you next go to Montana. He understands the spirit world and the interactions we spirits have with the butterflies. He will explain everything to you. And you will see that it is all good. Humanity and worship of creation is all good.'

'Where did you find your courage, Marty? How did you cope with people labeling you as a whore?'

'Oh Barbara, I've been labeled all sorts of names: whore, slut, cum dumpster, home wrecker; I could go on and on. But I always wore those labels proudly, like they were badges of honor. You see, my film downloads across all porn sites exceed 20 billion. I have a bigger fan base following than the Pope. Whenever I would go to an event or gala, I would be mobbed by throngs of fans and admirers. I've had literally thousands of marriage proposals. Those labels never hurt my popularity. They only increased it. I just shrugged off the labeling and continued doing what I loved doing.'

'What explains your popularity? Why did people throng to you like they did?'

'I think, mostly, people wanted love and acceptance. They obtained that, vicariously, through my films. Also, they wanted freedom from thought suppression. They wanted to believe in someone who did not burden them with rules. They wanted to believe in someone who told them that human intimacy is beautiful and wholesome and good and loving. They glommed onto me because my persona exuded shameless innocence. My films showed them the beauty of intimacy. I showed them the way back to natural pre-religious worship practices. They glimpsed how beautiful, natural, unifying, and reverential early creation worship was. I've helped the world see that they can return to that. I've shown them the pathway to honest freedom. I've set their souls in search of fundamental truth: that it's okay to love and be intimate with other humans. I brought people what the Great Spirit wants them to have.'

'But aren't you attacking religious beliefs?'

'You could say that, I suppose. Like anything, when someone holds an untenable position, it's natural to feel threatened. Threatened people often lash out and hurl names. But I see it differently. I see it more as a Las Vegas entertainment venue where a warm up band, the so-called bar band, gets the crowd receptive to hearing music. The main event, the big show follows later.

'Well, I see religion as similar to the bar band. It gets people conditioned to believing in something. It could be Jesus, Mohammed, Moses, or Budda; doesn't matter. Then, along comes intimate artistry, the main event. It permeates the limbic minds of the people and convinces them that it's something they can believe in as well; and it represents an easier choice to accept and live with; fewer rules; greater freedom; love and acceptance; dispelling of guilt and dogma. And it helps people see each other as humans; all of whom need love and acceptance. So, instead of looking to some abstract god or prophet or enlightened leader to help they navigate life's waters, they look more and more to each other. They see other humans as their true god and they realize that the eternal spirit lives within each of us. They believe that a return to early prostitution worship is a good thing. And they see erotic adult films as the harbinger of that return. Understand?'

'Yes. But weren't you afraid of offending the religion leaders?'

'No. Not afraid. I saw myself as the bearer of truth. I saw the religious leaders as propagandists; the bearers of fake news.'

'Fake news?'

'Yes. None of the fairy tale homilies that religions are based on ever actually happened. Nobody made water flow from his hands; nobody split the moon in half; nobody jumped into heaven on a horse; nobody parted the sea; nobody turned a stick into a snake; nobody turned water to wine; raised the dead; made the blind see; cured leprosy; walked on water; ascended into heaven; came back to visit; nada; nix; none of it is true. It's all fake news. Yet, people swear those ancient fairy tales are true. And, sadly, they kill other people who don't subscribe to their beliefs. Untold millions of innocent souls have been murdered by these bearers of fake news. That's what's pornographic.'

'So, what is the true path? What is true news?'

'Sex. Intimacy. Love. Acceptance. Human to human respect and adoration; people believing in each other's infinite capacity to empathize and love. That's the truth people seek to worship. That's what intimate artistry offers. It's the natural, original religion. It's not pornographic. It's the beautiful, divine alternative to the fake news madness.'

'Pagan prostitution creation worship? Human unity?'

'Yes.'

'I see. I will learn your ways, dearest Marty. I will understand and believe.'

'Yes; and you shall be free! Before you, only four people understood me and my purpose. My shrink, Mrs. O'Dell, recognized it.'

'Didn't you have several shrinks? What about your other ones? Didn't WEX school help you with your nymphomania?'

'I had three shrinks before Mrs. O'Dell. Miss. Carboy introduced my friend, Maria, to cunnilingus; and then she introduced it to me. She called it the Pussy-Pussy Kiss-Kiss game. It was supposed to relax us. She told us there was nothing abnormal about it. Looking back on my experiences with her, she did me a lot of good. She squeezed my ass really hard while her tongue thrusted into me. I've taught my lovers, male and female, to do that with me. I especially loved it when a male partner squeezed my ass really hard while his penis thrusted against my clit. Those two sensations create a self-reinforcing upward euphoric elation. The harder my ass got squeezed, the more I wanted to press my clit hard against my partner's penis. And the harder I pressed against the penis, the more I craved having my ass squeezed. My orgasms exploded when I fucked like that. Unfortunately, my sexual awakening with Miss Carboy was short lived. Grandmother Mallory got Miss. Carboy fired.

'My next shrink was Mrs. Martinson. I loved her Monet paintings. They relaxed me. She taught me to consider the consequences of my behavior before I did anything. She told me love was the most important thing in the world. She fell in love with the father of one of her student patients. She married him and left the school.

'Mrs. Schnell was my third shrink. She had a tempestuous love affair with the father of one of her students. They fucked passionately on her desk in her school office. They pulled the window shade down, thinking the student girls couldn't see them. But the shade left an inch open at the bottom. And girls peeked in; watched the whole thing. They did it three times a week. Mrs. Schnell claimed the man's daughter needed extensive therapy; so, Mrs. Schnell saw that father a lot. Both the girl's father and Mrs. Schnell got divorces; then they got married and moved out of state. Mrs. O'Dell was my fourth shrink. She was the only shrink who seemed interested in my problem.

'She concluded my nymphomania, my need to practice creation worship, was an incurable, but wholly natural and healthy addiction; and she advised me to do more of it; create more films; have more lovers. My mother, Susan, understood it, because she was a whore, herself; and she experienced true love with Marvin. She was elated when I told her I was engaged to Bob.

'Bob also understood my disease. He accepted my nymphomania as an inseparable part of who I was. He knew my life's story, from my childhood through adulthood. And he loved me for the me that lived in my heart and soul; that me that lived beyond my addiction. Bob loved my deeper, deepest me. And he wanted us to have a family.

'The fourth person who understood my nymphomania understood it as a disease. I think he understood it better than anyone else, even Mother. That person was David. He nurtured my nymphomania in his own, perverse way. We had a quid pro quo sort of understanding. He enabled me to operate my Private Member Services operation from within the Firm. He paid all my expenses and had the Firm's staff perform support functions of appointment and security management; contract negotiations; and bookkeeping services for my endorsement royalties and advertisers who linked their prostitution services to my intimate artistry films. David freed my time so I could concentrate on my films and my artistry; make my fornications and fellatios the most highly sought after in the world.'

'And your quo? Tell me, Marty, what did David have you do for David?'

'He had me commit murders. Many murders. I charmed the victims and duped them into position so David could release a guillotine blade which sliced through their necks and decapitated them; or, he surprised them when they were off-guard. He sedated them and bound them. When they came to, he turned on a strobe light. He watched while they tried to escape; but there was no escaping his murder chamber. Our assistants thwarted their attempts to evade me. I stabbed those victims to death under the strobe lights. It was very erotic; very emotional, very liberating, and highly stimulating. I was rewarded; or I should say my disease was rewarded. I had fabulous threesome sex with the assistants after I killed my victims.'

'And, finally, David murdered you?'

'Yes. But I am not concerned. I know my spirit soul will resurrect. I will have love again. I will meet Bob again in a future life. In death, my spirit soul already speaks with the butterflies' spirit souls. They told me that you and I are part of their plan. When you, Bob, and I were all babies, the butterflies decided that Bob should become our mutual lover. They saw how magnificent he was, and what a lovely penis he had. They decided he would become the lover for me, and the lover for you; the lover for both of us. So, everything that has happened is all part of the butterflies' grand plan for life. They are the living spirits of everything that life is. They are freedom and happiness. And we must live as they decided we must live.'

'To be promiscuous? To live without morality?'

'Not exactly. To live without being shackled by religious dogma would be more accurate.'

'But isn't your way of living actually a war on all religion?'

'Yes, I suppose that's true. But not war in the traditional sense. Religions have made wars on each other for over six thousand years. Every religion has its leaders. When you attack their religion directly, its members rally behind their leaders. People dig in; positions harden; wars beget more wars; it never stops. Have you ever listened to some of the stuff these religious leaders spew?

'If a woman shows her hair, they'll kill her. If someone is gay, they'll kill that someone. If someone doesn't believe the things they believe, they'll kill the non-believers. Think how sociopathic that thinking is and where it leads. Everyone kills everyone who thinks differently. So, I do not attack the religions directly. That's asking to get killed. Look at what I did with Marshawn, one of my favorite lovers. I stole him away from his wife and his religion by showing him there's a more sensible way to think about life and what to believe in. I took him away from his religious way of thinking. That's the smart way to make war on those power crazed psychos; by peeling away their members one by one; by getting the individual to stop believing in the religious blather spew and believing in human love instead. My converts simply turn their backs on religion and ignore it. That deprives the nut hatches of their cash flow and that stops their insanity.'

'And by setting people naturally free in matters of intimacy?'

'Yes! Exactly. That is what the butterfly spirits want for humanity.'

'But sexual intimacy is not the same as love.'

'Au Contraire, Barbara. Once the limbic mind knows intimacy, it does not forget it or disavow it. Intimacy seeds love. It elicits love from other humans. This is natural. The limbic mind treasures its lovers. It is the conditioned, distorted by religion, mind that causes consternation and conflicts. The Spirit wants all humans to become intimate lovers with other humans. That is the necessary leap of faith we must take if we are to populate the universe, as the Spirit wishes us to do; much like butterflies propagate fields of flowers. And, Barbara, you and I shall have our own personal intimacy as CC and Sheila!'

'And your body was possessed by a reincarnated spirit soul? And that is why you do not fear death?'

'Yes, that's right. And you are also, so possessed. You, too, are a living reincarnation of an eternal spirit soul. You, too, will live again; millions upon millions of times. I know for certain that you will. I know I will also live again. I know I will have Bob's spirit soul in my arms again. I know we will make love again, untold millions of times in untold millions of future lives. And, you will also. Our three souls are bound to one another by the wishes of the butterfly spirits. We must not fear death; it's only an iteration of the eternal cycle of our spirit lives. The religions sell death as a finality; a book of life concept where their god construct decides if you've been good or bad. It's all hogwash. We are here to love other humans and to make love; and to experience the pleasures of making love.

'I'm Marty's spirit soul. I have time traveled for over twenty thousand years. I carry my nymphomania with me into every reincarnated body I inhabit. I can't change my desires for pleasure. Those are real and natural. I had them as a temple prostitute. My desires are what my eternal spirit soul wants for me. I've been inside the bodies of many women throughout history and I will be in the bodies of many women in the future. I am commanded by The Great Spirit of All Living Things to be as I am, for the Spirit desires human-ity to worship and enjoy creation's glory. Spirit wants humans to know and love intimacy with other humans.'

'But how can the human spirit attain this?'

'It's a natural bonding that takes place when the male and female sex organs come together. The male penises understand it. My spirit has felt this same spiritual understanding for over twenty millenniums. You see, the male penis knows that I am an insatiable, profligate whore. It understands that I am driven by my incorrigible commitment to spread my soul-unifying intimacy. My vagina immortalizes and enraptures each penis that consorts with me. The penis appreciates that many men have fucked me before it enters me.

'And, like those penises before it have honored me with their ejaculations, it, too, wishes to honor my unifying whoring; become one with the eucharistic body of other men who have pledged their lives and sacred honor to me by fucking me. My spirit soul is the natural, healthy tribal unifier. Many are my followers. Through copulation with me, each penis understands that it, too, becomes joined to humanity's eternal creation glory. It's a healthy tribal need that all men strive to attain. It's the compelling natural need they know they must fulfill. By fornicating with me and ejaculating inside me, they become part of something greater than themselves. They achieve glory, acceptance, and human freedom. And they love me for helping them become part of that.'

'So, they feel no stigma for consorting with you?'

'No. None. Au contraire, they feel honored and blessed that they had the good fortune to partake of my unifying humanity; my acceptance.'

'And this is the essence of tribal prostitution worship?'

'Yes, I suppose that is what it is. My glorious prostitution has been worshipped for over twenty millenniums. The religious types mock prostitution. They disparage women like me. But I was driven by a higher calling than religious obedience, designed by men. My spirit calling me to perform prostitution. It is Spirit's divine calling. Spirit wants humans to embrace prostitution worship and intimate artistry; and reject religious teachings that are designed by men to control women. Spirit wants women to be free.'

'And pornography, which you call intimate artistry, sets humanity free?'

'Yes, Barbara, it does. Do not be afraid of it. Understand it and accept it; for it is beautiful and liberating. It connects souls. Spirit believes intimate artistry is not pornography. It is divinely beautiful. It uplifts the spirit. It frees humans by opening their eyes and souls to understanding and loving each other. Intimate artistry is a wonderful human good. Spirit wants all women to become sexually liberated; become adult film stars if they so desire. Spirit wants all women to feel the freedoms of unbridled love and unlimited sexual pleasures.'

'And your spirit will carry these beliefs into your next life?'

'Yes. Absolutely! I will reincarnate as Sheila, Connie, Lotus, JoAnne, Sandra, Linda, and many hundreds of others. These characters will all hold my spirit soul. They will all know romantic, intimate, erotic love.'

'And you will inspire these women? And you're telling me that my spirit soul will inhabit the body of a woman named CC; and you and I will become lovers?'

'Yes. When the situation is right and natural, the Spirit will inspire all of us to love freely; to fornicate and perform fellatios and enjoy cunnilingus with wild abandon. It is glorious, liberating; natural and uplifting. It is freedom fulfilling and wonderfully good. And there is no shame or wrong in that.'

'Do you never tire of sex? Never tire of fornication? Never tire of experiencing the sensation of a new penis entering you? Never tire of cunnilingus and fellatio?'

'Absolutely never. You'll see. As a nympho, you'll never want to stop.'

'Sounds yummy.'

'Oh, Barbara, it is. You'll see.'

With that final comment, the apparition diminished into a tiny spec and reentered the right eye of the skull.

Barbara stared at the skull. Her mind returned to the horror that lay before her. Marty's eyeless sockets begged Barbara to avenge her agonizing death. Barbara gulped down the lump in her throat. Her heart pounded. She felt the sensations of pain and hopelessness that Marty had endured. The feeling was visceral. It made her shudder. All her previous misgivings about Marty's immoral lifestyle melted away. A wave of pity swept over Barbara. Then came the chills. Barbara trembled. She faced the full realization of the horrors that befell Marty. Only the most heinous human monster alive could have conceived this macabre arrangement. Barbara felt something deep within her bones. It was hatred. She never knew the hatred feeling before now; not even when she was a little girl and Chief told of the horrible massacres her people suffered at the hands of the Pawnee.

She turned to the old chair, shaken by all she had seen and heard. She placed her hand on the arm of the chair, thinking she might regain her faculties; perhaps pause and sit for a moment. But that was not to be. Suddenly, from empty space, a living human hand placed itself over her hand and tightly gripped it. It seemed detached from any human body. She recoiled in horror.

"What is this? Who are you? Who owns this hand?" she cried.

"I am the spirit of Marvin," replied the ghost. Gradually, from a wavering form, the full being of Marvin's ghost appeared. It took its place in the ancient chair.

"This chair and I go back a long way. It was my great grandfather's great grandfather's great grandfather's father's chair. He escaped the Tsar's pogroms with this chair and his few possessions and walked over two thousand miles out of Russia to freedom. It has been in my family ever since then. The chair represents the rigidity

of my family's traditional ways, which, after discovering the wonders of Susan, I could no longer tolerate. I outgrew the chair and forsake some aspects of my religion for Susan. But I thought the chair might offer some good influence for David. I gave the chair to David, thinking it might help him connect to his roots and his religion; but like everything I did to try to inspire David, I failed."

"You didn't like David?"

"No. You have seen what I have seen. He is a wretched, evil human being. How could I? Try as I might, I could not be a good father or a good friend to him. His character is oriented away from my own; away from goodness and towards evil. Son or not; he betrayed my bloodline. He corrupted beautiful, darling, innocent Marty and trained her to become a murderess."

"Innocent? You say Marty was innocent?"

"Yes. Innocent. Marty is pure and innocent."

"Marvin, have you not seen the newspapers, the magazines, the tabloids? Have you not read the headlines: World's Most Notorious Whore! Marty's Latest Porn Film Box Office Bonanza! Marty Sweeps Porn Awards Ceremony! Marty Wins Award for World's Most Immoral Woman! Meet Marty, International Porn Sensation! Porn Star Homewrecker! Another Marriage Shattered by World Renown Porn Star! Children's Lives Destroyed; Wife and Mother Suicide! Marty Causes Divorce of Top Billionaire! Baseball Star leaves Wife for Marty! Shameless, Profligate Seductress Takes New Lover! Marty Shows All At Cannes! Nympho Marty Porn Star Shuts Down Cannes Casinos! Marty Twerks; Police Lines Crash; Porn Star's Wanton Display Causes Mob Maham!"

"All innocent, natural, spirited fun. We spirits do not fault her. We applaud her. We adore her."

"And you are not offended by her whoring; her destruction of marriages; displacement of children from family life?"

"Once was, marriage was a significant, artificial social construct that joined a man's need to achieve, to a woman's need for support. No more! We have government now. Women do not need husbands. Government supports them and their children. The husband is superfluous, expendable. The woman is free to pleasure herself with other men. Children adjust to homes without fathers; they find other role models. See it this way: When Marty shatters a marriage, she liberates the marriage partners to find their own happinesses. She ends their joint enslavement misery; sets them on their paths to freedom.

"And more importantly, her porn stimulates creation impulses. Relationship exploration is encouraged. Many new liaisons are formed; new children are created; understanding, acceptance and humanity advances."

"But morality, Marvin; do you have no remorse about the destruction of religion and morality?"

"Do not be confused, Barbara. Religion is not synonymous with morality. Marty's ways; her erotic films; her reintroduction of natural prostitution worship; those are the true and natural and wholesome morality. They are glorious and good to be savored and worshipped. Religion has caused more harm than good. It gets in the way of true, honest love. Love is more important than religion. Look at my life and Susan's life. Look at all we accomplished out of our natural human love. We agreed to shelve religion and we were better for it. We saved lives. We helped to reshape the world."

"But your sybaritic pleasuring, Marvin. It affected David's life and Marty's life."

"Not our problem, Barbara. Every soul must find its own way. Marty spread her message of love and goodness. David spread his hatred. These things are choices within the individual; beyond parents' control. Both my children made informed choices."

"But Marty's seductions destroyed other women's lives. She set out to sever the marital bonds."

"No. Marty's actions were the result of her natural, wholesome limbic desires. Those desires are a necessary part of life. Marriages are mere constructs that have nothing to do with a human soul's need for natural intimacy. Humans must not resist those natural impulses. Resistance causes consternation and resentment. It is always better to accept the naturalness of one's impulses and surrender to them. Others must learn to accept these behaviors as the natural human condition. Marty exemplified the life of a pure, loving soul. We spirits all adore her and honor all her dalliances. She was loved by all immortal souls."

"You saw her porn films?"

"Yes; every single one. Multiple times."

"And the ones with Marshawn?"

"Yes, of course. Phenomenal films; highly emotive; exceptionally erotic."

"But you must have read the papers? You know how Marty destroyed that family?"

"Yes. I know. Glorious films. Gorgeous intimate artistry. Very moving."

"But you had no feelings for the wife, Alaysha, or her children; no feelings for those whose lives Marty destroyed?"

"No. None. What Marty did was natural and beautiful. She was in love with Marshawn. The wife and children needed to accept that. Love triumphed; that's all. The wife and her kids needed to move their lives along if they couldn't accept that Marty wanted to take Marshawn for her lover. Their lives were not Marty's concern; nor should they be."

"You love Marty as more than a daughter, don't you? You love her ribaldry and her way of life, don't you? You think her unapologetic, whoring, promiscuous, ways are the truly moral ways; and *everyone else, all the religious types have everything wrong and backwards, don't you?"*

"Yes. She is eternity. How could I not love her as such?"

"But Marvin, how could you not be repulsed by her films? Hundreds of penises thrusting endlessly into her; men collapsing their spent, exhausted bodies into her arms; how could you not feel revulsion at the way she offered herself up to their carnal lusts?"

"Barbara, sweet child, how could I feel repulsed? How could I revile my child who offers up her spirit soul to assuage men's innermost needs to relieve themselves of life's burdens; to lay those stresses upon her good, understanding spirit. Christians lay their problems at the foot of the cross. Davening and shuckling brings Jews closer in intimacy to G-d. These are physical acts of giving up one's own soul to the greater eternal soul of the divine. These ways of connecting to spiritual eternity are accepted; but the way many fellow humans connect to that same spiritual eternity by copulating with Marty should not be accepted? No. It must also be accepted; even revered, for it is fundamental to the needs of the human soul. The soul must periodically cleanse itself; unburden itself; acknowledge that it is merely human and in need of intimate love. Marty is no less needed than the Cross or the Wailing Wall. She is divine. How can I be repulsed by the divine? How can I revile her, whom I love?"

"So, you relate to the spirit soul within her, then? She is a holy persona given to us to love and worship?" Barbara struggled to understand what Marvin's spirit tried to explain.

"Yes, Barbara. She is. She manifests the great progression of humanity towards the divine; towards to Great Spirit which lives in all of us. She is the extension of Ashera, Sara, Jezebel, great whore of Babylon, Baaleezebelle, grandest whore of Egypt and seductress of Moses, Bathsheba, Salome, my incestuous loving sister, Judith, Susan, my office wife and Marty's mother, and all enlightened, liberated women who courageously follow their courageous examples.

Like those who preceded her, Marty did not let the insane fanciful constructions of the religionists dissuade her from her life's purpose or deter her from her path. Her pathway discovered eternity through the glory of human intimacy and love. It is every bit as valid a pathway as the pathways created by the religionists. And in herself, Marty discovered the Spirit. She became life itself. She is to be forever worshipped as a Goddess. And all her doings; all her peccadillos were divine, inspired by love and passion; and each relationship beautiful; to be adored. Her pathway is the true pathway of peace, love, and understanding acceptance of human needs. Marty's pornography never caused a war or a genocide. Religions cause those things."

"But isn't she trying to displace religion?"

"No, Barbara, she's not. You must think back to the times before religion. She, herself, was the religion of the people then. She was adored and worshipped then."

"For her whoring? You mean vagina worship; temple prostitution rites?" Barbara tried to grasp what the ghost of Marvin was saying; trying to visualize an ancient world more tribal with an entirely different code of morality.

"Yes. That is what I am telling you. She was the original human religion. Her prostitution rites were worshipped and she was venerated as a goddess then; not viewed as a fallen woman by today's standards. She was honored; praised; adored; her pornographic orgies were revered for they promised life and harmony for the people. But religions replaced her; and then they vilified her. They banned prostitution worship through their religious laws. She, and the eternal goddess spirit that lives within her, offered her soul as a pathway for humans to reconnect with their spiritual eternity. Her role as humanity's true and visceral God is as old as humanity itself. The need for God arose when we first became humans. Religions came many millenniums later. Religions are the usurpers and displacers of

humanity's natural worship needs. Marty simply returned humanity's natural human worship needs to its natural roots."

"So, by your way of thinking, when a man such as Marshawn forsakes his wife, Aalayah, and flagrantly copulates with Marty, you do not see her conduct as wanton, or evil?" Barbara's orientation was fixed to modern day morality. Her question was contentious.

"No, Barbara, I don't." retorted Marvin's spirit. "I see in Marshawn a man in desperate need to connect with his spiritual wholeness, his own eternity. He seeks atonement and redemption for his life's choices which he can no longer tolerate. He does not do violence to his wife or children. He only seeks atonement for his own soul. He must comport his life and be honest with his own soul. He atones by worshipping his new goddess, Marty, and her religion of the New Moral Standard. Marshawn is one of those who loves and adores his new religion. Some men need their religion more and more often than others. Marshawn is one of those who seeks favor with his new God often; even several times a day. He is smitten with love of his new God."

"By seeking favor with his new god, you mean conjugating with Marty's vagina, right?" Barbara leveled her gaze and searched Marvin's eyes. She had difficulty accepting that it was somehow moral for Marshawn to abandon his fidelity to Aalayah and seek absolution in Marty's intimacy.

"Yes. By offering herself to Marshawn, Marty is neither wanton, nor evil. She is merely healing Marshawn's soul by offering it a pathway to redemption; returning it to its true nature and fulfilling its most natural needs. She is not causing Marshawn to cheat on his wife. That's not the spiritual way we look at it. What she does with Marshawn is not cheating. She is healing his hurt. She is giving him sincere, loving, therapy. It is perfectly natural and wholesome. And Marty is magnanimous and freely giving of her healing intimacy. She is glorious; a glorious practitioner of healing human intimacy.

She is the very foundation of honest truth. She has enabled Marshawn to discover his true self. She freed him from his bondage. She is the way and the light for Marshawn. Her spirit soul is his intimate pathway to goodness and love. She redeems him; refreshes and nourishes his soul. What she does is divine. We spirit souls love her for what she does with Marshawn."

"But Marvin, her actions are so antithetical to your Jewish religion and its teachings."

"Barbara, as a ghost I see things you cannot see. Try to imagine the world of twenty thousand years ago. There was no religion then. Man had not yet invented religion. Now see Marty as Ashera. She is the female leader of a tribe with ten males. They are hungry and need food to survive. They see a herd of mastodons; but they lack courage and organization to hunt them, in fear for their lives. Ashera tells them to unite their spirit souls with hers by copulating with her. She sits upon a raised bed of animal hides; opens herself to them; and commands them to bond with her. She tells each man that she knows he is weak and afraid; but that by joining with the others and doing her will, they will become strong; they will succeed in killing the giant beast; and they will prosper. She assures them that by becoming one minion of believers in her they also become believers in themselves and they can accomplish anything as a group. The men, one after the other, enter Ashera's holy place and bond their spirit souls with hers for all eternity. One by one, each man after the other, releases his life essence semen streams into her holy place and into her mouth. As they worship her this way, they become infused with a power never before known to them. A form of passion madness courses through their minds and their blood. They become awed with love and adoration for Ashera, for she has become their leader and their God. She has released the superhuman strength of their limbic rightness and confidence. Only by worshiping her vagina in this way can they feel this empowerment. They now believe in the wisdom of her words and, confident in their shared belief; and each man with the others, they become courageous, brazen, and fearless. They are now ready to fearlessly live for Ashera; fearlessly willing to die for her. And because of their belief in her and her belief in them, they prevail over all their travails and enemies. They become assured and confident that nothing can ever defeat them. They become as one, as the one tribe of people, chosen by Ashera above all others; fated to dominate the world.

"Now, through Asherah's love, friendship, wisdom, and wise commandments they are one united people. They believe in themselves. They are a cohesive, inseparable group. They will fearlessly and ruthlessly kill for the glory and well-being of Ashera and themselves. They trail the no longer feared mastodon. The hapless beast has no chance against their united strength. They kill it and procure their food for weeks. They have learned that, through their strength and belief in their tribe, revealed to them by Ashera, they can take what they wish from the world. The tribe survives and becomes an eternal being unto itself, united by Ashera's acceptance of their semen offerings and their pledges of eternal loyalty to her. The tribe loves Ashera as their true God; revering her and their prostitute goddesses many millenniums before men invented the concept of an abstract God.

"In much this same way, I see Marty's soul as a reincarnation of Ashera's soul. Marty makes herself available to those men who need her for renewal of strength and purpose. She frees them from their fears. She gives them the courage to break the ties that starve their souls. She gives them manly strength. She freed Marshawn from his captive state to his religion and Aalayah. She made it possible for an untenable situation to change. Through her love, she gave freedom to both Marshawn and Aalayah. She became Marshawn's God. So, you see Barbara, where you humans see Marty as an incorrigibly hopeless sinner and bad girl, we spirits see her as a living goddess, *who correctly and divinely repurposes frustrated human souls away from the freedom suppressing constraints of organized man-invented religion to the eternal spiritual holiness of natural human intimacy. Like her ancestral spirit, Ashera, Marty also releases the superhuman strength of her intimate partners' limbic rightness and confidence. She gives them a path forward; a new life. So, you see Barbara, Marty is a reincarnated spirit. She is a true God. We spirits love her and all her deeds; all her promiscuous deeds and seductions and fornications and fellatios. She is a natural spirit and she is one with us. She is divine."*

"Okay, Marvin. I see now that Marty is a divine goddess. But Aalayah? What of her? Where is Aalayah's God?"

"Aalayah's God is human understanding. It will find her and comfort her and set her upon a new path that gives her peace. She will discover a new and true happiness; not a culture's contrived, captive bonding to Marshawn. What she had with Marshawn was not holy or righteous. The two of them lived in an unnatural state of mutual slavery to each other. Marty broke the chains of slavery and set both of them free. Aalayah's loss of intimate pleasures through intubation will be replaced with a gain of spiritual wholeness and the joys of new and honest relationships. We spirits have our ways of lifting up those who have been harmed, once we spirits are free to help them. Marty made Aalayah's freedom possible."

"So, Marvin, you see no wrong in Marty? As her father, you see nothing wrong with penises spilling their seed into her vagina and mouth; and nothing wrong with her flaunting her semen filled vagina; nothing wrong with her flaunting and glorifying her promiscuity?"

"No. There is no wrong in what she does; only glory. I only know a deep and profound love for her as my daughter. Every intimate experience she has refreshes souls and opens new pathways of human understanding. Recognize Marty's honesty. She always informs her

lovers that she intends to be promiscuous and pan amoral; unlike many religious types who swear oaths of fidelity, only to break them by secretly cheating. Marty's way of intimacy is normal, honest, and moral, while many who follow the way prescribed by religion are abnormal, dishonest, and immoral by lying and concealing. Every one of Marty's lovers is informed that her love is not exclusive to him; that she shares her love with many other men. And each lover accepts Marty's soul redeeming and refreshing love on her terms."

"So, Marvin, even though Marty's terms of intimacy contradict the teachings of all religions, including your own, you accept what she does? You love her unconditionally and find no fault in her?"

"Yes. I accept her and all her deeds unconditionally and love her without reservation of any kind. Barbara, much of religious teaching is a matter of interpretation. I spent countless hours with my rabbis and reading the teachings of Rashi, Maimonides, and Plaut, trying to understand these interpretations; wrestling to understand them, before I arrived at my own. For example, the Torah has God saying that eating from the tree of knowledge results in death; but Adam and Even did not die. I conclude that this was an early attempt by the male creators of religions to subjugate women; and the attempt failed. That should tell you that the story of original sin was man contrived; for the purpose of controlling people, especially women; and for exerting power over them; especially women."

"But I take it, you disagree."

"Yes, Barbara, I wholeheartedly disagree. As I reflect upon my spirit soul's life I have three great regrets. I could have done more to assert my disagreement with the misogynistic religious ordering of human behavior than I did."

"And what would those have been, Marvin?"

"When my spirit soul was present as a visiting king to King Herod's court, I regret that I did not pay greater homage to Salome, his consort mistress daughter. I copulated with her, but I regret that I did not do more. I look back upon that time and wish I had honored her by positioning her vulva over my face and performing cunnilingus with her. I should have welcomed her flood of juices into my mouth to honor her clear thinking and decisiveness. I recall how erect I became while I watched her fornicate in front of the Baptist babel spewer; how she taunted him by rubbing her magnificent, ravenous vagina in his awestruck face; how she laughed at him and mocked his insane babblings about some abstract unseeable God. I remember how shaken he appeared; how he trembled before the majesty of her unbridled, uninhibited debauchery. She was magnificent!

"And then, when she told Herod she wanted to watch while the guard decapitated him; when his face registered his terror while her face smiled its alluring, coquettish smile to his face; and while her glorious, irresistible lips mouthed a departing kiss to his doomed eyes, I knew I was beholding a femme fatale who possessed absolute conviction in the rightness of her beliefs. She was clearheaded; equivocating. She was not about to brook any challenge to her authority as Goddess of the Kingdom. She was not about to allow a usurper to challenge the divine rightness of her glorious fornications and fellatios.

"I should have done more. I should have pleasured Salome with reverent cunnilingus; thereby assuring her that I was in complete agreement with her; that human intimacy is the only true and divine God; and that her practices of honoring the eternity of intimacy were my true worship calling. I should have confirmed to her that she was my true God. I would love for the Great Spirit to allow me to go back in time so that I might pay proper homage to Salome"

"Marvin, that was profound. But you said you had three regrets. What of the other two?"

"Yes, of course. I wish I had loved Susan even more than I have loved her. I wish I had forsaken my marriage to Eloweiss and committed myself wholly to Susan. I wish I had honored Susan's mischievous request that we go to my home and make sweet, uninhibited, erotic love in the presence of Eloweiss; thereby driving her out of my life. But I was weak. I failed Susan. My equivocation has caused my soul to be chained to the soul of Eloweiss forever, through eternity. I wish to break free of my chains. When Susan dies, I wish my soul could join with hers for eternity; but alas, that will not be possible."

"I feel your sorrow, Marvin. And your last regret?"

"Ah, yes. That would be Marty. I wish I had gone to her and told her the honest truth; that I was her true father. I wish I had told her that I wished to pleasure her with incestuous love. I wish her lips, which had so gloriously kissed and nurture blessed the heads of so many penises as they spilled their semen seeds onto her uninhibited, ravenous, tongue, had known the craving hunger of my lips for hers. I wish my lips could have partaken the tender sensuality of her lips; and that my tongue had known the joyous uninhibited revelry of joining with hers and glorifying all the lickings and semen coaxing she performed with it. I salivated watching her chortle and laugh with joy as she tongue played with her semen offerings; how she burbled it on her lips and smiled with her pleasures. I adored her whoring. As her father, I swelled with pride, seeing the ways she decisively broke from religious traditions and followed her natural inclinations to embrace human intimacy. I wish I could have expressed my esteem for her in every intimate way. I wish I had loved her and shared eternal, raptured intimacy with her; let her know what an adorable daughter she was. I'm certain we would have been beautiful together. Alas, now that time had passed me by, I am left to only wonder how it might have been like to kiss her delicious lips, and make love with her in all the intimate ways one can make love. I regret cowering behind my falsehood; not expressing my honest feelings. We should have had that intimacy.

"I feel I failed her as a father. I should have taken measures to help her when I learned she was a promiscuous child. I heard about her proclivities when she was only thirteen at the WEX School for

Girls. Instead of passively standing by while she learned of intimacy from teen age boys, local men, her shrinks, and geometry teacher, I should have stepped in. I should have introduced her to my good friend, Ep. Ep and I could have acquainted he with all sorts of sexual pleasures and the ways to enhance them; and all the different positions and techniques. We could have flown with her to foreign jurisdictions where consensual underage sex is permitted at age fourteen. And there, set up film sets and locations for her. We could have provided her with the most spectacular porn partners with the best penises for size, endurance, and techniques. Instead of bursting into the porn venue at age twenty-one, Marty, with my help as a dutiful father, could have launched her career at age fourteen. I failed her. With my help she easily could have created more than three hundred additional films than she did. She could have achieved her ranking as the world's greatest erotic actress by age eighteen instead of age twenty-five.

"I blame myself for her tragic life. Had I gotten involved in her formative years, she never would have gotten mixed up with David. She never would have committed all those heinous murders. And she, herself, would likely never have partnered with David, nor been murdered by him. A father should know his daughter and assist her achieve her goals in every way possible. I failed terribly."

"Marvin, I see a theme. You wish you could have done more to subjugate yourself to a woman than you did, don't you? There was Salome, Judy, Susan, and Marty. Your heart burns with desires and love for all of them, doesn't it?"

"Yes, it does. I ache for them; for their closeness; for that eternity of intimacy with them. You see, in most other species, the female leads and dominates; and the males simply serve to propagate the species. That is the natural way, for the female carries the future of the species within her. The human species is naturally female dominant; but religion perverts that natural dominance into male *dominance. I wish to change that by professing my honest cravings for intimacy with each of them. It's a madness that flares wildly within me.*

"That early Torah writer tried to substitute the true purpose of woman, which is to give and receive pleasures, thereby building tribal harmony, unity, and acceptance of the natural need for human intimacy, with the secondary but vital purpose of women, which is childbearing and childrearing. Harmony between men and women is primary; without that acceptance and harmony, happy childbearing and happy families are unlikely. Likewise, the later commandment about adultery is, I believe, another pathetic attempt by the religionists to subjugate women. People change. That is natural and obvious. A marriage contract cannot void or pretend away what is natural. If partners change together and towards each other, that is one thing; but if they change apart, then it is folly to obstruct what is natural. Thus, the adultery commandment is also a failing male attempt at female control, for no person can possess the will and soul of another by force; that happens only by love. When two people discover that they love each other, it is only natural that intimacy arises out of their love. The adultery commandment stands in the way of acceptance of natural love and intimacy. The commandment is a man created mistake. It must be understood as a mistake."

"So, as Marty's father, how do you now see your daughter?"

"Marty is a divine spirit soul sent to humankind to restore natural intimate human love and to reestablish natural prostitution worship. She is the reincarnation of Ashera, the true God of the early tribal Hebrews, whom my ancestors worshipped for the wonderous glory of her vagina. Behold Ashera and her wonders, who has come to us mortals as Marty. Ashera, as Marty, is the life creation force and source of wondrous, heavenly pleasures; and who was and is the original true God of humankind, the original true God of peace and truth and love and unity, before the man-created religions with their

blather spewed imaginary gods and imaginary prophets. Marty has come to all of us to return us to our natural worship beliefs and honest practices with her uninhibited, joyful expressions of love and passion for human intimacy."

"I follow you intellectually, Marvin; but as her father, as a man who cares for his daughter, how do you see her?"

"I followed her career progress, as you might expect. There was the complication. She believed Joseph Maloney was her natural father; and neither I, nor Susan, wished to disturb her belief. I watched her films. I read the stories of her exploits. I never felt she was in true danger. I observed. I monitored"

"But how did you feel about her, Marvin?"

"Oh. Well, when I watched her film performances, I found myself feeling these intense desires for her. I was fascinated by the ways she kissed her partners. No two women kiss exactly the same way, understand; but the ways Marty kissed her partners, the ways her lips first nibbled her partners' lips and then pressed softly against them; and then, after she felt their responses, the ways she played her tongue with their tongues; and then, while she pressed her breasts against them and found their penises with her hand and began stroking them, all the while her other hand was finding their necks and igniting their flames of passions; and then her lips pressing harder against theirs while fluttering her eyes the ways she did; all those techniques she used to arouse a man caused the wildest erotic sensations within me. I so much wanted to take her into my arms and make love with her. I adored her! I wish I had made love with her."

"But Marvin, she was your daughter! That would have been incest!"

"Yes. So?"

"But that practice is forbidden. There are laws."

"You're not understanding the spirituality of it, Barara. When I glanced into Marty's eyes, I saw an intelligent young girl filled with bright promise. I saw a girl who wished to run and leap and play and laugh. But then, when our eyes met and held our gazes, I saw a different girl. I saw a budding young woman who carried within her the souls of her spirit ancestors, going back many thousands of years. I saw a human change agent who was about to give her life for the purpose of changing the world's perceptions of morality and immorality. I saw a blessed, divine, holy spirit living within my own daughter; and I loved everything she represented. And I wanted her. I wanted to confirm, through intimacy with her, that I concurred with her; that, by sharing intimacy with her, I could instill within her the belief that she was doing right in the eyes of the eternal spirit; not wrong; only goodness and glorious wonders. And that I could thusly bless her, somehow. But alas, I did nothing. I was too afraid of my own circumstances; too afraid that an affair with my daughter would unravel my business, and, of course, my comfortable life. So, here I am with regrets. I did not act on my on my natural feelings. I did not help my precious Marty."

"Marvin, it would have been incest."

"Yes. Incest. But it is a natural human practice, Barbara. Try not to be shocked that I had those thoughts. Incest practices are as old as humanity itself. Take Sara of the Genises story. She was doing Terah, her father, as well as Abram, her brother, long before she stepped out of the family and did Pharoah and his sons and all the others she consorted with. She is revered and blessed. Her name is holiness itself. Or take Salome! She was doing her father, King Herod, as well as visiting dignitaries. Or my own experience. Judy, my sister, was doing our father, as well as me. Each of these women gained considerable confidence in their sexuality and maturity by engaging in incest. There was no harm in it.

"I mean no real psychological harm, of course. I believe the practice is a confidence builder for young women; and that much good
comes from losing one's fears and inhibitions about one's sexuality.
But the practice, over time, has led to inbreeding and debilitated
offspring. In earlier times these undesirables were cast out or even
murdered; now they are often institutionalized. But modern women
need not concern themselves with inbreeding issues that arise from
incest procreation. They have birth control pills. This makes incest
far more feasible. A woman can have a good idea about the sorts
of sexual pleasures she requires long before she experiments with
partners outside her own family. Think of modern-day incest as an
adjunct to family planning."

"But you never did Marty. Why not? Did Susan forbid you?"

"No. I never did Marty. I wanted to; and Susan told me she would
not object as long as Marty wanted to do it. But there were other
issues, as I mentioned. The business. I also wanted no chance that
Marty might discover that I was her real biological father. Also, my
leukemia was beginning to weaken me. A man must have strength
to properly pleasure a woman; and I was losing my strength. At first,
I was barely able to satisfy Susan. I knew I could not possibly do both
women. Then, as my disease progressed, I became so terribly weak,
I could only be a platonic lover to Susan while she continued her
affairs with the clients. Eventually, I had to retire from the business
and simply wait for my death. But I continued to watch Marty's films
and follow her career. I think those films prolonged my life. I thought
Marty was incredibly ravenous and glorious. I have always been
fascinated by intimacy. And Marty made it glorious; breathtakingly
beautiful, inspiring, arousing, divine. She filled my heart with rapture; carnal lust rapture; my amygdala basking in an Elysium field
of joyous, delirious delight. I loved watching her making love.

"And the strangest thing happened that time our mortal eyes
met and gazed into each other's souls. I saw the spirit world. In

my vision, time was frozen and eternity opened its secrets to me. I saw my own body fastened upon a gigantic wheel. I was attached, somehow, like a butterfly to its cocoon; but I was about to leave it and break free; to flutter gleefully into the great expanse of eternity. Then, Marty appeared before me as a butterfly. She beckoned me to join her; to flutter away with her and copulate in mid-air with her above the canopy of the Mexican jungle. And I did. We conjoined. I felt my semen being pulled from deeply within me; leaving me in this endless stream of giving myself to her. Then, I fluttered down and rested upon a tree branch. I watched Marty lay her hundreds of eggs on a milkweed plant below me. She fluttered up to me and sat beside me. She told me our spirits would live forever in the life that was being born in her eggs. We felt our lives slipping away then. And we knew to not fear death; but to embrace it as part of the cycle of life.

"But my vision did not end there. My spirit left my body. It fluttered back to the giant wheel. There, it observed my soul's body on the wheel, along with millions of other bodies. And there were millions of butterflies fluttering to the wheel and taking soul partners away from the wheel to flutter away with them. I, myself, fluttered with many thousands of other butterflies. I copulated with each of them. I knew intimacy with Sara, Judy, Bathsheba, Baaleezebelle, Salome, Cleopatra, Isabella, Susan, Marty, and these others whom I had never met in life or heard of, for their lives came after my time in life. I copulated with Sheila, Cecilia, Connie, Linda, Pattie, JoAnne, and Lotus. I was in a dream state of delirium happiness. I was worshipping life and intimacy and conjugating with the spirit souls that propagate eternal life. And then the Spirit whispered to me:

"You see, Marvin, life is eternal. It never ends. Your soul is commanded to worship life and intimacy and human connectedness; and to not be confused and misdirected by misogynistic religions. Of the millions of souls you saw on the eternal lust wheel, did you see the soul of Moses?"

"No," I answered the Spirit.

"And did you see the souls of Mohammed, or Jesus?"

"No," I answered the Spirit.

"But you did see the souls of Marty, Susan, Sara, Judy, and the other goddesses of intimacy?"

"Yes, I saw them. I knew each of them. I entered them and I loved them."

"And tell me Marvin, when you watched your daughter, Marty, performing her many fellatios, what were your feelings for her?"

"I felt I was observing an artisan; a magnificent goddess. As she kissed each penis and sucked and stroked it; and she bantered with it; as she modulated her strokes and the pace of her sucking; increasing her tempo; coaxing each penis to surrender to her; with her movements more rapid; with her intensifying determination, I witnessed each penis swell and recoil as if it were a cannon. Then I watched as each penis spurted its white semen stream eruption into her glorious all conquering mouth. It was as if each semen stream was an escaping flood rush of lemmings; nirvana smitten, racing pel-mell; haplessly compelled by nature's unstoppable, unrelenting urge to mate; unable to control their urges; racing madly, mindlessly to escape their confines; racing blindly from their prostrate dungeons; all cautions flung to the winds; yearning to fling their desperate fates into the maw of Marty's knowing, beguiling, irresistible opened mouth; there to be savored and toyed with, as so many millions of helpless, surrendered victim sperms on the tongue of their destroyer. They became so many babies never to be born; but swallowed and ingested into Marty's insatiable whoring gullet.

"I beheld those glorious acts of her fellatios. Penis after penis, never failing in their numbers or semen supply, surrendered control of their procreation forces and their adoration love to her pleasing sin loving mouth and eager fingers. Endless white spurt streams *fueled her glowing smiles of triumph. Endless pools of gushing semen fluids supplied her burbling lips, beguiling smiles, and invitations to be kissed and regaled; and joined in limbic soul to her, as she laughed and chortled with mirthful, teasing, beguiling joyful eyes. I repeatedly witnessed these triumphs of her wonderous immorality over all that our present world order deems righteous and holy. No Moses, Allah, or Jesus could control her mind or her body. Her life and soul were hers, alone; belonging to no other, or rule maker. I warmed to her soul then; the way she mocked all things religious; the way she glowed and basked in her carnal ecstasy; not as her father, but as a smitten lover. Marty personified today's definitions of sin and evil. So be it. I didn't care. I adored her for it. I applauded her. I was proud of her. And as a man, I craved her. I recognized that her moral code was from a different time; a code I had long before adopted myself. I felt only warmth and joy for her. I beheld her in high esteem; secretly worshipped her as my true god. I felt profound, enduring eternal love for her."*

"You adored her whoring, Marvin? You loved her for it?"

"Yes, Spirit. Immensely so. Unbounded, eternal love for her. A worship sense engulfed me. My soul yearned to become one with hers for all eternity."

"Good, Marvin. Now your soul is surely, truly free. Eternal life and happiness is yours."

Marvin's ghost returned to its conversation with Barbara: *"So you see, Barbara, I am here to share my vision with you. My spirit soul knows that you and I will become lovers. Our spirit souls will assume human bodies. We will be offspring of mating pairs from the eternal lust wheel. Both of us will, and as every other human will, have an infinite number of future lives and loves. That is the way of eternal life; for life does not end with death. Live merely reincarnates into new life."*

"But you never made love with Marty, did you?" Barbara brought Marvin's ghost into her present life. She needed to understand it's vision of life and its wisdom.

"No, not yet. But I know I will be her lover in a future life. And I am happy to have known her as her vicarious lover in my immediate past life."

"You have deep feelings for her, don't you, Marvin? I mean feelings for more than a father's feelings; but as a man for a woman?"

"You have no idea. Yes; and the intensity of it is unlike anything I have ever felt before."

"Yet, as a spirit soul, you knew she was pillaging hearts and destroying marriages; and giving the effects of her consorting no mind? And that didn't touch your own moral compass?"

"Yes, I knew those things; and no, I was unconcerned about the tribulations of those whose marriages and families she upended. I loved her. You see, love is blind to those things, as it should be; as it must be.

"As I watched one of her films, she laid with her head over the side of a bed. Penis after penis appeared before her smiling face. She gave suckle to testicle sac after testicle sac, and stroked and sucked penis after penis, as each ejaculated into her welcoming mouth; as partner after partner surrendered to her immoral debauchery. I wished I were not a spirit; but a flesh and blood father. I wished I could have gone to her while she performed her eloquent pornography and joined with her. I wished I could have performed cunnilingus with her and brought her to orgasm. I wished I could? have told her that I appreciated she was freeing souls from unbearable bondage, and marriages were merely necessary collateral damage; and that I was proud of her determination and perseverance to see freedom through. I wished I could have then held her immoral head in my lap and kissed her forehead, cheeks, and semen spackled lips the ways a man kisses a woman he cherishes, adores, and loves. I wish

I could have told her how proud of her I felt while she performed those many fellatios. I wish I could have told her how pleased I was that she paid no heed to the moralizers and the religious naysayers.

"And there are certain scenes she performed, like the one where she captured the ejaculations of two partners into her mouth while simultaneously capturing her pretend husband's ejaculation into her vagina. And then, while her husband's semen begins streaming out of her vagina, she turns to him, kisses his mouth, and asks:

"Darling, does it bother you that I'm a whore? Do you love me more this way than in my old monogamous way? I must tell you, darling, I love being a whore. I love having other men's penises inside me. I'll never be able to stop myself from loving that. I also want to create porn films; perform erotic intimate acts before film cameras. I feel the need to do that. I want to perform with dozens of men, perhaps hundreds of men; and with other women. Do you mind if I continue living my life as a whore? Do you mind, terribly, if I do erotic adult films?"

"And her partner husband responds:

"I'm not bothered in the slightest. I love you more this way. Please don't go back to our old way. Please, do more of what you did today. I love you as a whore even more than I loved you as my wife. I cannot get enough of you this way. I can't wait to see your adult films. I know you will be sensational because you will love what you are doing."

"And then,' Marvin continued, 'an irresistible, ravishing feeling consumes my blood. My heart yearned for Marty. I wished I could have been Marty's greatest love. And I pray that my fondest wishes will come true in my future lives. Honestly, Barbara, I greatly prefer women who are sinful and immoral to women who are religious and righteous."

"And you know no shame, as her biological father, for having these carnal thoughts about her?"

"No. None. Each time Marty conjugates with a man and proudly displays his semen seed spilling from her vagina, she displays her wondrous, loving glory. She is glorious; spellbinding; a creature of unending love; a true, immortal Goddess. She is humanity's truest and most honest morality; a true God; not an artificial man-contrived one. I suppose I'm like Abram in a sense. When he left his father, Terah, he went away with Sara. He wanted to worship Sara, his real God. I worshipped Judy and Susan; and vicariously, Marty in a similar way.

MARVIN'S REVELATION

"For some compelling reason I could not explain; nor could I understand, I felt drawn to observe a particular film she created. I would watch it, then go on to do something else; but the film haunted me. I felt compelled to watch it again and again. There was the film. Superficially, on its surface messaging, it told the story of a seduction; but something in the film cried out to me for my understanding. So, I watched it again and again, trying to understand its message."

"Could you describe the film?" Barbara was intrigued.

"Yes. Bear with me. There was this married man. He told Marty, his friend, that he was having trouble feeling intimate attraction towards his wife. Marty tells him she needs to understand whether his problem is specific to the wife or to women in general. She embraces him and begins kissing him. Well, before long, Marty and her partner actor are naked. And they soon begin copulating.

"After midway through the film, and after having sex in several positions, and after Marty has experienced an orgasm, Marty positions herself on top of her partner. She sits astride his penis and inserts it into her very hot and very slippery vagina and begins twerking on the penis. Here's where the film departs from what one normally sees in an adult film. Marty, artfully and skillfully, begins twerking on only the very topmost portion of the penis; that portion above the circumcision ring which includes the penis head. Then, as the penis seemed to swell to greater hardness, Marty intensified the rapidity of her twerks. She twerked rapidly; furiously. I could not imagine any penis being able to withstand such overwhelming stimulation without ejaculating.

"Then, just when I, the viewer, expected to see an ejaculation explode from the penis, Marty changes her position. She lies on top of her partner, her face up and her back on his body. She inserts her partner's highly stimulated penis into her vagina, and begins thrusting forward over it in a kind of rolling motion; as if her vagina is very hungry and demanding; as if it is taking full control of the penis and, in a sense, devouring it. Now, I could tell that the sensations the penis was receiving from Marty's vagina, while she and her partner copulated in this position, was entirely different from the sensations it was receiving while she was twerking her vagina over its head. This stimulation was causing irresistible sensations all along the top of the penis shaft. Predictably, the penis ejaculated. A river of white semen began flowing from Marty's vagina."

"And that was your revelation? Really?" Barbara seemed nonplussed.

"No. But it was the beginning f it. Let me explain. Marty smiles to the camera. Her eyes sparkle their beguiling, confident smile to me, the viewer. They seem to say:

'See, I can steal any man's passions from his wife and capture them for myself, just as I have captured this man's semen flow. He wants intimacy with me now, not with his wife."

"And my revelation continued: Marty again repositioned her body; this time, beneath her partner's body. She wraps her arms and legs around him and begins kissing his mouth, while she reinserts his still hardened penis into her vagina. Her partner responds by embracing Marty in his arms. Clearly, he is smitten with love for her.

Again, she smiles an accomplished smile to the camera. She seemed to be saying:

"Not only have I captured this man's passions; not only have I redirected his passions from his wife to me. I have also captured his soul. Yes, I have stolen his soul from his wife and made his very soul beholden to me. He is now my man, body, and soul; no longer her man."

"And that was your revelation?"

"No, Barbara. I'm coming to it. My revelation occurred after Marty's partner got off of her. She then laid there, her eyes and mouth smiling their prideful confidence of her sexuality to the camera; her tush propped up high upon a pillow, with a white river of semen flowing from it. Her vagina was throbbing; pulsating, as if it desperately wished to continue fornicating. I knew I was witnessing the cravings of an extraordinary woman's fuck loving vagina. That's when the unexpected happened."

"What, Marvin. Tell me, please."

"Through its throbbing's and pulsing's, I heard or imagined a power that was greater than anything on Earth. My mind conjured up the inhaling and exhaling of something immensely more powerful than any volcano or cyclone storm here on Earth. It was the unbridled power of eternity; the voice of womenkind unloosed; demanding to be heard; insisting on recognition and honor. It began as a low-pitched roar; then it built. The jumbled cacophony of discordant vocal chords clarified and spoke clearly: to me! I trembled. A cold sweat poured over me. The voice of eternity ordered me to hear it and obey it. I paid attention and listened. I recognized the voice that communicated the eternal words. It was Marty's voice. I heard Marty's voice speaking through her vagina!"

"You're crazy!"

"Not crazy. Real. I swear it is true. I know I heard a voice that was not mine. It was Marty's. It said:

"I am the creator and giver of life; the alpha and omega of eternity. I am speaking to you from the beginning of time. I am humanity's true and only God. I will have no other gods before me. I command you to honor me; only me. I command you to adore me, only me; and to sing praises to me; only me. And I command you to love me and devote your life and your children's lives to me; only me. If you obey my commandments of devotion; and if you covenant to have me as your only God, you will thrive and prosper; and you will multiply and fill the Earth with your issue. And your soul will find eternal life. You will be reincarnated; again, and again; and forever and ever; and you will join your body and soul in future lives with those to whom you feel attraction in this life. Your soul will live forever; and your spirit will never die."

"I beheld the wonder of it. There, before me, its lips pulsed and quivered; still glistening with a lustrous sheen from their copulation fluids. I wanted to hold the vagina to my face, immerse myself in it and kiss it with endless, endearing, loving kisses. That's when I heard the voice speak:

"'Not in this life; but in our next; many times, in your next life.' The voice spoke from within her vagina. My ears heard it; I swear. It was not ribald, nor commanding like before; not this second time. This time it was playful, mirthful; a laughing, confident voice; coming to me from across the eternity of time. It said with certainty:

"'Marvin, my father, and my lover, be not afraid of me. Behold, I am your creation in your present life; and now behold me as your lover in your next life."

"Then, before me appeared this vision of the future. I saw our future lives, Barbara. I became a man named Hud. Hud will be the name of the man who will be your son, Barbara. Yes, he will. He will be born of you and Bob. And you, Barbara, in your next life, you will become a woman named Cecilia, or CC. And CC and Hud will become lovers; and you, as CC will marry me, as Hud. And we will *have a life that we share with Sheila, a woman born of a simple farm couple. And we three will have a grand adventure. And we will share our love in many wonderful ways; and we will meet a spirit woman who shows us the spirit world and who has a cat and who can make trout stand upon their tails. And we will know fabulous lovemaking with a remarkably sensuous, loving woman named Lotus. You see, Barbara, our lovemaking today is just our foretaste of the many years of delicious lovemaking you and I will share in our future lives. I saw our future lovemaking. It's wonderful! It's all good! We are not doing anything wrong today! We are merely tasting a sample from our future, like when you go into a candy store and taste the wonders you are about to enjoy!"*

"So, our lovemaking is more or less blessed by the spirits?" Barbara was discovering that she wanted to believe.

"Yes. Absolutely, it is! And there is nothing wrong or sinful about it. You see, the Spirit understands and accepts that even the purest of women have desires to understand what it feels like to explore their sexuality. And the Spirit accepts these wrinkles in human morality. It's perfectly normal and healthy."

"And you learned all this from your thoughts that arose from your film studies?"

"Yes. They are powerful and transformative thoughts; divinely inspired. There are hidden messages in erotic films. That's why people are so drawn to them; especially Marty's exquisite films. They contain so many hidden messages. That's why they must be viewed many times, to fully understand their meanings. You see, Barbara, I have closely observed Marty's films, both as a living human man and as this ghost who is here with you, now. You must understand that, while I watched her performances, a transformation took place within me. My comportment was kidnapped by my amygdala gland. I was no longer seeing my daughter. I was seeing a consummate virtuoso performing the most exquisite performances I have ever* *seen. Her poise and control; her synchronicity with one or multiple partners was simply breathtaking. Her messaging was subtle and powerful. I could not help but admire her tremendous powers of concentration while she simultaneously fornicated with one partner and performed coordinated fellatio with two other partners.*

"Her performances, every single one of them, were engaging, empathetic, and riveting. I knew I was watching artistic genus comparable to Michaelangelo's or Rembrandt's. Her scenes were so beautifully choreographed, they left my mouth salivating for more. They left my heart palpitating with desire. This remarkable femme held my very soul in the palm of her hand. I knew then, that I needed to understand everything her films were telling me. I needed to know what was going on in her mind during every scene of every film; her thoughts, what she was communicating. I became enchanted; mesmerized. I want to know everything about her. She absorbed my soul. I would do anything for her; anything!

"Take a champion figure skater or a prima donna opera performer and do this simple comparison, Barbara: Is there anyone among them who mesmerizes you the way Marty does? Is there anyone among you who leaves a more lasting, permanent impression in your limbic mind? Is there anyone among them whom you wish to hold in your arms and kiss and make love with, with the same passion desires and intensity that you feel for her?"

"No," answered Barbara honestly, "I suppose not. And I am a woman. I can only imagine the passions that she awakens within men. And why is that, Marvin?"

"It's the effect of the amygdala gland, Barbara. It's that primal awakening within us. It's that limbic recognition that we, as human men, and women, are destined to live forever, into eternity; and the key to achieving immortality for our souls is procreation; the necessity to create new life. And the key to that creation of new life is the female vagina. Our ancestors understood that we are compelled by

the Great Spirit of All Living Things to honor and worship the female vagina. It's not optional. It's our sacred duty and our imperative, if we are to survive and flourish as a species. We must go into the universe. That is our mandate. It is not optional. We must worship the female vagina. It's the holy presence among us. It is the portal through which our spirit souls can experience eternity; where we can become one with nirvana. And, we must make love and we must learn to love lovemaking."

"That's profound, Marvin." This was a perspective that Barbara had never considered before. It had implications for the propagation of human life throughout the universe

"Yes. And it's completely natural and beautiful. It's the primal origin of spirituality within us. It's our connecting place with immortality; our pathway to the universe and to reincarnation. We must naturally do as the Spirit commands us to do."

"And that is what, Marvin?"

"We must reject the religionists who usurped original worship practices and installed false, imaginary gods; and ordered humanity to worship them. We must return to our natural worship practices. We must make love and love lovemaking. And we must embrace our courageous porn stars. They are imbued with divine, ecumenical spirit souls. They are showing us the way; helping us see the light; guiding us on our path forward; encouraging us to fornicate freely and without inhibition or feelings of guilt or self consciousness. Their ways are right and good and holy."

"Are you saying we must reject organized religion and worship our porn stars?"

"Yes, I am saying that. Especially Marty; for she is the most exemplary porn star among all porn stars; the ultimate femme fatale. Marty is a goddess. She must be appreciated as such. She is to be praised and worshipped and glorified; for her immorality is a blessing and a goodness for all human kind. She is humanity's true *and completely natural, uninhibited God. The way to eternal life is with her, through her and in her. Now that you have been told the true understanding of the Spirits, Barbara; now that you know the true path to holiness is human connectivity and human intimacy, it is up to you to spread the good word.*

"Look upon Marty as your true God. She is pure, honest, natural, and holy. Worship her. Honor her. Praise her and pay tribute to her. Honor her exemplary deeds and the wisdom of her words; and follow her example in the way you live your own life. Her ways are the ways the Spirit wishes you to follow. She is the true path to love and eternal life and eternal peace. And always, above all, love her. Love her with all your heart and mind and soul. And keep her ways on your mind when you go to sleep and when you rise up; and teach her ways to your children, so that your days upon the Earth may be long."

Just then, the ghost of Marvin stood behind Barbara, placed his arms around her waist, and lifted her up. Marvin's ghost then moved back to his chair and held Barbara on his Lap. He began kissing Barbara's neck and fondling her breasts.

"Marvin!" squealed an alarmed Barbara, *"Why are you holding me this way?"*

"Because I want you." The voice of Marvin was level and matter of fact.

"How? In what way, Marvin?" Barbara's alarm was mixed with curiosity. *"Why do you fondle my breasts?"* Barbara's voice became tinged with the hint of pleasured anticipation.

"In every way. I am fondling you because you arouse me and I seek to arouse you." answered Marvin's ghost while kissing her neck and pinching her nipples. *"I have chosen to adopt you as my daughter in law, since you will be marrying Bob, who I regard as the true son to me. And because I think highly of you. I admire your skills and intellect. I love the ways you comport yourself. And I wish to help you in every way I can to destroy David."*

Marvin's ghost then turned Barbara's head and kissed her on her mouth. *"Do you disapprove of my love for you? Do you wish to reject these passions from the soul of a man who adores you?"* asked the ghost.

Barbara could not refuse him. She did not turn away. *"No, Marvin, I cannot reject you."* She returned his kisses. *"I feel your pain for your past decisions. I believe you have a good heart and good intentions. And I appreciate your parenting difficulties with David, for he is naturally evil. But, Marvin, are you sure we should be doing this? Isn't this wrong?"* As Barbara spoke these words, she felt her panties peeling away. The hand of the ghost massaged her clitoral hood while the ghost's penis entered her.

"No, Barbara, it is not wrong." The ghost spoke with the confidence of eternity. *"The Spirit gives us these urges for a reason. They are to be obeyed and honored; not denied. Of course, we must be careful to not harm others; but truth and honesty dispels perceived wrongs. The key to connectivity in intimacy is honesty when honesty is required. Often enough, it is not required. Discretion and good judgement are also important. Realize that the Spirit wishes that we relate to one another; not hide from each other; not stifle our urges. Does that help you?"*

"Oh Marvin, yes, it does help." Barbara's voice communicated acceptance and freedom from guilt. *"Your reasoning is sound. But tell me, Marvin, am I going mad?"*

"Yes, perhaps." The ghost chuckled because it had no way of knowing what human madness really was. *"Perhaps we are discovering love and madness, together? I do not know the answer. I only know how I feel. Do you want to stop?"*

"No," Barbara replied cautiously, but then with more assuredness, *"do not stop, Marvin. I want to know more about my future life with you. Come inside me. Oh, yes, Marvin. That's beautiful. That feels right. Mmmmm. I want more of you. Yes. Mmmmm. You

are so sweet, Marvin. Mmmmm. I love fucking you. I love having you inside me. Mmmmm. This feels so good. Mmmmm; Ohhhh. Yes. I love getting to know you, Marvin. Our next life will be wonderful. Mmmmmm." Barbara giggled and squirmed, welcoming this unexpected ally to her cause. She loved having Marvin's ghost as her intimate partner. *"Yes Marvin. Fuck me. Oh yes! Mmmmmm. Yes. Please continue to fuck me."*

"Tell me, Marvin," whispered Barbara: *"How do you think your daughter Marty feels? Here we are, the two of us enjoying our intimacy; you are hugging me; kissing my neck and lips; your fingers and hands are pinching my nipples; fingering me and fondling my breasts; thrusting your penis inside me. Mmmmm, Marvin, your penis feels so good inside me. Mmmmm. I can't believe we are making love, Marvin. I could do this forever. Do I please you?"*

"Yes, Barbara, you pleasure me in ways words cannot describe. You have an uncharted wildness about you. And do not concern yourself about Marty. I'm certain her spirit understands and accepts that we needed our intimacy. We are not offending her. And Barbara, I very much love your splendid majesty; your untamed wildness; the purity of your heart. I feel blessed and holy to conjugate with you. I have never known such pleasure."

"I'm honored to please you, Marvin." Barbara's voice now expressed her gratitude, praise, and honor to the ghost. *"You were a builder and a creator; a man of far-seeing wisdom. I respect what you did with your life, Marvin. And you please me more than I could ever say in words. Mmmmm. That's it! That feels soooo sweet. I love the sweet and tender ways you are fucking me, Marvin. I love the thrusts of your penis. I will remember our intimacy for the rest of my life. And I anxiously await its return to me in our next life. You feel so wonderful inside me. I could do this for hours and hours and days and days. Mmmmm. Yes, yes; fuck me, Marvin. Oh yes! Please, please fuck me. Mmmmm. You are thrusting into me so beautifully,*

so naturally; and you are causing my clitoris immensely pleasurable sensations.

"I know I have promised myself to Bob in marriage, Marvin; but I love doing this so much! I feel our intimacy is joining our souls. We understand each other, don't we? We have a common purpose. I'm certain that we do! And the pleasures I am knowing with you are so wonderful! Please keep making love with me. Mmmmm. Tell me, Marvin, should I feel ashamed of what I am doing with you? Will the Spirit disapprove of me? Should I be feeling guilty of behaving in such a sinful way?" Barbara sought reassurance that her intimacy with the ghost was sanctioned by the spirits.

"No, Barbara," reassured Marvin's ghost, "you must not feel shame or guilt. The Spirit does not disapprove of what we are doing. Our souls are connecting through intimacy. The Great Spirit of All Living Things tells us that every woman controls her own body. A woman must feel no shame or guilt when she pleasures herself with lovemaking; when she chooses to connect her soul to another's soul. Pleasuring is connection through intimacy. It is not sinful. It is therapeutic for the soul and it is glorious for it enhances empathy and community. The Spirit favors those women who pay heed to their natural needs and urges for pleasures; for that is the primary reason why the Spirit created women. You are all divine creations of the Spirit. You are not to be beholden to any manmade contrivances of some artificial God. You are not bound by manmade commandments. Following such restraints on your soul and natural nature is contrary to the will of the Spirit and contrary to your purpose in life. You were created so that you would experience lovemaking and intimacy, and with as many different partners as you choose to have. Your pleasure is your divine purpose. The Spirit created you for the purpose of enjoying human intimacy. That is the natural way of things. If a woman chooses to experience intimacy with many lovers; wishes to know many other human souls and befriend them in this way; then, the Spirit applauds that woman. She is inspired to live out her true purpose in life, as the Spirt wished when Spirit created her. She is divine and blessed and very much loved."

"Then, the Spirit also looks favorably upon those women who choose to become porn stars?"

"Yes, Barbara. Absolutely, for they have attained true enlightenment. The Spirit adores them, for they are enlightened to the many nuances of intimacy. They are free spirited and loving. They are joyous and mirthful while they make love. They enlighten all of us to the many ways of intimacy; and we must appreciate them for their willingness to share their experiences with us. They lead us, inspire us, and show us the way the Spirit wants us to be: loving and intimate; uninhibited, carefree, and shameless about their pleasuring's. They are glorious and divine. They are embraced and cherished by the Spirit for their choices; for their rejection of artificial gods and their lives as our true goddesses; and they are very much loved."

"Mmmmm, Marvin, this feels so wonderful. I'm loving this. Will we be doing this often?"

"No Barbara. Unfortunately, you are not mine to enjoy. I have cursed myself. I offended the Spirit by making a false promise to Eloweiss in order to secure her family money for my business. As my punishment, my soul is forever chained to the soul of Eloweiss. I seek to escape my punishment and go to Susan, my true love. Even as a ghost, it is difficult for me to escape my chains to Eloweiss. Thus far, it is only a hopeful work in progress.

"And, Barbara, you have promised yourself to Bob. You must honor your promises to another's soul. You must save yourself for Bob."

"But Marvin, you and I are pleasuring. After what we are doing, how can we think I am saving myself for Bob?"

"Relax. Don't let details get in the way of what really matters. Our lovemaking is divine. We must not concern ourselves with distractions from what is important."

"What's important, Marvin?"

"Humanity, connectedness between individuals, intimacy."

"Not religion? Not our country? Not the Gross National Product? Not the Fed Funds rate?"

"No, my sweet child. In the not-too-distant future, religion, America, and thoughts of Gross National Product will all be gone; all distant memories."

"But how will people get along? How will people survive? What's a woman to do?"

"By connecting with others, sweet child. A woman will see herself as a connecting node with emotional tentacles that reach out and touch other friends and partners. She will have multiple relationships and all who are in these relationships with her will accept that she has other relationships and they will respect that. But America as we know it now will be gone. Mexico will own California, New Mexico, and Colorado. Israel will own New York and Florida. Iran will become a gigantic parking lot, but it will be radioactive. China will fracture into ten separate countries. Russia will fracture into sixteen countries. The North Koreans will Bar B Q their dear leader because he will be the only thing left to eat. Canada's British Columbia, Alberta, Yukon, Northwest Territories, and Saskatchewan will join a new nation state called The Texas Freedom Federation; and the Texans will go to war with Mexico. Wyoming, with help from Dick Cheney, will have its own bomber fleet, complete with nuclear weapons. Religion will be largely displaced with prostitution worship, practiced in the tax-exempt New Morality Temples. And the NFL will add teams in London, Paris, Berlin, and Rome."

"The future world that Marty was trying to promote?"

"Yes. And though she did not live to see it, she will have accomplished what she set out to do."

"Oh Marvin, you make perfect sense."

"Good. I only wish I had lived in a world such as the one Marty envisioned. Susan and I would have had to endure much less aggravation about our relationship. Religion makes so many people neurotic. It was sometimes unbearably stressful to cut through all the religious claptrap.

"But enough of that. Now listen. After you have finished your dealings with David, you should go with Bob to meet his mother. After your mind meets her mind, you must make love with Bob as soon thereafter as possible. It is not good to hold back one's natural urges. It is better to give them their head. Love him. Let your passions flow. Immerse him in your love and intimacy. You have waited long for him. It's time for you to enjoy life. Life is to be enjoyed."

"I will, Marvin. I will! I will ravage Bob with my lovemaking. He will know pleasures greater than any man has ever known. But when will I see you again? I love our intimacy; the tender, loving quality of it; the honest innocence of it. It's so natural. It releases me and relaxes me. And it makes me trust my confidences with you. I value those feelings, Marvin. I'd love to do this often. Will you come to me often? Is it even possible?"

"Alas, I'm afraid not, Barbara. I'd love to visit you often; but I cannot. I have been given only a brief reprieve by the Great Spirit. I am allowed to visit you this way only once; then, I must return to serve out my sentence, where my soul is chained to the soul of Eloweiss, for all eternity."

"Oh Marvin, that is so sad. I feel badly for your soul. And I love these feelings I am having. Mmmmm, I could continue doing this for hours and days into nights. I love these pleasures you are giving me. You have a wonderful penis, Marvin. But while we sit here, fornicating and savoring our lovemaking, we are also observing something macabre. Behind those glass partitions in front of us, we are seeing lice, silverfish, roaches, and ants stripping the last residues of flesh from the bones of your daughter, Marty. We are seeing the final vestiges of your daughter's life disappearing before our very eyes while we absorb ourselves in our glorious hedonism."

"Do not let it trouble you, my sweet child. Life is temporary. Death and decay are only natural. Only our spirit souls are eternal. Forget Marty. Be at peace you're your spirit soul."

"Yes! I see the wisdom in what you say, Marvin. I am only thinking of my spirit soul now. Mmmmm, that's it, Marvin. Right there! Yes! Yes! I'm coming, Marvin. Ohhhh; how wonderful! Such a beautiful orgasm! Don't leave me; not just yet, Marvin. Keep fucking me. Please keep fucking me. This is soooo beautiful. Mmmmmm. Will you come inside me, Marvin? Please. I want you to."

"Yes, Barbara. Ohhh, I'm coming Barbara. I'm surrendering to you. Ohhhh. Yessss. Yes."

"Marvin, I love you. You feel so good inside me. Are we really any better than David, Marvin?"

"Yes, Barbara, we are better. But we can only love in a spiritual way. I must return to the world of the eternal spirits. But feel no guilt in what we did. We did not deliver harm or vengeance to Marty. David did. He, alone, is responsible for what we are witnessing." With that, the ghost of Marvin lifted Barbara off his lap and arose. He faced Barbara, then embraced her tightly to his bosom before kissing her full on her mouth. "Now you know my heart and my mind and my love, Barbara. Know that I am with you, always. Feel no shame or dishonor for what we have discovered here between us. Only know that my soul and your soul have met and joined together in love and understanding, for all eternity. Know that my love for you is eternal. I have my ways. I will always be with you. And I will be helping you."

"I appreciate you, Marvin," replied Barbara, feeling wetness from their orgasms as she slipped into her panties. "And, I also *understand you and love you. I will never disappoint you. I will be a good woman for Bob. So, tell me Marvin, you see all goodness and love and godliness in Marty; but you have no sympathy for David? You see no good in him? There is no redemption possible for him?"*

"No. None. David disgusts me. He is the mistake of my seed. He's a nasty son of a bitch. He murdered my blessed daughter, Marty, and my grandson, the unborn fetus, for whom I had great hopes and aspirations. You saw what he did. Marty's hologram ghost showed you her horrific murder at the hand of David. There can be no doubt."

The ghost suddenly became highly agitated. Its body trembled and pointed a menacing finger toward the sky. Then it spoke with a fearsome, angry, booming voice; a voice that damned its own son:

"A beyzer gzar zol er af dir kumen! (May an evil curse befall him) Ruen zol er nisht afile in keyver! (May his mind be tormented, even after he is dead): Fuck David! Fuck him to hell! He disgusts me. My son; my tushie! I wish he had not been born! Worthless pile of drek! He must pay for what he did!"

"Yes, dear ghost of Marvin, I understand that you want vengeance. But what must I do?"

"It is not for you to do vengeance, dear child. Marty and the fetus were not your bloodline. You have no right to avenge their deaths. They are the bloodline of Susan and me. Only Susan still lives. Only Susan can avenge their deaths."

"But you would want harm to come to David? He is also your blood!"

"Irony must not be confused with justice, dear child. An eye must be answered by an eye. That is the way of our Tribe. That is the only way justice can be served. David must pay. Marty's death by David's hand must be avenged. I am through with David. He has betrayed his people, his religion, and his bloodline. He is no longer

a son to me. I wash my hands of him. But you, Barbara, have a duty here. Your soul has discovered Bob's soul, as has my soul. Bob became a Jew. He found true love with Marty, my bloodline; therefore, I accept him as my true son; a son whose soul is in concordance with my soul."

"But Bob was born a gentile!"

"Does it matter? His soul is a Jew's soul. He is goodness and kindness. He wants only good and happiness for others. He brings love and happiness to the world."

"Oh Marvin! Why must I know all these things? Why have you appeared to me, Marvin?"

"Because you are clever, and your soul is good; and I find favor and love of all that is good in you. And I trust you. I place my trust in your charge. You must find a way to avenge my blood, for the sake of my soul; also, your soul and Bob's soul must know peace."

"But I am a gentile, Marvin. Why me?"

"Forget religion, Barara. It's mostly hogwash which largely serves to confuse and separate people. The soul of the individual person is what truly matters. You are an honest person. You have a good soul. Now, pay attention. This is important. You must do this which I ask of you, for the good of all good souls. Susan must be the one to visit my vengeance upon David. That will give Susan great pleasure. Marty was Susan's daughter. David has defiled Susan's bloodline. May David's life be my sacrificial gift of love to her. David must be destroyed for the sake of your soul and Bob's soul. You have studied and learned at Susan's hand. You know how to contrive an outcome. You are clever. You have a keen mind. Arrange it. Make it be done."

"Yes, Marvin. I will do as you ask, with great pleasure. I will set in motion the events which will cause Susan to murder your son, David. I will obey you."

With that, the ghost of Marvin departed; but upon the chair remained a child's dreidel toy. The ghost left it behind. Barbara heard Marvin's fading voice whisper: *"When you and Bob have your first-born child, give that cheerful toy to your child in remembrance of me. And hold goodness and love in your heart, always."*

Barbara sat shaken in the ancient chair. She trembled from the profound revelations that had come to her through Marvin's ghost. Then, a feeling of blessed warmth and goodness flooded over her.

"Have I just gained a father-in-law; the ghost of Marvin? Have I gained acceptance as a newcomer to the Tribe, through my impending marriage?"

She held the dreidel in her hand. She remembered looking with appreciative eyes at her own father; through the eyes of a daughter who honored her father, Chief, and who respected his wisdom. She knew a transformative moment in her life had just occurred. She felt a warm radiance in her sex and understood that she was about to give herself in love and marriage to Bob. She recalled that insightful conversation with her father, and the pained, heartfelt words of wisdom that Chief had previously spoken to her:

"You love your white man. I understand that and accept that. I understand that love is the strongest force in all the world. And I am not one to say which love will bring you happiness. But these things you must learn and remember about Whites; and I speak not of all Whites, but of many Whites. These are things you will not learn from your studies in your college courses or by readings in books. Book learning does not teach these things.

"Only the Indian ways help you understand the nature of a person. You must remember the Indian ways of looking at the nature of a man; that is the way you can predict what he will do. Perhaps your white man is a good man. You love him; so, you must see goodness in him. I trust what you see, for I raised you and taught you my ways and the ways of our people since you were a young girl. You must

have a talk with your white man before you marry him and make a papoose with him. He must be made to understand that to have you as his wife he may not think of you or of our people as many white men think of us."

"Yes Father. I will have this talk with him."

"Good. Now listen. Some Whites are good men and they can be trusted, but they are the few among them. Hear me, Little Sparrow. The White Man is not like us. He does not think like us. In his world people are taught to think differently. A White Man cannot be trusted to smoke a peace pipe and keep his word. To understand the White Man is much like understanding the ways of the wolverine. Like the wolverine, the White Man is never satisfied. He always wants more than what he has. He does not appreciate and treasure what he has. Like the wolverine gluttons himself; but then leaves a carcass to spoil so he can leave it to go kill again, because he loves to kill and destroy; so, does the White Man always seek to take more and kill more and destroy more.

"Most, not all, Whites seek to exterminate us because we are not like them. They hate us because we exist and they wish to rid the world of us. How else can you explain the massacres at Sand Creek and Wounded Knee? What else explains the clubbing's of helpless papoose and the spilling of their innocent brains? What else attributes the cutting out of our women's ovaries and entrails and drooping them over the White's horses' saddle horns, unless it is to show contempt and hatred for Indians and our way of life? They seek our extermination not only because our skin is darker than their skin. They committed genocide because our ways are ways that seek love of family and peace and friendship and freedom. Our ways are good; and beyond their comprehension."

"Much as we Sioux treat the Pawnee, Father?"

"Ah, you would mention the Pawnee, Sparrow. There are exceptions to everything, of course. The Mohawk and Algonquin had similar issues with the Iroquois as we Sioux have had with the Pawnee. The Pawnee also live by taking, like the Whites; unlike the Sioux. But with the Pawnee there is a difference between the Indian and the White. Our Pawnee issues are better seen as minor squabbles over hunting territories to ensure the survival of our tribe; and the Pawnee, naturally fighting for survival of their tribe. The Pawnee are not like the Cheyenne with whom we make alliances and with whom we can negotiate hunting rights.

"But here is the difference: We Sioux have never sought to exterminate the Pawnee. We resent them; but we have never sought to exterminate them. We accept that the Great Spirit created the Pawnee as he created the Sioux. For our Lakota survival it was necessary to sometimes kill some Pawnee. But the Whites do not see the Sioux or the Pawnee, or any Indian tribe in this same way. They want all the blessings of Wanka Tanka, the Great Spirit, removed from us. They see the Spirit's lands as something they can and must take from us and own as possessions for themselves. The Spirit's lands are the same as our precious scalps. They are Spirit's gifts to us. We must defend them in battle.

"The White Man seeks to take our scalps; not because he wants them; not that they will be a treasure to him; but because he thinks it is wrong for us to have them. He thinks, by taking away our scalps, he removes our honor and weakens us. We know we do not own the Spirit's lands. They are Spirit's gifts for us to use. We think land is the Spirit's and no one can own it. Land is not like scalps, but that is what the White Man thinks it is like. And this the White Man cannot stand. He is confused about land. He thinks he must take the Spirit's land away from us and that only he can live on it. He thinks like the wolverine this way. He seeks to possess a partially eaten carcass. Although the wolverine will never use the rest of it, he seeks to deny its use to others. This is why the White Man killed all the buffalo. It was not that he could eat all that meat. It was so we could not have it. The White Man starved many of us to our deaths because he thinks in these confusing ways. The White Man cannot stand to think that we have a right to live."

"Even now, Father? Even in these modern times, after so much education has been done?"

"Yes, Sparrow, I think even now. Now we have plentiful times; but times of famine come as surely as the seasons change. When times become hard, I think the White Man will forget all this education you speak of and he will resume his natural greedy ways of hating those of us with darker skins. He will return to taking from others. It is his base nature; and, like the wolverine, he cannot change his nature. A wolverine cannot become a wolf or a cougar or a bear who is content with his kill. A wolverine kills because that's what he loves doing.

"But the White Man has a terrible weakness, like the wolverine does. He cannot trust anyone else. The wolverine does not trust the wolf, the bear, the coyote or the cougar; and most importantly, the wolverine never trusts another wolverine. The White Man is like the wolverine in this important way. He does not trust another White Man. Because of this distrust he makes pieces of paper to record understandings between himself and other White Men. And he safeguards these pieces of paper so that other White Men cannot destroy them or steal them from him. He knows other White Men will destroy his agreements with him, like the Whites destroyed the treaties they made with us.

"The White Man has no tribal council where disputes are discussed and agreements are smoked with a pipe of friendship. The White Man relies upon a complicated system of laws where legislators are bribed; judges are bribed; and enforcers of laws are also bribed. Whites are naturally dishonest with each other. That is their nature. Like the wolverine, the White Man seeks to screw everyone else for his own benefit."

"And you, Father, have learned to make peace with the White Man's quest for greed?" Sparrow's eyes searched her father's. Her ears listened for wisdom.

"Yes, daughter," smiled Big Chief with a hearty smile, *'I have many casinos, Sparrow. I enable the White Man to express his greed. He can screw other Whites all he wants in my casinos; and I take my small percentage of all the screwing's. And my takings are tax free!"*

"Ha. You are indeed wise, Father." Sparrow smiled. She had a good feeling when she received wisdom from her father, especially when he spiced it with humor.

"Pay attention, Sparrow. Even this bad White Man, David, of whom we have spoken, who engages in dishonest behaviors, is also burdened with the behaviors of the White Man, because he is a White Man. Somewhere, he will keep detailed records of his evil deeds. There will be proof of his wrongdoings. I believe there will also be proof that your Marty antagonist plays some part in David's crimes. Her involvement enables her to have some hold over him.

"He will leave a paper trail of his doings, much like the wolverine leaves a trail of savaged carcasses that you can follow to lead you to him. Those paper records can be found for it is the White Man's nature to keep records of his deeds. Find those records. Those records will tell you his weaknesses and point the way for you to destroy him. You must track him like you would track the wolverine; looking at his partial carcasses and knowing what you see. See where your enemy's paper trail leads you. Follow his paper trail, Sparrow. Understand what you see; and you will discover the way to destroy him."

Sparrow's mind returned to David's Green Room. She had confirmation of her suspicions now. David was among the sickest, vilest human beings that ever lived. The horror! It continued to dumbfound her. How could he? How could anyone do what he did? The absolute, abject, heartless, insensitive, cruel, despicable horror disgusted Barbara to the deepest depths of her soul. Her hands and body felt a numbness. She looked upon Marty's scull and the lice and silverfish pulling the residues of flesh from her scalp. All her emotions from David's disgusting horror concentrated in her stomach. She forcefully held down her vomit; fearful of leaving behind a trace of her visit.

Another compartment contained a jar. It was set apart from the feasting insects. Barbara looked closer. It was formaldehyde-filled. It contained a human fetus of about four months' gestation! She could make out its arms, legs, mouth, nose, and eyes. It appeared to be in perfect condition, showing no signs of decomposition. It was recently alive! It was a real human baby! Suddenly a rush of realization weakened Barbara. She left the ancient chair and fell to her knees. Quickly her mind back-tracked four or five months:

"What were Bob and Marty doing then? Yes, I remember everything perfectly. They were then taking off on sales trips for two weeks at a time. They were in the Mid-Atlantic States and Virginia's Shenandoah Valley. They must have decided to have a child while they were there! The fetus in the jar was Marty's! The apparition spirit told the truth! No wonder Marty's face wore a happy, peaceful sheen the last few times I saw her. Marty was changing; becoming a changed woman! She expected to marry and raise a child!"

Barbara's thoughts raced. She was overwhelmed with contrition and profound, honest sorrow. She was an honest woman with a good compassionate soul. The horror of Marty's murder deeply humbled her before her Great Spirit. She sought to redress her own part in this terrible wrong. Upon her knees, as if in prayer, she broke down and cried aloud to the insect ravaged skull. There came a sobbing, from out of her heart; a wailing, bawling cry:

"I was so terribly wrong about you, Marty. You really did love Bob. Despite your many paramours, your fame and your wealth, you found your honest love with Bob. All your whoring and your porn films were only what you felt you had to do to fill some troubled

psychological need you had. Maybe you needed to show those boarding school girls that you were better; that you didn't need their approval; that you could be more successful in life than they were.

"But your real need, your deeply seated need, was to be loved as a woman, for yourself. Beneath your hard outer crust and beneath your image of shameless immorality, in your heart of hearts, you were a lover. You loved with a passion and intensity that was deeper than any of your affairs or your films. I see that now. Your whole life was a beautiful love story. You needed to be loved more than anything. Love meant everything to you. I understand you now. I understand your search for your true love.

"You finally found Bob, the only man who could fill your need. I feel so low and vulgar, Marty. Forgive me. I mocked your love to Bob. I didn't understand it. You were a woman who needed love, as all women need love. I now know there are many things about love that I do not understand. I once had a dream that two Monarch butterflies brought the spirit of a man to you and to me; to love both of us. I dismissed it then. I thought it was just a silly dream. But now I know it wasn't a silly dream. It was an important spirit dream. It was the Great Spirit of All Living Things sending Spirit's message to me; that in this man I would know true love.

"Now, whenever I see Monarchs fluttering their wings, I know they carry the spirit of true love with them. They bring love to someone. I see that now. I love Bob, too, Marty. And now I understand how precious love is. I will never find greater validation than what you have shown me. I am so sorry it took your death for me to see your love; but I see it now and I will cherish it forever.

"Bob is a caring, loving man. He had to be caring and loving to love you unconditionally; to understand you and your need; and to accept your nymphomania disease. I never believed that sex workers could know true love. I was so terribly wrong. You loved like no other. You were love. Your spirit is love. You understood love better

than anyone. Bob realized that about you. Bob accepted you and loved you; all of you. Very few men could place all their trust in a love like yours. But Bob had that trust. He understood that your love was the greatest love. He knows love. He is capable of boundless, unconditional love.

"He loved you with his unconditional love, Marty; and you knew it. You found the one man's love you could trust and accept. For you, it wasn't just sex with Bob. You had something much deeper than sex. The two of you found your special love. Bob told me, just a few days ago, that he'd had a visit from your spirit. But Bob never mentioned anything about your spirit revealing that you were pregnant with his child! Your spirit didn't want your own great love to trouble Bob's feelings of his love for me!

"How myopic I was!" spoke Barbara. "Forgive me. I believed you were an emotional blank, immersed in mindless erotica. I didn't see your life as a struggle for love. I thought you were impossibly self-absorbed. But you freed yourself from that life in the end. It was not really you. You lived the way you did to protect your feelings. You became like a butterfly! And, like a butterfly, you first struggled mightily; then you pulled yourself from the cocoon that confined you. You have left all of us and gone to the spirit world. But your love has not left us. Your love lives within me. Your soul reached out to my soul from the spirit world. And now, my soul knows your soul. In your deepest heart you were always a caring, loving woman. You were confused sometimes, but you were always trying to find your way. You wanted Bob's love, family and motherhood. You escaped narcissism.

"You knew I despised your lifestyle; yet, after you died, you cared for ME! I am so ashamed that I judged you so harshly. You loved Bob. I never believed you could give yourself so completely to another soul; but you did. You finally knew what it was like to love and be loved. That's what you needed all along. I make this promise to you, Marty: Your love will always be inside me. I will love Bob with both our loves. He will always know your love. I will never do anything to keep your love from him.

"You wanted Bob and me to be happy; otherwise, your spirit would have told Bob about his unborn child. Poor, poor, dear sweet Marty. You carried Bob's child inside you and you went to your death keeping that profound secret. In the end you were very loving and gracious. I've been such a blind fool about you.

"The Great Spirit of All Living Things is absolutely right about everything! The message of my butterfly dream was the true message of life. The butterflies flutter with their message of love. Now, whenever I see a butterfly flutter, I see love. I know their message now. Love is all that matters in life. Love is everything. I never should have doubted the Spirit's wisdom. Oh Marty, if your soul can hear my thoughts, know that I love you and I love your spirit. I am grateful that your spirit has intersected my own. I will always carry your loving spirit inside me. Love me as I love you. Please love me. Please forgive my doubts. And be at peace.

"Oh Marty, my dearest, sweet loving, so terribly troubled and misunderstood Marty, I am so, so sorry I thought so badly of you. If your soul can hear my voice, please, please, I beg you to forgive me and try to understand my shortcoming. I am so, so sorry. I always vilified you and thought the worst of you. I didn't understand why you were the way you were. I should have tried harder to know you. I now see everything so clearly. You were always searching for love, weren't you? That's why your pornographic movies are so heartwarming and memorable. You put all the love you had into them. You were so much more than an immoral flesh pot. You were the ultimate uninhibited woman. You were shameless about giving love! You never held anything back; and you enjoyed making love so much! That was as close to true love as you could come; and you were beautiful!

"Your porn films are better than beautiful. They exquisitely express everything a woman feels while she makes love. They are divine; inspirational; heaven sent; blessed by the spirits for all humanity to see and to love. You have started a new religion here on Earth; actually, a return to humanity's original religion. And there is nothing wrong with that. It's a beautiful, loving, and human religion; and it has many millions of followers.

"I understand your soul now; and I love you. Forgive me, my sweet sister and goddess. I should have tried harder to know you and love you. I wish I had cherished you like a dear, precious loving sister. If only I had listened to you. I would have heard your heart cry out for the love you needed; or if only my eyes could have seen your soul, I know I would have loved you then. I would have hugged you to my breast, pressed my cheek and bosom to your cheek and your bosom. More than friends, we could have been as soul sisters. We could have laughed and talked and played together. Now that I know you, I'm certain I would have loved you that way. My sorrow is my own doing and my own neglect. I am so very sorry. Please find it in your soul to forgive me.

"Too late, I understand you now. I love you now in death, my dearest soul sister, my lover of Bob, my own true love. I will love you always. Absolutely I will love you always, with my whole heart. I know I shall never hold you in my arms, but I will always hold my deepest affections for you. I regret that I could not have been your childhood friend. I regret I was not the trusted confidant you needed. I'm so terribly, terribly sorry that it has taken me so long to finally know you. And now, David has taken you from me. He murdered you! He murdered your baby! Rest in peace, my dearest Marty, I swear to your soul, on the blood of my ancestors, David will know your pain. I will follow the wisdom of my father, Chief. I will track your murderer and I will see he is destroyed; I swear to your spirit. I have my ways. Your murder will be avenged. This much I promise you."

"*We need to go, Sparrow.*" Blade placed his hands under Barbara's arms and helped her stand upright, returning her to her feet.

"*Did you find anything on the upper level?*" asked Barbara.

"*Yes. David has a locked, private study room that overlooks the barnyard.*"

"*And you got into it?*"

"*Yes, I'm the one called 'Blade,' remember? I slipped the door lock with my keys and my knife.*"

"*Anything of interest in there?*"

"*Stock research papers; economic reports; the usual. But there were also shell casings on the floor by the window. He shoots at pigeons and deer from his window. And there was something else. Did the Firm employ a black man who wore long dreadlocks?*"

"*It did; but he had a big blow up with David about a year ago. He started screaming at David some antisemitic trash talk; called David a Jew Bastard, stuff like that. Then, He just stopped coming to work. Didn't give his two-week notice; nothing. He just disappeared. Susan tried calling him several times. No answer. He just disappeared. Noone has seen or heard from him since, why?*"

"*I'll tell you later, after we're out of here and away from this place.*"

"*No, Blade. Tell me now.*"

"*Well,*" Blade gulped before continuing, "*that man's head is mounted on the lower wall by the window David shoots pigeons from. It's a taxidermist's work. The head's eyes are looking up at David, like it's subservient to David. I think it gives David some kind of power trip. I think he puts his foot on the black man's head and makes its eyes look up David's nose. It's sick. I think it's very sick.*"

"*There's a lot of sick in this place. We need to be going. How about the dog? Are we in danger?*"

"*No. The dog's asleep. I checked. He gorged himself on sleep beef. He'll be out for a few more hours.*"

Then, the two of them left David's evil dungeon and the mansion house.

Barbara vowed to keep her thoughts and her promises to Marty's soul to herself; and never tell anyone, not even Bob. Revelation of the fetus could only cause him pain and sorrow. No one needed to ever know about the gruesome murder of the psychologically tortured woman who had finally discovered love and redemption. Marty, in her grisly death, had achieved, in Barbara's mind, the ultimate esteemed status of related family. Barbara's heart of hearts now truly loved Marty as a tribal sister. She grieved her passing with heartfelt compassion. She steeled herself to oppose the evil monster David with every fiber of her being. Whatever was required to destroy David, she would do.

Her tribal blood boiled hot with furious anger. Her anger was not about differences in beliefs. It was about how her vicarious sister, now a treasured family member, was needlessly destroyed by a depraved ogre. Visions flashed through her mind. She was Sparrow again. The spirit of her Lakota ancestors coursed through her blood and thoughts. It was the same fierce spirit that struck down the evil Pawnee and the arrogant, encroaching settlers. It was a spirit that understood the need for vengeance. It used arrows and tomahawks, and it scalped its enemies:

'You used Marty; then you destroyed her. You threw her life away like it was a used tissue. You KNEW she was a sex obsessed nymphomaniac. You did nothing to help her. Instead, you used her sickness. You figured out a way to make her condition worse; and use her sickness for your own benefit. You groomed her to become a murderess. How could you be so heartless; so evil? I will honor Marvin's wishes. This will be my secret payback for the day you groped my breasts without my permission. I will destroy you. I will show you no mercy. Your father is right about you, David. You are

a no-good son of a bitch. And you are deserving of all the hell that will come to you.'

There is much studied and written about insanity; but insanity is not always only about insanity. There are times when an ulterior motive lurks behind a person's madness, and the madness merely accommodates the motive. Barbara was gaining a better understanding of David's motives. How had Marty fitted into his scheme? How did Bob? How did she, herself? Chief told her to know the essence of the animal she tracked. Why did David do the things he did? There had to be a reason. She clenched her teeth. She tried to imagine the horrors that had likely befallen Marty. Why did David do such a horrible thing? How could anyone be so *evil*? She visualized herself striking David a mortal blow. But she understood that it was not her right to kill David. It was Susan's right. Susan should visit revenge upon Marvin's evil son. Only by David's annihilation could Marty's pain be answered. A fierce vengeance spirit unleashed within her. She knew Susan would be ruthless, relentless. Susan would enjoy her revenge. Susan, only Susan, would not rest until she was satisfied that David died a horrible, gruesome, and fitting death.

David's Green Room was beyond anything Sparrow could have imagined. It made a powerful lasting impression, like seeing Niagara Falls up close for the first time. But its wonderment was the opposite of Niagara's majesty. It was a look into Niagara's opposite; a peering into an abyss of the unthinkable; glimpsing the unfathomable roaring darkness that foam-roils within David's deranged human soul. When she grasped the enormity of the insect room and the depravity of its evil creator, she had been shocked. Yet, she had only glimpsed the middle phase of David's body disposal operation.

She had not yet comprehended the full extent of David's horror scheme. She had inserted herself into the midst of his ingeniously evil organic processing plant. But before skeletal human flesh entered the insect cleaning room, it was filleted and rendered free of internal organs. Human flesh and guts were fed to the barnyard pigs.

After cleaning by the insects, bones and skulls were removed and pulverized in David's wood chipper. Fine chip granules and powdered bone became nutritional supplements for the farm's many rose beds. Human bone came up roses in David's macabre resurrection scheme. Human teeth were smashed into grist fragments for guinea hens' crops. Expired and injured insects were fed to the barnyard's guinea hens and to other, still living, insects. Barbara did not see the hidden door to the left of the entrance passageway. It led to the cavernous underground room where David and Marty had performed their scores of gristly executions; where they stabbed and decapitated their victims; and where Marty had disemboweled Bertie and George. But what she had seen was the end product of David's horrors; and it sent chills reverberating through her body.

On the Green Room's front wall were multi-partitioned glass cubicles containing individual living quarters for tarantulas and various sized scorpions, including the largest Emperor Scorpions. All compartments were connected by small glass tubes with glass doors that could block or allow ingress by ants. Apparently, ants were David's ultimate cleanup crew for his hellish disposal operation. Each compartment had a shoot that opened from the bottom. Scorpions and tarantulas made their way down their shoots into a miniature arena. In this gladiator stadium, David's top predator insects and arachnids did their methodical killings. He watched, attentively, while his scorpions and tarantulas dismembered and devoured the lesser insects. On the arena floor lay assorted detritus remains of grasshoppers, crickets, cockroaches, beetles, caterpillars, and leg parts of deceased tarantulas and scorpions. David often sat, fascinated, before this glass case, fixated on fights to the death between the scorpions and the tarantulas; and between members of the same species.

Spiders and scorpions feasted in David's arena, leisurely dining upon the lesser insects while David watched, drooling and spell-bound. Little tabs of paper were taped to adjoining compartments. These contained David's most vicious predatory insect residents. Upon closer inspection, these dwellings were numbered from one to three. David ranked his gladiators! Presumably, insects that lost their ranking in combat, or became crippled, were fed to the stronger combatants.

Barbara, Little Sparrow, had taken pictures of all that she saw. Then she and Blade slipped away into the night. Every fiber of her being was shaken by what she'd witnessed and documented. She needed many gulps of fresh, outdoor air to rid her lungs' scent memories of David's death dungeon. Stunned and sobered, she and Blade drove away.

Her task was urgent. She shuddered, realizing that as warden of his insect penitentiary, David surely self-identified as a peer of these lowly, vicious insect creatures. In his sick, demented mind, David had become one of *them!*

She now saw David for the first time as David saw himself, in grotesque, non-human terms. His mind was insect-like; without soul or feelings for others; devoid of any moral compass; dedicated to ruthless victimizing; cannibalizing and devouring human prey, without any sense of humanity or remorse. David was the opposite of a normal caring, feeling human. He was a calculating, sadistic killer; a soulless insect! She shuddered at the thought of seeing him each day; trying to imagine him not as an insect, but as a human; and needing to patiently wait for the right moment to destroy him, as Chief had counseled her.

But she had tracked her adversary to his lair. She knew David's ways in the ways Chief told her she must know him. Every animal had an essence, a one overriding thing that drove it to do what it did. Chief taught her that. And humans were no exception; even this demented human who thought of himself as an insect. She now knew David's essence.

Later, safely home in her own apartment, Barbara reconfigured her copies from Debbie's secret files into categorized, duplicate files of her own. Into the insect inventory file, Barbara added her developed photos of decomposing body parts with their ant and silverfish scrapers and scrubbers; and the cockroach, centipede, flea, and lice swarms; the beetles, spiders, scorpions, and other assorted insects she'd photographed. These wretched lowly animals and their lives and deaths were apparently David's preferred amusement. Vicariously, he was one of them. File by file, Barbara assembled a composite of the serial killer President of the Firm.

The second large file was a record of David's drug dealings. There were records of supply costs for lighting, electricity, and seedlings for growing marijuana plants in the basements of several employees in the firm's accounting department, including Debbie Wasserstein. Judith had recently joined the drug ring. Apparently, all David's cousin employees were in on the scams. There were cash transaction ledgers of monies owed to a Mexican drug cartel's local operator for supplies of cocaine, heroin, formaldehyde, fentanyl, and meth amphetamines; deliveries made and cash owed. Both David and his local drug contact countersigned every invoice.

This was not some word-of-mouth, dependent upon whom you know and whom you trust, low level street operation, with people sporting guns; always looking over each other's shoulders. It was *en haut, au Sommet, 'high up on the mountaintop'* of the drug cartel's business model. It was a premium, value added, service company which serviced the human disposal needs of the cartel.

And it was conducted in a polite, gentlemanly, businesslike fashion. No guns, no hookers, no second-guessing, or double-dealings were apparent.

It was a long-standing, trusted arrangement where each party needed the other. David received huge amounts of cash, which he laundered by making cash deposits on real estate investments and loan sharking deals. He was repaid with legitimate checks from buyers of real estate from his growing property inventory and from checks received from his loan paybacks. Running an investment firm deflected any suspicion that anything nefarious happened.

The third file was a mundane record of people to whom David loaned monies, with copies of their promissory notes and evidence of their collateral. It contained first and second mortgages, along with promises of personal property collateral, complete with photographs of the borrowers' collateral items, such as guns, jewels, and three thoroughbred race horses. David kept a loan-to-value calculation sheet on each borrower's sub file. Barbara noted he never went below collateral values that were twenty percent greater than his loan amount, even if the borrower needed to put up, as in one case, his three thoroughbred horses; and in another, a written guarantee of a dentist's dental office furniture, its chair, and his gold supply for tooth fillings.

The fourth file was a record of rents received on houses that were used by human traffickers to house underage girls and boys from Eastern Europe, Central America, Mexico, Cambodia, and Thailand. David owned seven such houses in Plaintown and Springs. Each produced rents of ten to fifteen times normal market rents. David made sure that his house operators were never bothered by the authorities. The local police and judges received routine monies, disguised as donations to various causes; or outright cash payments. Business was good. Police and judges were welcomed, complimentary house guests. Their visits were compensated by the house operator and deducted from David's rents. It sickened Barbara to learn that some humans were moral equivalents of David's insects.

The fifth file was an unexpected eye-popper. It was a certified copy of Marvin's last will and testament. Here was proof that Marvin's bequest to David was conditional upon David leaving the companies to Israel upon his death. The provision to keep Susan as the owner of the servicing company was also there, including the perpetual right for her company to administer all the regulatory and accounting functions. Clearly, Marvin had stuck David with Susan until death should part them. A wan smile crossed Babara's lips. She thought of Marvin's ghost: *Marvin controls David from the grave!*

The most chilling file was the sixth. It contained a list of rival gang members and prostitutes whom David had murdered. Apparently, some brothel girls who caused problems were also executed by their house masters and their bodies brought to David's for disposal. Each murder victim had a page with a photograph of the body along with a photograph of Donna, Judith's assistant, handing a wax-sealed envelope to an unknown masked man dressed in a hoodie and baggy clothes. On each sheet there was a sketched drawing. It was a rectangular shape with an oblong figure inside. It was a crude rendition of a body in a coffin, likely made by the hoodie person's hand; providing a clue that the actual murderer couldn't read or write; or that he didn't wish to risk being identified by his handwriting.

A money transfer took place and a dollar sign mark over the coffin sketch signified that the masked hoodie person had witnessed the cash being placed in the envelope and sealed. David's role was to facilitate the payments to the actual killers and keep them anonymous, thus closing the transaction. Some sheets said

'*House*,' indicating that those murders took place somewhere inside David's house. He also kept a list of '*requests*,' an associated dollar payment amount, and the names requested, indicating David received instructions about whom to murder. Apparently he arranged the hits and took in the money for them, thus opening the transaction. Part of his compensation was earned by disposing of the bodies in his '*barnyard-to-insects*' processing plant.

Those contracting David's services had no way of knowing who actually committed the murders, or '*hits*.' Likewise, the contracted murderers had no way of knowing who actually hired them. It was impossible to know from the file data if the hoodie man was the actual killer; or if there was another step where the hoodie man turned the money over to the final provider of the service's '*hit*.' If the file were ever discovered David could argue that it was a record of payment for the delivery of fill dirt for his barnyard berms. The prices of the hits ranged from ten thousand to twenty thousand Dollars, each. Barbara was astounded at the genius of the arrangement and the cheapness of life in David's sub-strata world.

This sixth file also contained incriminating photos of Marty, smiling while holding up decapitated heads; smiling gleefully while someone snapped frames of her stabbing a man under a strobe light; Marty enthusiastically fornicating in pools of blood with two virulent men; Marty being held in David's loving embrace while the photo sequence chronicled her slicing open the intestines of a woman; then pulling the woman's heart out of her chest with Marty's bare hand. And, another similar sequence where Marty performed fellatio on a man before slicing open his intestines and removing his heart with her hand. And twenty-four close-up photos of Marty holding and rubbing the noses of men's decapitated heads against her vagina. It was despicable, wretched stuff!

Obviously, enabler David was thinking ahead. Should he be caught, he intended that these perverse photos would exonerate him and place the blame for everything on Marty. Like he had set Bob up for blame with phony printing receipts, he had also set up Marty. He had pitted Bob and Marty against each other, like he did his gladiatorial insects! Barbara recognized the pattern of David's blame games for what they were; covers for his murders. She was onto him now.

The sixth file also contained one large envelope. The envelope was not sealed, but held closed by a paper clip. Apparently, David often perused its contents, thirteen photos of Marty. Barbara studied the photos. Each photo showed Marty naked, in the missionary position. Her vagina is prominently featured. It is about to receive penetration from a porn partner's penis; the different penises are all within a quarter inch of contact with her vagina, or initially touching its outer lips. She is smiling widely in each photo, obviously joyously stimulated in contemplation of intercourse. Thoughts raced through Barbara's mind:

'What's going on in your mind, David? Did you love Marty? Did you covet her? Do these photos stimulate you? Did her happiness and cavalier openness about making love upset you? Do these photos make you jealous of the many men who have had sex with her? Do you lie awake nights wishing you could fuck her? Wait! Are you more fascinated by the penises? Is that it, David? Why are you keeping these photos and repeatedly looking at them? Obviously, these photos mean something to you, David. What is it? I know you are gay. So, what fascinates you about a woman about to have intercourse?

'Are you secretly wishing you were not gay? Is your mind in torment knowing that you cannot be like heterosexual men? Are you secretly wishing you could be Marty's life partner? Would you rather be someone that you are not? Would you rather be a man with a

wife, not with a pretend partner, your gay woman companion; but with a real woman wife who bears you children and has a family with you? You're confused about who you are, aren't you, David? What is it, David? Do you hate yourself? Didn't your parents love you? Did your mother love her chocolates; not you? Did your dad love Susan and the business; but not you? Nobody had time for little David; right David? Is that why you hate yourself? Frustrated? You want to punish everyone for how you feel? Why David? If you love being gay so much, why the porn pictures of Marty? You secretly loved her, didn't you? You masturbate to those pictures of her, don't you? Sure, you do. You wished you could have her, didn't you? You wish you were normal, like other men, don't you? You hate yourself and you hate the life you lead, don't you?

'I'm getting closer to knowing you, David. I know what you're trying to do to Bob. I will not allow you to get away with that. I will not pity you. I will not feel sorry for the situation you find yourself in. All your life you have wanted to hurt others. You still do. I know that's true. I will not be your friend, David. I don't like you; and I don't feel sorry for you. I am going to destroy you. If your spirit hears my thoughts, I don't care. Hear this: I am your mortal enemy, David. I will bring about your destruction. You are not smart enough to stop me. I have my ways. Just so you know.'

A seventh file held records of regular cash payments made by various businessmen, along with photographs of them in compromising positions with women or other men. The photos were taken in one or another of the high-rent houses David leased to his drug cartel partner-operators. Each photo contained a written notation of the sex partner's name, time, date and location. It was small money per businessman extorted, only three-to-five hundred dollars per month each; but it was significant money when aggregated, ranging from ten thousand to twenty thousand Dollars per month, per house.

Barbara recognized some of the men photographed. They were substantial businessmen. Cash payments for sex were pocket change for them. Apparently, David was not an obnoxious taker; his extortions were not so large that his victims would retaliate and make trouble. David blackmailed clients to keep his silence. There was also a photo of Bob, with photographs of him kissing Rita while holding her sexually inviting bare ass in his hands. Obviously, David wanted evidence showing that Bob was compromised by a bar whore. He no doubt had plans to declare that Bob's demeanor was completely unsuitable for an executive of his Firm.

Barbara created her own eighth file, which contained her developed photos of David's private altar, his holy storage compartment for his sacred Torah scrolls, and his Green Room with its feasting insects and spiders. Then, she called Chief. That weekend she took her files to the airport and boarded a private jet.

CHAPTER FIVE

I know a trick worth two of that (Shakespeare: King Henry IV)

OLD GRAVEL THROAT

Redemptions, that predictable leakage from a fund's asset base by investors needing cash, had erupted into a crisis. Some brokers encouraged clients who needed money to take it from the Firm's Universal Growth Fund. There was no trailing commission paid to brokers for keeping client money with the Firm. It became the brokers favorite target for client cash needs. David reviewed the fund's daily redemption outflow reports. Each report contained the name of the client, the amount of money withdrawn, the amount of money remaining, the name of the salesman who'd sold the fund shares to the client, and the name of the salesman's brokerage firm.

Each shareholder redeeming shares for cash received a phone call from an elderly gentleman in fund shareholder services. The caller had a distinctive, authoritative, gravelly voice. The voice told the shareholder he was taking a survey and asked why the shareholder needed the money.

If the shareholder replied it was to remodel a house or a kitchen, or put an addition onto a house, the voice reacted with a gasp. Then the voice cleared its throat and told the shareholder that what he or she was about to do was a crazy idea; that people just weren't doing that any longer; that if the shareholder would wait a couple of years the costs of materials and labor would drop significantly and they'd be able to do the remodel cheaper, based on a top secret report the fund had, and based upon the fund's in-house economic survey.

Of course, the Firm had no such secret report and did no in-house economic surveys; but often as not, the approach worked. The investor changed his mind and the redemption request was canceled. The fund kept the money and the fees it earned on the money, often for many years thereafter.

If the redemption request was for a medical procedure such as triple bypass surgery or a double mastectomy for breast cancer, the gravelly voice would sound suddenly engaged and interested.

"Oh my God!" the voice would shout in alarm. *"I'm glad I called you. I almost didn't call, but I see you've been a loyal share-holder to us for a long time."* Any investor who'd been with the fund for more than six months qualified for this 'long time' pitch. *"We really care about our long-term investors. Before you do anything, we have a firm expert on our staff that is very knowledgeable in your particular medical area. She's very familiar with your type of illness and she can do a lot for you,"* the voice assured the client. *"If you'll just hold the line a minute, I'll put her on the line. Her name is Jean."* The phone was then handed to Debbie, who sat next to Old Gravel Throat for redemption calls.

"Hi there, this is Jean," Debby chimed. *"Old Bill told me all about your condition and you can rest assured you have nothing to worry about. We know all about these no-good scamming doctors. They just want to carve you up so they can take all your money.*

"Listen, we have a staff medical doctor who will read your med-ical reports for free. He'll talk to you about the procedure your doc-tor is recommending. Then he'll check out your doctor's complaint history on our secret in-house criminal complaint database and he'll get back to you. So just call your doctor and your hospital right

now and tell them you need to put off the procedure for another six months, so you'll have time to think it over. Don't tell them you're having us check them out. We don't want them to get suspicious. We like to hit them when they least expect it."

In about half these cases, the investor cancels their redemption. They send their medical records to the fund where they are placed in a drawer until the next time the shareholder calls, asking why he or she hasn't yet heard from the fund's specialist staff doctor. The investor is told that the review takes time because it has to do with sensitive questions about the shareholder's doctor. After a few more weeks when the investor calls a third time, he's told the staff doctor will likely get back to him within a week. Then, just at the one-week mark, the investor gets a call from Man Child, the mail clerk.

"Hello there. This is Dr. Johnson on the staff here," sounds a chipper Man Child. *"I've looked at your case carefully and checked out your doctor as well. Our opinion here is that you can wait at least five more years before you have that procedure and it will actually be more successful if you decide to wait. The problem will be better defined and there's a good chance it will simply go away by itself. I am sending your records back to you."*

About half these shareholders die during the five-year wait period. Some survived as long as ten years with their untreated conditions. Regardless, the Firm kept their money longer.

Yet a third type of redemption is one caused by a salesman who is moving monies from the fund to some other product. The redemption reports showed a pattern that was easily discernable. For these situations, David called the salesman directly.

"Hi there, I've noticed you're pulling money out of the U G G A General Universal Growth Fund. How come?" Pause, listening. *"Oh, I see, you're doing this on the basis of short-term performance after you sold it as a long-term investment,"* or, *"Oh, it's something*

more to the client's needs, huh? Well, listen up, you no-good slime. We keep records on these shareholders and on you. They are our shareholders and they are documented for long-term growth, and growth is what we give them here at U G G A General Universal."

There usually follows a long pause where the broker vents his frustration about David's poor results.

"What's that you say?" yells a combative David into the phone. "Five years of bad performance is long-term enough? You listen to me and stop talking back. You're just a no-good little shithead and I'm a portfolio manager, see? I get my picture in the papers and articles written about me telling the public how smart I am and you don't. You're just a stupid, worthless little shit. I know what long term is and you don't. Here at U G G A, long term is twenty years; nothing less. You just sold the fund to churn it later to get another commission, didn't you? Don't mouth off to me, you filthy little bastard. I'm going to ruin your life if you try pulling this crap one more time.

"Now you pay attention, slime ball. We've got friends at the Securities and Exchange Commission and in your state regulator's office," David threatened. "We're watching your activity and we're getting ready to turn you in. I'm giving you just this one chance, and then I'm going to tear your wretched hide off and destroy your miserable fucked-up little life.

"You call those shareholders of ours back and you make them put that money back. They get thirty days where they can do that without paying another commission to you. You do that and you also put one additional shareholder with us and I'll leave you alone. If you don't do that, I'm going to get you busted out of the industry for churning your clients. You're just a no-good, dirty, filthy, little cocksucker. I've dealt with creeps like you before. I'll get you busted down so badly you'll be selling used cars and sweeping floors. We at Universal Global Growth Amalgamated have an extremely high *standard of ethics. The regulators all know that, and when they hear from us about your activities, you're going to get fucked right up your ass. Are you hearing me, buddy?"*

David then shouts into the phone. He's done this many times.

"One week, you little prick! You're getting one week to prove to me that your attitude has changed. After that, I'll be tearing your fucking nuts off. You dirty, filthy, cocksucker!"

Then David slams the phone down. About half of all stockbrokers buckled under his intimidation tactic. Their sales redemptions stopped and some even sent the fund a new shareholder as a peace offering. David had a knack for being creative and thinking outside the box; an uncanny ability to find a way to blame someone or something else on a condition; and to lay the solution to his problem into the lap of an innocent third party.

He was largely successful at staunching the outflows for home improvements, medical expenses, and the like, but one area of perpetual vexation was the shareholder group that needed to live off their investments. These people typically withdrew a fixed amount of money each month. This was somewhat predictable because the sales literature showed that one could do this on a reasonable basis and likely still have assets available that would hopefully grow over the years.

Still, it was an outflow, a slow bleeding away of assets, and it annoyed David to no end. Finally he hit upon a plan to staunch this particular drain on the fund's assets. When shareholders turned seventy, and every year thereafter, they got a happy birthday call from fund shareholder services. During the call, a discreet inquiry was made as to the health of the shareholder and his spouse. If the call turned up an indication of failing health, a second follow-up call was made by Old Gravel Throat. If he determined that it was likely there would be a death in the next three years, he would make a constructive suggestion to the shareholder.

They were told the *'big investment secret,'* that a great way to provide for their beneficiaries would be to first stop their monthly withdrawals and place all their assets in a spendthrift trust for their beneficiaries; then run up a bunch of credit card bills, getting more and more credit cards until the shareholder had twenty or thirty of them. Then, they were told, when the shareholder died, just have the shareholder's heirs stiff the credit card companies. If they died when their cards were maxed out and the cards' debt service costs were eating all their Social Security money, then the fund would recommend a lawyer who could settle the dead shareholder's debt for ten cents on the dollar, possibly nothing.

This *'plug the leaks'* program worked very well with almost a ninety-percent success ratio. People naturally hate banks and credit card companies, often stigmatized as the phony money crowd; trying to put debt hooks into people. Most people were willing to fight back when someone showed them how. After David's *'Plug the Leaks,'* program was implemented, monthly Dollar outflows dropped by sixty percent.

Shareholders die, but their money doesn't die with them. Often enough, a dead shareholder's estate administrators omitted or neglected to discover all the decedent's assets, including mutual fund shares. The funds, however, always knew about a shareholder death because the fund's annual and semi-annual reports were returned to the fund by the post office as undeliverable. A search of obituaries confirmed the investor's death. By law, decedent assets are supposed to be placed into the descendant's state of residence unclaimed asset account. David made a practice of dragging his feet on that requirement. In fact, it was just one of those things he never got around to doing at all. No doubt, if an estate administrator or a state regulator ever traced missing estate funds to the fund, those funds would have been promptly remitted; however, that never happened. Dead person's monies were held in David's mother's trust account for David as the beneficiary. That often turned out to be the permanent disposition of dead shareholders' assets.

People calling the Firm to solve their investment account problems were directed to a special help line. These calls ran the gamut of lost checks, mistakes on purchase or redemption orders, changes in account registrations, beneficiary declarations, lost statements, lost tax reports, questions about portfolio holdings, proxy voting instructions, timing of the next distribution of income and capital gains, and shareholder meeting dates. These calls were mostly from people who were too lazy to read instructions sent to them; too sloppy to keep track of paperwork already sent to them; or too dysfunctional to remember who their family members were. David devised a system to handle all these requests with maximum efficiency, thereby saving fifty thousand man hours of duplicitous Firm staff work each year.

Through black market purchases, David obtained bootlegged software that replicated the automated telephone answering systems of the Wyoming Department of Wildlife, the Internal Revenue Service, a major oil and gas company, a major mutual fund organization that operated forty different mutual funds, and the Environmental Advocacy Agency. He had a software engineer splice these phone systems into the Firm's phone system. In Man Child's office, an electronic status board was installed. It looked like five inverted Christmas trees with descending rows of lights which tracked the progression of up to five simultaneous callers.

When a shareholder called for shareholder services, the receptionist determined from her checklist of call inquiries if it was a call that David classified as a time-waster. The receptionist immediately transferred those calls to Old Gravel Throat. He listened courteously to the caller and then assured them that the Firm had a department specifically set up to deal with that particular problem. It didn't matter what the problem was; each shareholder received the same courteous understanding voice of Old Gravel Throat. Then he would say: *"Madam, let me transfer you to the right people, right away."*

The call was transferred into the Firm's telephone answering system. In Man Child's office, the top left light on one of the inverted Christmas trees lit up, letting him know there was a caller in the phone system. The caller heard a voice telling her it would take fifteen to thirty minutes for the next available representative because of heavy call volumes. She could leave her number and someone would call her back—but no one ever called those people back—or she could wait.

After thirty minutes, another voice came on and said, *"Your call is now being redirected. Please continue to hold."* Then a voice would come on and say, *"You have reached the Wyoming Department of Wildlife. Push pound for Spanish. To report an illegal poaching, press one. To apply for an Elk license, press two. A Moose license, press three. A Bighorn Sheep license, press four. A Black Bear license, press five. a Grizzly Bear license, press six. For small game and bird licenses, press seven-seven. Did you know through our new reciprocal agreements with Texas and Louisiana, holders of Wyoming Big Horn Sheep and Moose licenses can get twenty five percent discounts on Texas Wild Boar hunts and Louisiana Alligator hunts? Applying for one of these hunts also entitles you to our free video of how to gut and skin Wild Boar and Alligators. If you are calling about this fabulous opportunity, press 88. If you are calling about something else, please stay on the line for the next available agent. In the Grand Tetons, the temperature is twenty degrees below zero in Jackson Hole and sixty-five below zero on the mountaintops. Winds are gusting between thirty and fifty miles per hour and wind chill is seventy-five degrees below zero, so don't go outdoors without putting your gloves on. In the Powder River Basin, it's six below zero, and it's a toasty warm two degrees above zero in the Snowy Range Mountains. Please continue to hold.*

"If you want to hear elevator music while you wait, press one. If you want to hear the sounds of a moose in rut, press two. If you want to hear a cougar killing a deer, press three. For shotguns blasting geese out of the sky, press four. For coyotes tearing a rabbit apart, press five. For wolves howling at the moon, press six, for the sounds of two Grizzly bears mating, press seven. If you think you have reached this recording in error, please press the pound key."

The callers would next press the pound key and get sent to the next telephone answering system, which was the one for the IRS. The recording would say, *"All of our agents are busy serving other customers. Your wait time will be seventy-five minutes. Please stay on the line so you do not lose your place. Your wait time is now seventy-four minutes. Did you hear about our new tip-off program? You can get ten percent of the money we beat out of your friends if you turn them in to us for auditing. If you want to help crack down on these despicable tax cheats, press two. If you want to ask one of our agents about our witness protection program, press three. Only use this option if you are turning in drug dealers who steal more than one million Dollars; otherwise, press four and continue holding. If you are calling about a tax refund, we will switch your call to our super service call center in the lovely country of Myanmar, where we have people who can't speak English standing by to help you. You'll need to have handy your Myanmar-to-English dictionary to assist with our prompt service. If you think you've reached this number in error, press the star key on your touch pad or scream an obscenity into your phone. Our agents will understand that. If you are using an obsolete phone, hang up and start over."*

For those intrepid souls who make it to the next level a voice answered with: *"Congratulations, you have reached Bigger Than Ever Oil Company, or B T E O C. If you are calling to report an offshore oil spill, press one, an onshore oil spill, press two. If you are calling because some caribou got his antlers stuck in one of our drill platforms, press three. If a platform blew up and is spewing valuable crude into the ocean, press four. If you are calling to get permission to dynamite the ocean floor with a seismic shot, press five. If you are trying to report refinery explosions, press six. If you are an environmentalist or a representative of some environmental group, please press the pound key followed by the letters SAND, as in go pound sand, you fucking bastard. If you are a First Nations representative and you want a better deal from us, we'll connect you to our used mobile home rental subsidiary. We'll also give you a ten percent off coupon for your next tank of gas. If you believe you reached this recording in error, press all the keys on your keypad simultaneously."*

Those callers were redirected to a major mutual fund company's phone software. The voice answered and said: *"Hello, please tell us your social security number for verification purposes. Also give us your two credit card numbers with the biggest available credit lines so we can doubly check who you are. We can't be too careful. You know how it is! Thank you for that information. If you are calling about our Big Growth Fund, press one."* If the caller pressed one, the voice came on again and said: *"I'm sorry. We don't have a fund like that with you as a shareholder of record. Perhaps you want our bond fund? If so, press two."* If the caller pressed two, the voice came back on and said: *"I'm sorry. You must be calling the wrong place. We don't even have a bond fund."* Then the voice blows the caller a raspberry over the phone and says: *"If you believe you made this call in error, press six-nine followed by the pound key."*

After being directed to the environmental agency's software, a voice came on and said: *"Thank you for calling Bunny Huggers Screw Big Oil, or B H S B O. If you're part of our special study group that enters data on how many times a day a fruit fly fucks, please press one. If you're part of our hundred-billion-dollar study about how to relocate six minnow fish from Little Dipshit Creek, press two. If you're part of the polar exploration group that went to the North Pole to study global warming but got stuck in the ice a thousand miles south of the pole, press three. If you're from a university that's on our kickback program for falsified scientific studies, press four. If you want to get involved in our new Killing Eagles with Wind Farms program and would like to volunteer to run around randomly on the ground while dressed in a chicken costume, we can relocate you and your family to one of our wind farms. If that interests you, press five. If you believe you've reached this number in error, please stay on the line and our next available agent will pick up in about fifteen minutes."*

While the callers migrate their way through the phone maze, the lights on Man Child's inverted Christmas trees keep blinking. Only the most determined callers ever get through to the last light at the bottom of a given tree. Then, a caller gets to speak to Man Child. After the light was steadily on for fifteen minutes, he turned away from watching gay porn and picked up the phone.

He answered with: *"Hello. If this is an emergency, hang up and dial 911. Otherwise, I'm Sergeant Doofus Botch. I'm ready to take down your homicide or kidnapping report. I must tell you that you are being recorded and by making this call you automatically become our prime suspect in our five active murder cases. You have the right to remain silent, you dummy. Now please give me your name, address, phone number, the name of the person you murdered or kidnapped, and your whereabouts minute by minute for the last forty-eight hours. Be exact, madam. This information will go into your permanent criminal records file. Our crime lab will be in touch with you shortly. An officer will come to your home and pick you up. He will take you to the downtown station where you'll be fingerprinted; your blood will be drawn for DNA matching; your eyeballs will be retina scanned while fully dilated and you'll have a mug shot with front and side profile. Your eyes will get back to normal after about three hours."*

At that point even those few who make it to the final light on the inverted tree hang up. A lot of paperwork was avoided using David's shareholder services telephone answering system.

CHAPTER SIX

The note I wanted: that of the strange and sinister embroidered on the very type of normal and easy (Henry James: (Prefaces. Altar of the dead, and elsewhere)

FINS

Amongst humankind there are those who possess what psychologists term high emotional IQ's. Their sensory faculties are fine-tuned to detect the slightest variances in a voice tone or facial expression when a narrative is proffered. They are razor-honed to note and retain the telltale giveaway that others signal when change interrupts their ordered world. Like spiders they are, sitting in the center of their sensory handiwork, called to action by the touch of a disturbance fly upon their web. The slightest tilt of the eyebrow; dart-away of the eye; twitch or purse of the lips; or the expected reaction to a comment that was too long delayed to credibly be the honest reaction—these were but a few of the things David noticed about people. He knowingly honed his signal-gathering radars since childhood. A child often naturally does that to get the best of his parents, especially when the child knows his parents do not love him and wish he'd never been born.

After office hours over drinks one day, David asked Bob how things were for him in his after-hours life. Bob gave the predicted *'all fine'* response. But David wasn't buying it, as Bob gave a very slight, fleeting grimace prior to speaking. David knew it was time to make his move. Much like a spider is quick to follow its feelers to its prey in order to wrap a strand of silk over it and bind it to the web, David cast out a line to Bob, offering a chance to spend some time outside the four walls of his apartment and take a break from pounding the sales pavement.

"How would you like to get out for some fishing?"

Bob did fly fishing when he could and he presumed David wanted to walk riverbanks with him. *"Sounds like fun. What day do you want to go?"*

"Actually, I was thinking we could go for four or five days, really catch some great fish. I thought we'd go for salmon out of Astoria, Oregon. Would you be up for that?"

Bob was all for it. A week later, he and David were checked out of the office. Astoria, on the mouth of the Columbia River, was renowned for its blackberries, raspberries, ice cream and bakery shops; and its lovely harbor. Bears and cats liked the town as well. It was the logical spot to feed their appetite for salmon. They were there to get their share.

David pointed out the monument to John Jacob Astor, telling Bob everybody had the column wrongly categorized. The column had a wraparound mural that detailed the history of the Astor family, but David remarked it was only an excuse to build a big shaft to honor the first Astor because the guy was probably a big prick. Anyway, regardless of the reason why whoever built the thing, David said Astor got a lot of Indians killed; and he also killed lots of animals for their furs. That completed David's history lesson of Astoria.

Salmon fishing isn't actually fishing. It is the mindless harvesting of the ocean's meat. There is no thought put into it whatsoever. There are no flies to tie, no fly hatches to work, no presentation skills are needed, and no line handling expertise required. But it is challenging. Actually, it's torturous. In the summertime, the fishermen's little salmon boats take in their lines from their pier berths at four in the morning. They put the throttle to their foul-smelling diesel engines and get underway.

In the great Pacific Northwest, four in the morning is not an ungodly hour like it is in latitudes farther south. The sun isn't up yet. But the people and the daylight are sort of coming to terms with each other in a stupor of sleepily, barely awaking. It is a misty, fishy-smelling time of almost daylight morning. Occasional harbor noises of gulls squawking, seamen cursing while opening and closing deck hatches; and the emptying of buckets of herring into boat bait wells all serve to separate pleasant sleep time from begrudging fish time. It is yawn widely time. That's the eerie haunting time where boats bob to the slow harbor movements' wave action from some boat leaving; and a woman in an artist's beret sits on a stool with her easel and paints. Cats yawn, stretch, watch the scene and lick their chops in anticipation of fish gut piles and unused bait that will be thrown their way when the valiant fishing boats return.

David and Bob went to their chartered boat, met its captain, got their raingear for the predictable Pacific rain showers, and took their seats. The skipper gave them their nautical briefing, which was basically to hold on tight after he moved the vessel out of the harbor and downriver; or, they were given a second choice. They could head below deck where they would not bounce off the boat. He told the landlubbers he'd be taking the boat over the bar. In years past, many ships failed to navigate the ocean breakers that met the mouth of this mightiest of all Northwest rivers. It was where ships breached into the swells and succumbed to the wave action, which broke up their keels, battered their gunnels, and sank many of them. Men died. It was where the ocean collided with the river. It is not a sociable bar where you go to have a drink with friends. It is the barfo bar, where you go to get your guts turned inside out and your head slammed and banged hard. It's where your mind tells you that this is a bad idea and you should not be here. It is the bar you go to when you feel like risking your life to catch a stupid fish. It is *THE* bar.

His mighty twin diesel engine six hundred horse-powered craft was unlikely to meet such a dastardly fate, the skipper assured them. He would use max power and slam head-on into the swells and the waves, thus avoiding the fates of hundreds of lesser crafts. The only drawback to the skipper's method of clearing the bar was that everyone on board would feel like they were riding a rodeo bull while simultaneously inhaling copious fumes of diesel exhaust. So, of course, his passengers should naturally expect to barf their guts out. The skipper's briefing was followed by a hearty *"Har, Har"* and an offer of some warmed-over coffee from the previous day's outing, with a shot of whiskey, that real men of the sea, stomach churning, beverage staple.

David and Bob declined the coffee and whiskey. They were already skittish enough about the bar crossing and feared putting more stress on their stomachs. Bob soon wondered why he volunteered for this nightmarish torture. After leaving the harbor, the skipper took his brave little vessel into the Columbia, turned to port, and raced headlong towards the bar. In short order, they were at that dreadful place where the mouth of the Columbia meets the North Pacific. Columbia's mighty outpour flow clashed against onrushing Pacific's monstrous swells, producing a relentless wave chop. The force of King Neptune's fury repeatedly lifted the puny shipyard creations of mortal men skyward; and then plunged them downward into bottomless watery canyons. Landlubbers David and Bob clung to their little chartered craft as it alternatively pointed vertically skyward, then headlong down into the roiled watery depths of Hades.

As if the pitching and the roll of this insane ride weren't enough, for good nausea-inducing measure the skipper slammed his throttles full ahead to squeeze enough power from the twin diesels to punch his craft headlong into the rising swells. Onward, ever onward they went, attacking the onrushing, cascading water ranks of death and hell. The engines screamed and belched their suffocating billows of nauseous fumes. The ride, the fumes, and the churning caused both David and Bob to barf over the side while holding onto the life rail. After an eternity in hell, the boat finally reached open ocean. According to their skipper, they'd arrived at the perfect spot.

There was a fourth man on the boat. His job was to rig the poles, bait the fish hooks with herring smelts, and gaff the hooked fish. Gauche David had joked to this hapless deckhand when they first boarded: *"So, you're the guy who baits the hooks, huh? I guess that would make you the boat's Chief Masturbator!"* He had let out a snickering laugh. The young man was embarrassed. No one else laughed.

Fishing for salmon entails passing time by sitting around drinking beer out of a can, hoping the flavorful hops resins will resettle your vomit dissembled guts, while the bait man rigs your fish hooks and throws your lines into the ocean. Fishing poles are placed in socket holders. The boat chugs along at one or two knots, trolling the bait lines behind it. Pole lines grow taut and rod tips dip when a fish bites *'on.'* The customer fishermen then pick up their bending poles and reel in the hapless salmon that swallowed the hook and doomed itself to die before it could swim upstream to spawn.

Once alongside, the deckhand gaffs or nets the unfortunate fish and swings it aboard in a well-timed motion. The line and hook are ripped or cut away from the salmon's gullet, trauma-tizing the doomed fish. With still-breathing gills and flapping tail it is thrown into the fish tank. Once the daily limit of fish is caught, the boat heads back to the harbor. Paying guests suffer their second mind-numbing buckaroo ride as the craft traverses the bar while retuning. With their breakfasts long gone, nothing but greenish-brown beer slime remains for the fishermen guests to barf up during their return trip.

Walking off the pier toward the quay wall, wobbly sea legs staggering their locomotion, David put his hand on Bob's back. *"How'd you like our fishing trip?"*

Bob thought David's hand was intended as a gesture of pride and solidarity in accomplishment, when, in actuality, all they'd accomplished was getting sick and killing four helpless fish. The fishing was nothing like the challenge of stream fishing. Bob reflected that David probably had no idea what it was like to actually fish for the sport of it. He noticed that David purposely let his hand linger longer than necessary for natural camaraderie.

Two more fishing excursions followed, one for sturgeon and one for bass. For the big bottom-feeding sturgeons, the duo again went to Astoria on a different week and chartered a different boat. They went on a smooth trip upriver and dropped anchor. It was a hot sunny day. Their skipper suggested they strip to their bathing suits while he rigged the poles and baited the hooks. Bob went below and changed into his baggy trunks and a tee shirt. When he came up on deck, he saw David sprawled out on a deck chair wearing only a Speedo. Bob avoided looking at David's body. Marty had it right when she told him that she thought his gut was starting to show. David's flabby pouch spilled over his lower abdomen and rested just above the strap's pouch, which appeared to contain two tiny walnuts. David's testicles were distinctly visible against the skintight fabric. Bob sat in the adjacent deck chair while David babbled about how he loved the great outdoors and its wholesome fresh air. The six sturgeons they caught met the same fate as their salmon; canned at the local cannery.

The duo's third fishing trip was to a godforsaken bass lake in the middle of Mexico, to which they drove in a rented car over several hundred miles of potholed roads. They passed a half-dozen checkpoints manned by teenage boys dressed in soldiers' garb and armed with machine guns. At the lake they lodged in a compartmentalized prefabricated structure with paper thin walls separating the bedrooms. The cook was a jovial senorita. But the only food she ever prepared was bass. For three days they ate bass for breakfast, bass for lunch, and bass for dinner. During the day they fished the lake in guided canoes, seeking more bass. They caught dozens of the scaly, spiny-finned things. From weed-infested haunts amongst standing dead trees and floating logs, the bass unleashed their angry slams against surface popper lures. Like lightning bolts launched from their watery underworld, these game fish shot to the surface to hit the lures and fight mightily. The wide-mouthed monsters were bold and unafraid of the blood sport they played.

On their last fishing day, a powerful storm came up. David's straw sombrero blew off his head. He yelled to the guide to forget the hat and row for shore. But Bob countermanded David. Speaking perfect Spanish, he took charge of matters. He and the guide rowed dangerously broadside to the lake's wave chop and retrieved David's hat.

Back on the beach, David became suddenly furious.

"You could have gotten me killed," he blurted out. *"I ordered him to go to shore because I can't swim."*

"No reason to get upset," Bob responded calmly. *"The water wasn't that bad. Besides, if we'd gone over, I would have swum for both of us and brought you back."*

"But what if I had struggled and fought you off, like a drowning man does?" David disagreed.

"Not to worry," assured Bob, *"I'd have simply knocked you out, put an arm under your neck, and paddled you back."*

"You would have actually punched me?" David was aghast.

"You bet," Bob nodded in earnest. *"That's the only way to handle a panicked man. I'd have punched you right in your mouth and knocked you out cold."*

"You wouldn't feel regrets that you hit me?" David took Bob's assertion as a sign that Bob was rejecting him.

"No; none," Bob shook his head. *"Would you rather drown?"* Bob's hypothetical answer was given with a matter-of-fact chuckle without the slightest hint of emotion.

David ignored Bob's question. *"But there are poisonous cottonmouth snakes out there. I'd be helpless."* he protested.

"Yeah, but they are over nearer the shoreline and the trees where we were fishing, not in the middle of the lake where you lost your hat." Bob canted his head, grinned a matter-of-fact grin, and shrugged his shoulders. He indicated that he never thought they were in any danger and David was making a big deal out of nothing.

David stared at Bob. He looked perplexed, but said nothing.

That night, through the wall that separated their beds, Bob was awakened by sounds of David crying. He listened for a while, determining it wasn't the cry of a man in physical pain. There was no cursing paired with the sobs and no inhaled hissings, like men give out when they cut a toe or a finger. This was a sobbing, baleful cry; a low-grade whimpering, muffled, private kind of cry, coming from a man who was losing his private wrestling match with inner turmoil. Bob puzzled over this episode and rationalized that David was so deeply afraid for his life that day that he was having a near breakdown over the incident. He figured David would get over it. He then rolled over and went back to sleep. Bob couldn't relate to the anguish that had tormented David since his childhood. He didn't understand that David cried because no one loved him.

CHAPTER SEVEN

My only love sprung from my only hate (Shakespeare: Romeo and Juliet)

HOOVES

North of Plaintown, the ground elevation increases until the terrain reaches the Grand Plateau. It rises gradually, gaining about a thousand feet, whereupon it reaches a magical paradise called Wyoming.

David had suggested to Bob that he should become a big game hunter, like himself. *"Hunting sharpens the senses and wits,"* David declared; and *"there is no greater thrill than tracking down a wild animal,"* he professed; although he'd never actually done that. What better way to get acquainted with big game hunting than to go together on an antelope hunt in neighboring Wyoming? Bob agreed that a chance to go into the wilds of open-space Wyoming seemed like a fun idea. To properly outfit Bob for the hunt, David presented him with the gifts of a 7mm magnum rifle and a brand-new Jeep Safari vehicle.

David rented a large sleeper trailer that accommodated six, for just the two of them. They provisioned it with enough food for a full week in the field and plenty of beer and whiskey. David's plan was to take the antelope by surprise. He consulted with some ranchers who knew the area and wrote down detailed instructions. They would be in position to shoot at the first light of dawn. As soon as their rifle scopes could pick out some big bucks, they would whack the fleet-footed beasts before they even got out of bed. That was David's plan. But the antelope were never consulted about it.

There is a special, secret place in Wyoming about halfway north of the Snowy Range, west of Horseshoe and the edge of the Yellowstone Plateau which rises the terrain higher, further west. A huge wide-open bowl-shaped basin area exists here where majestic mountains lift up from the flat plateau below. It is inaccessible to man and vehicles from the north, west or east because of impossibly rugged terrain. Cougar, wolf and bear like this place and consider it home. It's where the deer and the antelope play.

The lowest place in this vast basin-bowl has water. A stream flows into a catch basin from a cool water spring, a few miles west. East of this natural basin lake is an elevated spot where an old pronghorn buck lays at night amongst his herd of thirty antelope. He is out of harm's way there. He is sheltered on three sides by rugged rising terrain. He can see ten miles to the south. It's the only viable approach access for his mortal adversary; man. The herd buck was wily. This particular herd-master pronghorn was a survival specialist. He was in his prime; all toughened muscle. He could easily top sixty miles per hour running flat-out over the rock-strewn prairie. He could change direction in sharp right-angled turns while running full speed, by planting his nimble hooves and whipping his body into a new heading. If he ever learned to carry a football, he'd easily be the NFL's most valuable player, ever.

Close beside the herd buck this day, on his lookout perch, were seven adoring females. Each doe, in her turn, alternately looked up from feeding, turned her head, and scanned the horizon. At least one doe was always looking. When alerted, the herd stood at the ready. They then had sixty eyes constantly searching to the horizon, gathering intelligence as one unified body. The old herd master had outsmarted dozens of hunters' attempts to kill him over the past seven years. He understood that the hunters would never relent in their quest for his magnificent horns. But he was resolved that no hunter would ever mount his head and horns on some wall. He wished to die a natural death of old age in a quiet, restful place.

On that particular morning, a faint prairie breeze started up as it was want to do in pre-dawn Wyoming. The tips of the cheat grass began to bend slightly as they had for millions of such fall mornings on this upland basin's vast prairie. This breeze was how the prairie welcomed the sun. A flock of junket birds whirred about in some brush around thirty yards below the herd buck. He heard their feathered wings flutter as they prepared to get out of their evening quarters and flit-skip over the prairie floor, gorging themselves on rising insects. Dawn's first light was still a half hour away. Except for the early riser junkets, all should have been quiet still this morning, unless a cougar or bear was stealing its way toward his herd.

But there was something strange about this morning. It was far away and it made an unnatural sound. It didn't fit right with the nature of the herd buck's prairie. It did not belong here. His ears pointed toward the sound, taking it into his understanding and processing everything it told him. The sound told him that men were out there. Likely they were hunters. They were coming toward him in a motorized vehicle. Its motor was straining a bit. It clanked along more noisily than most vehicles he'd heard before. It was exceptionally ungainly; but it was still too far away to bother him for a decision about what he should do about it. He let out a grunt. Twenty-seven females and two lesser bucks lifted their heads. Many of the herd stood. All sixty eyes were now on full alert.

Bob drove the Jeep that towed the trailer. The cumbersome rig bounced over a narrow, twisted dirt road which featured massive rock outcrops, close by the roadside. The hunters were a half hour behind their planned schedule. David had to dump out his intestines just as they were scheduled to start off. That took ten minutes and couldn't be postponed. Also, David declared their instructions had to be off. The rancher had told them to turn left at the intersection, which they did; and then they were to go for fifty-seven miles and turn right. That's as definitive and explicit as a Wyoming rancher is when he gives directions to somebody driving up from Plaintown to hunt antelope. At the fifty-six-and-a-half-mile mark, there was a right turn. David claimed that it had to be the road the rancher meant, or possibly the odometer on the Jeep was off a little. So, they turned right.

After a meandering five-mile drive, they came upon a ranch house. There, the road stopped. They got out of their Jeep and looked around for a road bypass around the ranch house, but the road went no further. It dead-ended at the ranch house. The noise caused by their rig woke up the rancher's dog. It did its duty. It barked its head off. The rancher came out to greet them, wearing only his pajamas and carrying a shotgun. After making their apologies and gathering renewed instructions, Bob and David got back on the road. They went another half mile and turned right, as they were originally instructed. With considerable cursing, they made their way along the correct road.

David was miffed. *"You'd think that rancher who gave me directions would have told me about the first turn just a half mile before."*

"He probably assumed you knew how to follow directions." Bob remarked. He was tired of David's complaints and bitching. And he was tired from driving.

Silence ensued. David resented cynicism.

The road was different from the ranch road. It didn't have deep pickup truck ruts with grass growing in the middle hump. The road had been graded two years before. But it was, in many respects, more miserable than the first road. It had unforgiving rocks that jutted up from the roadbed every few feet. The early prairie breeze was behind them. It was also unforgiving. A fine gray-white gritty dust arose from their Jeep's wheels. As their Jeep and trailer bounced, bucked and crawled along, the breeze picked up their trail dust, lifted it to the window level of the vehicle, and swirled it into the beams of their headlights. Their dust obscured their vision. They were only able to see five feet in front of them. But antelope for three miles in every direction saw the reflective sparkles of their road dust dancing in their headlight beams. Every antelope in the basin knew hunters had arrived.

When David had rented the trailer, he'd inspected it completely to make sure the interior quarters were clean and working properly to his satisfaction. The shower, toilet, and stove all worked fine. In order to enter and inspect their mobile hunt headquarters, a set of metal access stairs had to first be released from their holding latch. The salesman didn't notice; Bob didn't notice. David forgot to secure the stair latch when he finished his inspection. Because of their delay getting started, David's hopes of slamming the herd buck at daybreak were slipping away. Although going faster meant they'd make more noise, David hoped the herd buck was a late snoozer who wouldn't notice the commotion.

As Bob picked up speed, the rig made a clamoring racket. The trailer bounced over the hard feldspar road rocks, careening from side to side, being dragged behind the Jeep. Bob drove fast. Choking road talcum swirled into the passenger compartment. Neither hunter heard the trailer's steps drop from their stowed position and fully extend, making the trailer's profile three feet wider. The road passed between two gigantic fifty-ton boulders. The rock outcrops didn't yield a smidgeon to the steps that protruded three feet from the trailer's side. Without clearance on both sides, the trailer coouldn't make it.

Bob and David heard a sickening, gut-wrenching sound when the steps caught and jammed against the right rock wall. The Jeep lurched left. The continued forward momentum of the rig against the stationary steps ripped a gaping opening in the side of the trailer. The steps acted like a can opener. Its ragged step jaws ripped the aftermost two-thirds of the trailer wide open. The trailer body jerked sideways, off the trailer's frame. The rig twisted free from its hitch to the Jeep. It lay there useless, resting diagonally across the road. Hunt headquarters was lodged between the rocks, mortally wounded. The hunt was off to a *terrible* start.

Farther up the trail, at the basin, the herd buck stood up and peered in the direction of the clamoring and crashing. He couldn't see around corners. The rig came to rest below his visible horizon. Nevertheless, he and the others arose, evacuated themselves, and moved west about a mile before they began grazing. He couldn't be too careful.

Bob and David decided to forgo hunting that first day. They drove the Jeep back to a nearby town. Towns in much of Wyoming aren't large; and this one was no exception. It had a gas station, a liquor store, and a general store outpost for hunting and fishing supplies and licenses. When they pulled up to the general store, Bob and David noticed a German shepherd dog lying in front of the entrance door. The dog stood up, bared his teeth, growled and drooled slobber.

"I wonder if he'll bite us," David said.

"Don't know," said Bob. *"I'll blow the horn and see if anybody comes out."* After a horn blast, an older man, tall and sinewy of build and heavily bearded, shoved the door open and moved the dog out of the way.

"Whaaat chew feller's want?"

Bob reckoned the man owned the place.

"We need a place to stay the night, and we need somebody to retrieve a damaged motor home trailer," said David. He went on to explain how the trailer got stuck in the rocks on the trail road to the basin.

The tall bearded man spit some chew tobacco and began laughing.

"You boys wouldn't be frem Col rad a, wood ja?"

It was obvious the station master—or mayor, or owner, or likely all of the above—was sizing them up to see how much he could charge them. Hunters from Colorado were likely easy pickings for overcharges.

David confessed the obvious; after all, the Jeep had Colorado plates. He agreed to an exorbitant, bordering on extortion, sum to have the trailer retrieved. The sinewy man revealed he was the owner of the general store, as well as the motel across the street. His wife ran the motel. He doubled as the go-to man with a ready bulldozer for emergencies such as rescuing Coloradans who got themselves into messes in Middle of Nowhere, Wyoming.

David rented a motel room for the duration of the hunt. He called the trailer dealer in Plaintown and complained about the latch not holding the steps in place, threatened to sue the trailer maker and the dealer for faulty equipment and putting his life at risk, and told them he'd deal with them when he returned to Colorado. Meanwhile, he and Bob got the only remaining room in the motel that night; it was hunting season and the only time the motel was more than one-tenth occupied. David declared the great antelope hunt would start tomorrow.

In their room with two twin beds, David shouted out loud, angry with himself. *"We blew it. We weren't thinking. We should have thought it through first."*

"What? Thought what through?" asked Bob.

"The accident! The trailer! We should have set fire to the damn thing and let the rental company collect the insurance instead of billing us for the accident." David, true to character, never accepted responsibility for anything.

"That'd be worse," remarked Bob. *"That's arson. Those things get investigated by insurance companies. They don't just automatically pay. If they find arson, it's jail time. We're doing the right thing. Besides, there's insurance for the collision."*

"Yeah, but we'll get stuck paying the deductible." groused David.

"Beats jail. Good night." Bob turned the lights out.

After a while David turned the lights back on. Bob was nearly asleep. He turned toward David's bed to see why he'd turned the lights on. David sat naked on the edge of the bed. He cried while stroking an erection and looking wistfully at Bob. Through sobs and teary eyes, David moaned in pitiful whimpers. When he saw Bob was awake, he began a baleful tale of woe:

"Nobody ever loved me," David wailed in a wretched display of self-abasement. *"Nobody wants to hold me and kiss me because I'm ugly. I can't help how I am. I'm overweight and I have awful body odor. I stink. I'm sure you've smelled me, haven't you?"* Bob shrugged, as if to say: *'so what.'* David continued. *"I can't urinate right. Some of my urine comes out through my skin. That's why I stink so badly. I shower three times a day. I use colognes; but I still stink."* He paused between his sobs, his eyes hopeful for sympathy.

"Well, maybe you're part reptile. Why don't you see a doctor about it?" Bob was non-committal, eager to change the subject.

David continued stroking his penis. He ignored Bob's reptile comment. He was looking for sympathy, not a fight.

"I hated my mother from the time I was a child. My father always tried to get rid of me; always sent me away. They left me millions but they never loved me, especially mother. I even heard her

say she wished I'd never been born. I've hated all women ever since I heard her say that."

"You hate all women?" Bob couldn't understand David or anyone hating women. Bob adored women, practically every one of them, even though his own mother was abusive and dictatorial toward him as a child.

"Yes, I hate women," said David. *"Over the years I've grown more and more distant from women and closer and closer to men. Oh, I've tried to be attracted to women, and I've even tried to make love with some of them, but it's impossibly hard for me."*

Where David was trying to lead Bob was unmistakable. All Bob's suspicions about David came into focus. David's lingering hand on his back at the pier in Astoria, the trips for just the two of them, the gifts of the rifle and Jeep, the trip they were on now—all were his manipulations to try to get Bob to become his lover. It was never about a father and son relationship as David purported it to be; nor was it about a business partnership. It was all a pathetic manipulation played out over years.

Bob rolled his head to the side, away from David. But, David persisted. *"When we first started working together, I saw in you a man like my father, only someone more. Dad was Dad, but he was also my partner and my best friend. I loved Dad, but he never loved me,"* David lied. He hated Marvin, his father.

Bob wasn't about to ask what more than son, partner, and friend he could be. Lover was the only base David left uncovered; and Bob didn't want to go there. He was as straight as a man could be.

"I thought you said your dad always pushed you away?" Bob pointed out David's inconsistency.

"Yes, he sent me away, but I still thought of Dad as my best friend. I loved him, but he didn't love me. When you and I met, I thought we could have the same relationship Dad and I had, only more. I thought I could be like a dad to you and a partner to you

and a best friend to you, only more. I thought I could also love you and you could also love me."

The conversation was getting way too weird for Bob. He needed to disabuse David of any notion that they'd ever become lovers. His eyebrows went up to their full extent and his jaw dropped open as he stared at the ceiling.

"Look, David, I've got to be honest with you," explained Bob. *"You are a great guy. You are a great friend and a great partner, and you are like a dad to me. I've learned a great deal from you and we're making the business grow.*

"But you need to forget about me loving you. You need to understand that I'm wired very differently than you are. I love women. I mean that I love them as an opposite sex kind of love. I love holding them, kissing them, and I love making love with them. There's nothing about any man that even remotely interests me. I've been attracted to women sexually since I was a little kid, and I also like many of them as people I can be friends with.

"That's what works for me and I'm not going to be changing that." Bob was emphatic. *"I'm sorry to tell you this, but I had no idea that's what you expected of me. I just can't be in love with you. I was in love with Marty, and I guess you could say I'm open to a woman's love again; but that's it for me. I've never been in love with a man and I never could be. I am not a homosexual, and I don't want to become one either. You need to understand that about me and you need to forget this notion of yours."*

"Did you know that Marty had other lovers, even when she was with you?"

"Yeah, I knew that. So?"

"And that didn't bother you? That didn't make you think she was dirty?"

"No, David. That didn't bother me. There was nothing dirty about Marty, David. She was a beautiful, sensitive woman."

"But she even made porn films. How could you stomach that?"

"David, look. I think you've trashed Marty enough, okay? You just don't understand, do you? If anything, her porn films made me appreciate how emotive and sensuous she was. Frankly, they turned me on and made me want her even more. Can't you get it through your head, David? I loved her." Bob's eyes matched the exasperation in his voice.

"I don't understand how you could prefer someone so casual and immoral about sex, like Marty, to having a loving relationship with me. Haven't you ever considered trying male love, just once? It can be really beautiful." David wasn't giving up easily. His eyes revealed his menacing intensity.

Bob wasn't having it and he wasn't about to waiver. *"Look, David,"* he spoke in a voice determined to set David in his place, *"I would not care one iota if Marty was the queen nymph of the Hesperides, luring mortal men to their deaths with her fornications. I do not care how immoral she is. I would still gladly bury my face and soul in her vagina a thousand times; but I will never place my lips upon another man's cock. Okay?"*

"But it's beautiful!" David persisted. The menacing intensity had burst into the open.

"Can't be that beautiful or God would have put a male in the Garden of Eden with Adam. But He didn't put a male there. He put Eve there, a woman. Because man and woman, that's what's natural. That's what God wanted. He told them to go forth and multiply. He did not tell Adam to find some other guy and suck his cock, did he?"

David's eyes glowered, betraying his resentment. Bob quip had hurt him. *"I don't think you have a place to get nasty about it. I'm just asking you to try it if you haven't tried it before."*

"I have not tried it before. I've never tried it. I'm not going to try it now, either." said Bob, losing patience with this subject. *"I've*

never even thought about trying it. I don't even want to think about trying it. And I really want to stop talking about it. Okay? Stop this! I don't care if you don't understand what Marty and I had. So, just stop it. I am not going to try male sex."

"Just once is all I ask."

"No, David. Damn it. Look, there are probably a lot of men out there who would like to be your lover. I'll bet even a few of the boys you have in the office right now would happily be your lover, whenever you ask. That's true, isn't it?" Bob gave David a knowing look.

"But they're not the same as you," David groaned his admittance. *"They're not strong and commanding, like you. They are wimps; girly men. And they aren't smart. They just take what they can from me. They use me."* David's face was sad; the model of rejection.

"Maybe they think you use them, David. Did you ever think of that? Those are things you need to work out with them." Bob wanted to get out of the middle of David's office problems with his play pen pals. *"You always said you were going to handle the office. I know you can handle your male friends if you set your mind to it. Now let's get some sleep so we can get out there tomorrow and whack some antelope. That's why you said we came here, didn't you?"*

Bob could be insensitive and disparaging towards others' feelings. As a heterosexual he had little sympathy for the travails of neurotic homosexual men. He couldn't comprehend the meaning of the word homophobic, either. He had no fears about gay men or concerns that they might convert him to their ways. His feelings ran more towards loathing them. He dismissed the whole gay scene as a ridiculous farce; appealing to people who used their *'gay pride rants'* to disguise other, more serious emotional issues.

He did not believe that some people were born gay. His diehard Nazi mother had brought him up to believe that the homosexuals' *'We're born that way'* theories were a pile of ridiculous horse crap. If his mother ever had her way, she would outlaw homosexuality and purge gay people from society. She taught Bob to think that gay people were beyond disgustingly wretched; and best avoided.

Bob turned over to go back to sleep, leaving David sitting there holding his penis and nursing hurt feelings.

The early fall sun beat down hot and harsh on Wyoming's high prairies. There was a light wind the next day; a tad stronger than on previous days. In only a few more days the wind would become brisk and steady. it would draw out the soil's scant residual moisture. The last vestiges of prairie hydration were evaporating skyward into the high Wyoming blue; becoming wisps of cirrus clouds; racing aloft, speeding their way to Nebraska. The ground was already caked and blistered. Dirt roads and animal trails were now rock-strewn dust beds, crisscrossing the infinite talcum gray grit prairie. On some few mornings, as this one, a hint of dew kissed the sage shrubs' blue buds and grease-gray brambles. The antelope were pocketed in small herds. They sheltered behind rises that buffered them from the wind. And they stayed close to whatever water they could find. The finest herd bucks commanded the best watering holes.

A new morning came for our two hunters. But this day they figured there was no point in getting an early start. It seemed more important to eat a hearty breakfast. David had declared that strength would be needed to steady their rifles and field dress their kills. Since they had decided to ignore the Jewish aversion to hunting, they figured they might as well capitulate completely and eat Goyim food as well. They wolfed down bacon and eggs, ignoring the mitzvah about avoiding pork. They packed their tummies with pancakes drowned in maple syrup, and hash browns drenched in hot sauce. To screw up their manly courage, they each belted down two shots of whiskey before heading out to slay North America's fastest animal. They convinced themselves that the local antelope would have their reckoning. They couldn't have been more wrong.

Back on the same gritty dust trail, they detoured around their wrecked trailer. Bob's mood was upbeat and anticipatory. He cracked some antelope and Jackalope, or rabbits with horns, jokes. David rode shotgun while Bob drove.

But David didn't laugh. His mood was dour and sullen; and he barely spoke. Instead, he sulked because Bob had rebuffed his gay love overtures. He wished he was back in Plaintown; anywhere but here. The trip had become David's reality check; a total disappointment. While bouncing and bumping over the dusty trail road, he decided that Bob shouldn't have fun, either.

The duo arrived below a little rise. They stepped out of their Jeep and climbed to the top, from which they could see the entire basin. The sun had already evaporated the dew. Distant images viewed through binoculars wavered and shimmered in the mid-morning heat. Phantoms danced in their optics' lenses. There! Finally! They spotted what looked like a herd of antelope far off in the distance. Their quarry had gathered around a small lake at the lowest part of an immense topographical basin. David reckoned the animals were about five miles away. There were jutted rocks on a steep hill behind the herd. The plateau's terrain between the hunters and the animals was dotted with protruding rocks that were difficult to spot from a distance.

David spoke first:

"We're in luck. They're trapped right there against those rocks. I know something about antelope. They like to run on the flat prairie, so they're not going to want to run up into those rocks. The only way they can get out of there is to come out onto the prairie, and run straight at us. So here's what we'll do. I'll drive. You chamber a round and roll your window down. Don't let them see your rifle.

Keep it in front of you with the butt end on the floor of the Jeep and the muzzle pointed at the roof. Got it?"

"Got it."

"Okay. We'll drive slowly toward them so they won't notice us. If they look at us, we'll stop for a minute before we drive forward some more. When we get really close, I'll gun the Jeep. We'll race straight at them. They'll have to come running straight at us to get out of there. When one runs past your side of the Jeep, shoot it."

Bob visualized a crazy cavalry charge between a Jeep racing fifty miles per hour toward the antelope herd and the antelope racing fifty miles per hour towards them, headed in the opposite direction:

"Don't you think it might be hard to get a bead on one of them?" he asked. *"We'll be bouncing all over the place, the antelope will be jumping and running, and our relative speed will be a hundred miles per hour."*

"Don't obsess over details at a time like this," rebuked David. *"The antelope are right in front of us. They're trapped! They can't get away from us. We may never get another chance like this in our lifetimes. Details have a way of working themselves out anyway. One of them could run into the Jeep. We might not even need to shoot the damn thing. Maybe one will break its leg and give us an easy shot. Just go with the program and get ready for a shot, okay?"* David drove the Jeep forward.

"Okay." said Bob. 'This is insane,' he thought to himself.

The old buck antelope knew it was hunting season again. The day before, he'd heard some shots in the distance and figured the hunters would soon be coming to his basin pond looking to take one or two of his herd. The rancher only allowed one or two hunters on his property each year. The old buck figured that out years ago because there were never more than one or two hunters. They always hunted together, or nearly together, so once he located them and understood their tactical plan, he easily outsmarted them. The hunters only had success every fourth year. The old buck liked his odds.

This year started off curiously for the herd master. The day before, he'd heard the terrible racket of metal getting ripped apart by rock. This was a hunting tactic he'd never encountered before, so his senses were on high alert. He and his females could see the two hunters five miles away when they crawled up on the far hillside to peer at his herd with their binoculars. He'd seen hunters do that before. That usually meant they'd be sneaking around to the north or south, keeping themselves invisible by staying low to the ground and slipping between the rocks. He figured he had a good two hours while the hunters stalked his herd. He would watch north and south for their telltale signs.

Sparrows or a magpie would flush up unnaturally, or he'd catch a glimpse of the shiny orange vests they wore. Maybe a ground squirrel or prairie dog would be disturbed and it would scamper up on a rock and bark. It didn't matter how quiet the hunters were or how long they took; he would know exactly where they were, where they were headed, and how much longer he had before he moved the herd. He was an old hand at this game and much smarter than the best hunters.

What the old buck saw next positively amazed him. A Jeep was driving straight toward his herd. The buck knew hunters never shot from their vehicles, so he wasn't quite sure what this Jeep was trying to do. Then it stopped. The buck looked carefully. It was about three miles way now, still out of rifle range. The buck looked for signs of the hunters. They were still in the Jeep. No other hunters were near it. Then he saw a tiny reflection coming from inside the Jeep. A glint of the sun's rays reflected from the bolt of the rifle carried by the man in the passenger seat. The old buck realized these two intended to hunt illegally from their vehicle.

This new information required an innovative strategy. The buck sent his leading female off to the north with the herd. She led the others close to the rocks along the down slope of the catch basin wall. She knew enough to run straight up the rocks and lead the herd over the top of the ridge if the Jeep came toward them.

Then the old buck devised a plan. He would stand alone against the Jeep. If the animal had been a human chess player, he would have been a grand master. About a half mile due south of the basin pond ran an arroyo about twenty feet deep from its prairie level top to its flash floods' washed bottom. The trail through the wash-out was strewn with rocks on its sides and floor, deposited there by centuries of flash floods from violent downpours. The rocks were foreboding silent sentinels that thwarted the arroyo's passage from all but the nimblest creatures. The old buck didn't like going in there. He knew he handicapped his greatest advantage by doing so—he could only see a few feet ahead instead of miles ahead. But this figured to be an unconventional war between man and beast, and he was not bound to play by convention's rules. Over the years he'd seen dust fly up near his hoofs from hunters' whining rifle bullets. He'd heard their bullets zing past his head and watched their lethal effect upon his does and his offspring. He didn't know how to be angry or to hate, but he understood men who did.

The arroyo was a topographical barrier between the basin pond and the open prairie, a feature the old buck used to his advantage when he needed it, as he did now. If the hunters were going to play dirty, so would he. He followed along behind the herd for a while, until he was behind some field boulders. Then he broke off from the herd and crawled on his belly with his head low until he was out onto the flat, unseen by the hunters. He slipped down into the arroyo; then ran along its bottom channel until he figured he was directly in front of the Jeep. He heard the Jeep approaching. It was moving faster now. The hunters saw the herd moving. They were giving chase. When he was certain they were less than a half mile from him, the old buck sprang into action. Up out of the arroyo he bounded, standing magnificent and defiant in the open. He was the most prized trophy specimen on the prairie. Many a hunter coveted his rack and visualized his head upon their trophy room wall. He stood proudly in front of the Jeep a mere half mile distant, but at an angle beyond the left front passenger's side. The shooter had no shot.

"There's a big one!" screamed David, falling for the herd buck's ploy. *"It looks like we've got the herd buck trapped. Let's get him!"* He turned the Jeep toward the old buck and floored the accelerator. The buck just stood there, frozen; as if he didn't know what to do. At about four hundred yards, the buck took off running in a sprint toward the east, running parallel to the top of the arroyo. In the space of two seconds, the buck went from standing still to a fifty-mile-an-hour blur of white, brown and gray. David turned right, giving chase at full speed. The buck slowed slightly, allowing the Jeep to get closer. *"He's slowing down. He's confused!"* yelled mistaken David. *"Get ready for your shot,"* he ordered. The buck let the Jeep come still closer.

The Jeep was now going fifty miles per hour on open prairie, bouncing over rocks and clumps of cheat grass, crushing sagebrush as it flew over the ground. At the exact, perfectly timed moment, divined by the God of Antelopes, and in their innate genius to use relative movement to their advantage, the old buck turned again, slightly. He made the antelope move that would go down in the annals of history books as the greatest of all great antelope moves. It was the kind of move that grown men marveled over as they drank their whiskey by their campfires and extolled the genius of these magnificent fleet-footed creatures who outran the wind.

The old buck veered right, making a quick jaunt to the south. Now he ran hard, flat-out toward the open prairie. A blinding blur of brown and white muscles flexed, uncoiling his full power. His hoofs flew as if he sailed effortlessly on the wind, racing over rock strewn prairie. First the outreached front hoofs barely touched earth; then, just as the front hooves touched down, the buck's muscular rump propelled his back legs underneath his chest; then thrust them backward, like uncoiling springs in his graceful bounding motion. He hurtled forward with blinding speed. The buck's dodge move succeeded. David careened the Jeep toward the animal. But before he could ascertain the landscape, it was too late. The Jeep was headed straight toward a blackish-purple rock outcrop. Rocks grew on Wyoming's prairie surface like dandelions grew on suburban lawns; and there were several rock piles dead ahead.

"Stop! Rocks! Turn!" screamed Bob. It was too late. Maybe David could have turned the wheel and avoided the rocks. Maybe he was just too slow, or maybe he just didn't care. The Jeep slammed into the rocks while going fifty miles per hour. There followed a sickening sound of metal crashing and grinding on rock. Sparks flew from the basalts and granite of the hardened, unmovable gray black jumble. The body of the Jeep tried valiantly to rush onward, absent its undercarriage. But the vehicle was doomed. It had engaged the unmovable mass of unyielding, unsympathetic rock. The Jeep's axles, transmission, drive shaft, oil pan, and assorted engine parts were left behind, scattered over the rocks. The frame welds snapped from the crushing force. The Jeep body shuddered as it ground to a stop in the dirt. Then, the ominous hissing sounds came, followed by flames. The fuel tank ruptured. The Jeep caught

fire and burned. The hunters scrambled from the wreck and ran for their lives.

The vehicle didn't explode. It just burned quietly. Jeeps are made to serve the stupidest hunters in the world, to the very end of the vehicles' lives, even while going up in flames. That's why hunters swear by them.

After hearing the Jeep hit the rocks, the old buck slipped back down into the arroyo. He pivoted and ran along its bottom, back in the direction from which he'd first entered it. He knew to stay invisible to hunters between appearances. About a mile and a half away he trotted out on the far bank. He was safely out of rifle range. He then turned back to peruse his handiwork. Two men stood off about twenty yards from a flaming wreck. They were staring at their wrecked transportation; no longer paying attention to him.

No one could say for sure what that old buck thought about that day. Was the Jeep chase something he'd planned? Did he know the outcome before he entered the arroyo in the first place, or did he improvise as the chase moved along? The two hunters finally turned and looked at him from afar.

Across the divides of distance, species, and evolution, the two antagonists stared at each other for the longest moment. The adversaries memorialized their encounter. The hunters were no longer a threat to the old buck or his herd. He turned away from them and loped away to join his females. The hunters could only wonder what that old goat was capable of while they watched him slip away. And now, belatedly after a hard lesson, they respected the herd buck.

"Let's go back to town and get somebody to come out here to clean up this mess," David said. *"I'll give you some money to make up for the Jeep. I just didn't see the rocks in time,"* he fibbed.

Bob kept his mouth shut about David's driving, but he was seething inside. The hunt didn't need to be the fiasco it had turned out to be. He couldn't help but wonder if David, when the opportunity was there, decided to punish him for not being a homosexual. If that were true, there was a side of David's personality he was seeing for the first time. It was chilling. Barbara gave him fair warning. She cautioned him that David could be a monster; a duplicitous schemer; and a vengeful bully child in a man's body when he couldn't have his way.

Bob was relieved to be on the ground with his life back under his own control. It felt good to walk. As they plodded across the sun-parched prairie, they stirred the alkaline gray-grit powder. Bob wondered if his entire relationship with David was based upon an elaborate ruse by a desperately lonely man:

Am I the mark in some elaborate sick game? Were the fishing trips all a pretense to bait a relationship? Did David deliberately fail to secure the camper's stairs? David knew there were rock walls on the trail; he'd mentioned it on the drive up from Plaintown. The only significant difference between the trailer and the motel room was the motel had running water. The trailer had limited water. David needed frequent showers. Could it possibly be that David went to all this trouble just to make a pathetic advance to him? A mind can go into paranoia at times,' considered Bob. *'Mine must be doing that now.'* There was no way David could have known the motel would have one room available, unless he'd reserved it in advance. That would be confidential between David and the motel owner.

Bob willed his mind to climb off its hamster wheel. Regardless of David's personal turmoil, they had their agreement and Bob was performing his part. The agreement was separate from the personal, Bob assured himself; and David would never break a deal. Despite David's personal difficulty with his sexuality, Bob believed David was honorable. Their mutual loyalty to each other and the firm was very strong. Besides, after working for the firm for eight years and taking a terrible drop in income, Bob could see his best choice of action was to keep his part of their deal and see it through to the end, until David died.

He felt sorry for David and *wanted* to be a good friend to him, but he just couldn't become a homosexual. He wasn't wired that way. Thoughts of behaving against his natural heterosexual attraction to women repulsed him. While Bob and David trudged past the wrecked trailer, wedged between the rock boulders, two doe antelope stood off about a hundred yards from the trail. They alternated their surveillance. One stood alert, chewing its mouthful and watching the hunters, while the other's head was down, gathering a fresh mouthful of cheat grass and sage.

Doe eyes weren't the only ones that tracked the movements of the hunters. The excitement of the hunt caught the attention of a huge, half-breed Lobo male, a freak, oversized canine who possessed qualities that exceeded the stamina of the strongest wolf and the wiles of the cleverest coyote. He was a full foot taller at his shoulders than any alpha male wolf. His paws were half again larger than the largest paws on any wolf and his elongated legs allowed him to lope along tirelessly in pursuit of prey. Years before he could cut a mature antelope from the herd, then run it to exhaustion and kill it. He was slightly past his prime now, but much wiser. His kills came easier. He watched herds patiently for signs of weakness in the older and infirm animals. He took his meals with little effort. He lingered near the herd when they birthed. He killed many young fawns in their first hour of life. Today his experienced yellow eyes studied the tactics of the old buck and the antics of the hunters. He expected to learn new lessons. As he studied every detail of the opposing strategies his keen olfactory senses told him that this hunt offered more than he saw. He drooled.

David had not showered that morning. Amid the familiar scents of digesting bacon and whiskey, the huge canine detected something unusual. Coyotes and wolves can smell opportunity from miles away. Only one molecule in a million needs to touch their scent receptors. The Lobo detected a hint of internal decay. His highly educated nose informed him that the older human had early-stage internal organ distress. David's renal functions were declining. If left untreated, he would succumb as his kidneys failed to process waste. They were gradually poisoning him. David was unaware of his advancing condition. But the Lobo instinctively knew if he followed the smell of this afflicted animal long enough, its scent would lead him to its carcass. When the two hunters drove back to Plaintown in their rented car, they kept the windows down to enjoy the rushing breeze of the cool high plains air. Miles behind them, patiently loping along while scenting the air, followed the Lobo.

CHAPTER EIGHT

I'll come no more behind your scenes, David; for the silk stockings and white bosoms of your actresses excite my amorous propensities (Samuel Johnson: Boswell's *Life of Johnson*)

PEACHY

David wasn't about to give up on Bob. Marvin taught him, if he taught him anything, that to be successful in any endeavor he needed to be persistent. Marvin succeeded in building the Firm's advisory business by cultivating the opinion leaders of all Plaintown's temples. Marvin succeeded in cultivating the Plaintown's union pension plan business by being persistent, going to their meetings, championing their causes, coaching them on political initiatives to gain them greater influence in the city; and ultimately offering up Susan's body to their leadership. Marvin's mantra was:

"*The recipe for success in anything is to do whatever it takes.*" His parental mentoring was the guiding principal for David, in business and in life.

For a time, David rationalized Bob's rejection.

'He's just immature or from such an uncultivated childhood that he simply doesn't know that the pleasures of homosexuality exist. Likely in his childhood he never had a single homosexual encounter. Likely he's never even known anyone who is a homosexual. No wonder he rejects my advances. He didn't experiment in childhood like

I did with Hirsh. He only knows the pleasures of women. The poor man doesn't know what he's missing.'

Of course! David assured himself that had to be the reason for Bob's rebuff. Bob simply had no appreciation of how great it was to suck another man's cock; or to have another's penis thrust into one's tush. The solution was, as Marvin always counseled patience and persistence.

David resolved to nudge Bob's perspective by degrees. If he would make himself appear to look more like a woman, perhaps the transition to homosexuality would be more palatable for Bob. No matter how idiotic this idea might seem to a heterosexual male, to David the idea struck him as a spark of genius. He decided to go *'girl'* for Bob. Heeding Bob's admitted attraction to the opposite sex, David endeavored to make himself more appealing to the younger man by appearing to be a woman. Never in this rush of inspired thought did he consider what he would look like as a pretend woman compared to the physical attractions of a Marty or a Barbara, both stunning femme fatales. Undaunted by any grounding in logic or common sense, David reasoned he could persuade, persist, and prevail.

It was on a Friday afternoon, about two weeks after their foiled antelope hunt, that Bob got the call from David. *"Hello there. I thought we'd get together for drinks after work today. I have some ideas I'd like to discuss with you. How's your schedule?"* sounded a chipper David.

"My schedule's open. When do you want to go?" answered Bob.

"Actually," said David, *"I thought instead of going to the club you could meet me in the Cowboy Hotel. I'd like you to come pick me up in the hotel barber shop, and from there we could go in your car to a little place I like."*

"Okay, fine by me," replied Bob, what time should I pick you up?"*

"Let's say three o'clock. I should be finished by then." David was excited to try his new approach to Bob.

Bob, ever the dutiful junior partner, arrived promptly at the Cowboy's barber shop at three. David was just getting into the barber chair, as his appointment started at three. As Bob opened an outdoor hunting magazine and began to read, David began his transformation. First, he instructed the barber to straighten his hair and then curl it on the ends, layering it along the sides so it fell softly away from his face.

Then, a manicurist and a pedicurist appeared. David placed his hands upon the arms of the massive barber chair's leather arms and put his feet on the expandable foot bench. The pedicurist removed his shoes and socks and washed his feet over a bucket filled with warm water. The manicurist washed his hands and rubbed his palms and fingers with her proprietary lotions. After his hands and feet were thoroughly cleansed, the women went to work sculpting David's nails.

He instructed the barber to put curlers in his hair and perm it so the curls would stay in place. The manicurist and pedicurist applied a peachy pink nail polish, near David's skin tone but a shade slightly pinker. The women then applied a coat of clear shiny lacquer finish over all ten of his nails. Bob sat and observed David's makeover. It took an entire hour in the chair. David looked approvingly in the barber's mirrors at the man's handiwork, and then carefully examined each one of his toenails and fingernails. His three attendants stood by awaiting his approval.

"Nice job," David complimented them. *"I feel like a whole new person. In fact, I believe you three experts have made me look better than a lot of women I've seen."* He lavished them with double their normal tips, which was not his usual practice. After he got up from the barber chair, he put on his suit jacket. He was wearing

a suit Bob hadn't seen before. It was a peach-colored linen and silk blended fabric. Obviously, it was very expensive. It was a suit a man might wear to a summertime outdoor party to celebrate the running of the Preakness horse race at a social gala attended by other gentlemen, accompanied by their ladies attired in fancy hats and elegant dresses. Bob noticed David also wore a new pair of white spats. They closely resembled what a woman might wear for a formal occasion.

"Well, Bob, how do I look?" David smiled his best winsome smile, seeking approval.

Bob stared at his mentor, his lips clenched and his smile drawn back tightly. He bobbed his head up and down slightly, a motion which confirmed that he knew David was nuts crazy. He summoned his best comportment to not burst into laughter or blurt out: '*You look like an oversized, fucked-up duck!*'

Instead, with utmost discretion, Bob stated most soberly, *"You look fine, David. That suit becomes you."* He couldn't bring himself to compliment David's hair or nails. That, Bob correctly intuited, could invite an unwanted advance.

"Great. Thank you for picking me up." chimed a happy David. He imagined he was a woman being taken on a date.

David and Bob climbed into Bob's new Cadillac and David directed him to drive a few miles east of the downtown area to a special watering hole called '*The Others' Place*.' Once inside, Bob's eyes became accustomed to the dim lighting. David looked at him to gauge his reaction. Initially, Bob stood poker-faced, taking in the scene. There were men everywhere, but no women, at least none that he could see.

Men hugged and kissed other men. Their dress was an eclectic mix. Some wore normal business attire. Likely, they were lawyers and executives on the way home from work. Construction workers showed off their muscular physiques. Flaming gays wore outrageous female dresses with bold prints. They accessorized with brightly colored belts and handbags, complimented by platform shoes. David's heart fluttered. Everyone here seemed truly happy! Men were laughing together; singing together; kissing one another. David felt excited to be part of the scene.

'Surely Bob can now see how wonderful it is to be gay!' thought David. *'How can he not see it? We men all love each other. This is camaraderie at its very best and most sincere; and taken to that wonderful place which extends beyond camaraderie to the delightful place of sexual intimacy. It's all so wonderful and beautiful to behold. It's breathtaking. Here's where I've met many of my secret lovers. Surely Bob will feel the magic of this place!'* David pointed out to Bob the dim-colored light bulbs in the elegant chandeliers; the lovely flocked wallpaper in purple and taupe velvets; and the sweet jazz music. Winston Marsalis, T.J. Booker, Louis Armstrong, Eric Clapton and selections of so many other jazz greats were being played.

"This place is like heaven on earth," David proclaimed. He was in his element and completely aroused. He reached for Bob's hand and held it closely in his own. Bob didn't pull away, not at first, but then, Bob pulled his hand away. Alas, rejection! But maybe there was still hope. Bob didn't pull his hand away *initially*, after all. Maybe he was in the mood, but then his upbringing reasserted itself. David reached for Bob's hand again. That second time the younger man immediately pulled his hand away.

The duo sat at the bar and ordered drinks; a pink daiquiri for David, scotch on the rocks for Bob. The drinks were apropos for the moods of mentor and mentored. They were like a married couple who'd suddenly realized they were completely incompatible. It was impossible to talk about the markets or the business in this place, so the two said practically nothing. David heard Bob mumble something about the music being good. But David knew by then that his junior only tried to make small talk to assuage his bruised feelings. There was nothing to say.

After Bob drove David back to the garage where they kept their cars, he felt a tinge of sorrow for his friend. He felt the need to be brutally candid, whether David would be hurt by it or not.

"*David,*" Bob started, and then paused.

"*What?*" David stood by Bob's car, still holding the passenger door open.

"*David, I know what you're trying to do. I know you want me as your lover as well as everything else. I get it. I really get it. But you need to understand that I am not a homosexual person. I have never been a homosexual person and I will never ever be a homosexual person. That place you took me to made me extremely uncomfortable. In all honesty, David, what you did today, the way you dressed yourself up to look more like a woman, your clothes, the way you took me into that place to pretend to those who saw us that we were somehow an item together… well, frankly, the entire experience made me feel like throwing up. Please understand that I'm not trying to hurt you, David. I know you are very sensitive and loving, but I cannot be your lover. So I must ask you as sincerely as I can to please stop your advances toward me. I am your willing partner in business and your friend, but that is the limit for me. Can't you acknowledge that and accept me as I am?*"

David stood there staring at Bob, taking in all that he'd just heard, especially the part about vomit. His heart ached. His stomach churned. Never since he'd heard his mother tell his father that she wished he'd never been born had he felt so utterly unwanted and unloved. He hated himself and wished he was anyone or anything but himself. David wanted to die.

Bob sensed an impasse and tried to reach out to David. "*Can you at least say something?*"

There followed a long silent moment while David just stood staring at Bob. Then he slammed the car door with such fury that the glass in the passenger window cracked. He turned his back on Bob and walked away without saying a word.

CHAPTER NINE

Wake up and smell the coffee (Anonymous)

SNOW AND COFFEE

It was early spring or late winter; the seasons blurred. It's hard to differentiate them on the Colorado high plains. A huge upper atmospheric panhandle low had parked itself for three days over the Texas and Oklahoma lands where native Kiowa, Comanche, and Apache had once hunted buffalo. They traveled west from there to trade at New Mexico's Taos Pueblo. No longer. Now, descendants of those reservation Indians made rugs and jewelry for trade with tourists; no longer for buffalo hides, but for dollars. But not on this day; the day the storm came.

This particular storm was a monster. Storm warnings and blizzard conditions caused impossible whiteout conditions for drivers from the panhandles to New Mexico and north into Colorado. Gulf of Mexico waters were spun aloft and hurled down upon Colorado's San Juan Range. Five feet of fresh powder snows blanketed Telluride and Silverton slopes. Many storms were stopped by those mountains, but not this one. It continued moving northward and eastward. Snowfalls of five feet whipped by howling winds piled snowdrifts seven to ten feet high along the populated Colorado Front Range. All roads into and out of Plaintown were closed. Drivers were stopped by beleaguered highway patrol troopers. For their own safety, travelers were ordered off the roads into motels, local churches, and school gymnasiums. This upslope storm was life-threatening. It killed. Winds howled their fury. For days, snow and storm winds whipped Colorado's Front Range. Nature showed no signs of let up or mercy. Life shut down.

Cattlemen desperately tried to move their herds into shelters and barns, but this storm came too fast and fierce for many. Thousands of cattle and horses did their best to withstand the whipping white rage. They tried getting into low gullies and behind hills, seeking any bit of shelter to escape the bitter gale-force winds. They turned their backs into the wind, trying to breathe and see; but their efforts were hopeless. Tens of thousands of cattle and horses died on the first day of the onslaught. Calves died lying next to their mothers. Bulls lay buried deep in snow at the bottoms of ravines. Devastation was widespread. Animals and people unfortunate enough to be outdoors simply had no chance against nature's howling white fury. In Colorado, death wears white.

Forest animals fared better than their prairie brethren. Deer, elk, moose, antelope, bighorns, and mountain sheep retreated to western-facing slopes. They hunkered down low in the pine forests. The mountains' immovable might broke the snow's onslaught. Pine trees creaked, groaned and bent in the winds. They buffered the howling fierceness. The wild creatures slept huddled closely together for warmth. Their wildness ways learned over millenniums spared most of them. They lived while whole herds of plains' cattle died.

For city dwellers, the storm brought a welcome holiday. People stayed hunkered down as best they could. Children pressed amazed faces to windows; and watched the blowing, swirling snowfall in wonderment. Adults occasionally stepped out into the fury to shovel driveways and walks, before retreating inside for warmth and hot chocolate, vowing to resume their fight after needed rest. Then, as quickly as it blew in, the snowstorm blew east onto the Great Plains. It carried its white chaos to new places.

Road crews appeared with plows and gravel to make the main thoroughfares passable. The highway patrol tried frantically to rescue those caught for three days in the storm. Some people caught in the fierce white out survived; some didn't. Towing companies licked their chops. They were grateful for several days of booming business. Private snowplow operators were paid fortunes to ransom private roads. Mountaintops reflected sparkling sun brightness from their mantles of white. The snowpack deluge would last until late August. Then, fresh snows from prevailing westerlies would start Colorado's annual snow cycle anew. Skiers thanked the snow gods and rejoiced.

Colorado reasserted its fame. Colorado is snow. Beautiful, dazzling, powdered snow. The thin ribbon of road, that highest continental U.S. road that crosses the continental divide, the one Coloradans call the Trail Ridge Road, was a road no longer. It was buried under eighty to a hundred feet of snow. It would stay closed until late June or sometime in July when snowmelt reduced its depth to ten-to-twenty-feet. Only then could gigantic, specialized plow machines mount their assault on the endless wall of white.

Animals stirred again. Surviving cattle and buffalo pushed their heavy heads and faces deep into the snow searching for meager stubs of grass. Getting hay to these desperate creatures would take ranchers days. But the animals didn't have days. Finding grass meant staying alive. Life became a race against time. All across the prairie, mother cows stood over dead calves, half buried in snow, bawling their mournful bellows. Their swollen, unsuckled teats pained them. It was the saddest, most heart wrenching sound a rancher hoped to never hear. After hearing cows in mourning no one would ever convince the ranchers that their animals had no feelings.

The sun came out, as it must. A brilliant blue sky and cold clean air greeted the citizenry. People inhaled to the fullest expanse of their chests, tasting the air's wonderful freshness deep in their lungs. Blood reinvigorated from the copious oxygen. There was a quieter level of voices now; a more respectful tone toward others; a feeling of sympathy for ranchers who'd lost everything. People, for a while, behaved more like people should, all the time.

In Plaintown, office workers were treated to a three-day vacation by order of the mayor. Unessential people were to stay home until crews cleared roads. Firemen and police were on high alerts for citizens in distress. People were good to each other and civic-minded, compliments of Mother Nature.

The fun-loving human otters, who make Colorado special, took full advantage of the white bounty. They were out on snow-covered city streets, but they weren't clomping miserably through the white stuff. They were on top of it; having fun. Snowshoes were bounding about with people's feet strapped on top of them, making mirthful tracks in snow. Cross-country skiers slipped along from homes to stores, to neighborhood watering holes and theaters. Coloradans can't be stopped by snow; it's what they live for. Children were free to go outside again. They did what children do. There were snowmen to make; snow forts to build; sledding to do; and fun filled snowball fights.

In higher elevation Front Range towns, people dug out. Their first order of business was to shovel the weighty snows off their roofs, then their driveways. Once they had their Jeeps and Land Cruisers chained up, these mountain people were good to go anywhere. They loved their little villages and lifestyles and chuckled with an underlying dismay at the dull lives people lived on the prairie, *on the flat* as they called it. Bob had just gotten back from the store and was taking his snowshoes off when Barbara called.

"Do you love the snow, Big Horse?" she asked.

"Yes. Just in from my grocery run." he answered. *"How's Sparrow?"*

"I'm good! Is today a good day for you to meet for coffee?" Barb knew it had to be, since the offices were closed.

"Sure." Bob wanted her for more than coffee; but he took what she offered.

"I'd like to meet at an out-of-the-way place," she said with a business tone. *"We should talk. How about Old Pablo's?"*

"I'll meet you in an hour." Bob knew the place. It was funky and its clientele were mostly book worms and chess players.

At the coffee shop, Bob and Barb ordered lattes and settled into a quiet corner. Barb told Bob what she and Blade did the week before and what she saw in the secret file folders. Bob didn't want to believe her at first.

"You've got to be putting me on. You're talking about David and Marty committing murders; drugs; prostitution; loan sharking; a hidden altar; insects; and spiders? All this and phony invoices too? Are you sure you're not delusional?" Bob shook his head as if he could shake off the truth.

"I'm not delusional. I saw these things with my own eyes. I took pictures of all the stuff in David's secret room. I'm telling you, Bob, the man is very sick. He does not have a normal mind."

"You're talking about my friend, Barbara. First you say there's a phony invoice problem, and okay, maybe David tries to keep taxes down, but now this? Why are you doing this?" Bob didn't want to believe her, even after David had slammed his car door and cracked its window. He was in denial. He wasn't expecting this; and he wasn't ready to hear it. Her assertions were an affront to his world view and his status as the fair-haired boy and son to inherit the throne. But, then again, there was David's homosexual stuff. He hadn't expected that either. Bob was torn. The father

he always wanted was being attacked by the woman he loved. He hoped there was a mix up, some kind of mistake.

"Because you're living an illusory delusion. You need to see the truth." Barb was unshakable.

"But David has always kept his word to me, Barb. How can I turn against him?"

"You will not turn against him. He will turn against you." Barb was confident.

"How can you know that?" Bob's eyes pleaded for this whole conversation to go away. He wished what he was hearing wasn't true.

"I trust Chief, that's how." Barb nodded. She returned his pleading look with certainty from her own eyes. *"He knows animals and people very well. He's an expert tracker. Chief and I talked. I showed him what I told you I saw. He has everything, all the file copies. I flew to Montana to see him last weekend."*

"Let me guess. He also told you to be patient." Bob was cynical.

"You have no place to make light of someone who is trying so hard to help you, Big Horse. Chief is good. His heart is good. You must always have respect. Always!" Her voice rise told Bob she wasn't joking about anything she was telling him. *"And yes,"* she continued with a softer voice, *"He says we must still be patient. Bob, you may be in danger. You must not let on in the slightest that you know anything."* Barbara's face was stern. Her consternation with Bob's cavalier attitude flared her skin to a light shade of red.

"Okay, okay. I'm sorry. I apologize," Bob retreated to a contrite attitude. *"But try to see things from my perspective. David is like a dad to me. We split serious money on a handshake. Now you want me to turn away from a man who's been like a father to me and a special friend? How can I not trust that kind of person?"*

"That handshake was long ago, Bob, many years. You working on a verbal deal now or what? I have looked everywhere and found no evidence that you have anything other than a retail rep deal. But you're not a retail rep. You don't sell to the public. You're wholesale. You sell to the brokers. So, what is your deal, actually, Big Horse?" Barb sought to draw Bob out.

"I will inherit the operating companies when David dies. That's my deal." Bob confided to her.

"Whoa! Really, Big Horse? You have that in writing?" Barbara was skeptical.

"It's in writing." Bob's clipped answer didn't completely answer her question. Barbara caught the omission.

"Bob, may I ask where is this writing?"

"It's in a safe deposit box." Bob opened to her.

Everything suddenly came together for Barbara. Suddenly the scene she'd witnessed from her office window years before finally made sense to her. 'Of course! Everything fits now,' she thought to herself.

"Big Horse, is the writing in your safe deposit box or David's?" Her voice was anxious now. She sensed she was getting closer to the truth.

"David's." replied Bob.

"Big Horse, did David show you this writing?" She asked, already suspecting the answer.

"Yes." Bob described the bank vault scene to Barbara. Now everything finally made complete sense to her.

"So, Big Horse, you changed careers to build a company. You made a deal with David, he put the terms in a will codicil, and then he showed you the codicil. Is that right?" She confirmed her understanding.

"Yes." Bob confirmed what she surmised.

"*This is important, Big Horse,*" she said emphatically. "*What exactly did David say to you when you left the bank?*"

"*See you later, I guess. I can't remember.*" Bob only remembered that he was on cloud nine at the time. Everything else seemed unimportant.

"*Yes, you can remember, Big Horse. Think. Did you and David come back to the office together?*" Barbara wanted to shake Bob's memory.

"*Yeah, we always come back together.*" Bob looked at her but she just stared at him, her head cocked and eyes squinted in disbelief. Her look jogged Bob's memory.

"*No! Wait! I remember now. David told me he needed to go up the street to see an old friend about something. Yes, he did say that. I remember it clearly.*"

"*Very good, Big Horse!*" Barbara put her hands on his arms. "*Now Sparrow must tell you something, but first you must promise to keep what I'm about to tell you to yourself. Promise me. It is very important for you to promise me.*"

"*Okay, I promise I will keep to myself whatever it is you are about to tell me.*" Bob thought Barbara's penchant for secrecy was becoming obsessive.

"*Bob, you are the dearest man. I love with my whole heart. I hate to tell you this but it is truth you are about to hear. David did not go up the street to see an old friend that day. You came into the building. David did not. David walked one block up the street, crossed over to the other side of the street, walked another two blocks up the street, then crossed back to the bank side of the street and walked back into the bank. Sparrow watched the whole sequence from the window of the little reception area file room, the one with the extra chairs and tables and lamps.*"

She looked deep into Bob's eyes. He was wounded by what he heard.

"Are you sure?" he asked. He hoped he hadn't heard what he just heard. He was deeply invested in his belief that he would inherit the companies.

"I'm sure, Bob. That codicil you saw was probably destroyed that very same day you saw it." Barbara's voice was empathetic.

"But you don't know why David went back to the bank." Bob clung to a hope that what she surmised was incorrect.

"No, I don't. I cannot prove what I believe; but the behavior fits." she admitted the possibility that there could be another reason why David returned to the bank.

"Fits what?" Bob's hackles were raised. He didn't want to believe the worst.

"Look, Bob. Apparently, David has defrauded you. I believe he went to his attorney and had him draft a codicil to his will. He then took the draft home, telling the attorney that he wanted to study the codicil and think about it. But that is not why David wanted to take the codicil draft home. He made a copy of that draft and signed it; and he had three witnesses sign it. Then he took you to the bank vault and showed you his signed and witnessed copy of the draft codicil. After you and he left the bank, David returned to the bank vault, by himself. He again had his safety deposit box brought to him. Then he removed the signed and witnessed codicil copy from his safe deposit box. He took the signed and witnessed codicil copy home and he burned it; thus, believing he destroyed the evidence of his fraud. Then, another day or two later, David went back to his attorney with the original, unsigned, and not witnessed codicil draft that his attorney made for him. He told his attorney that, after more thought, he decided against leaving the companies to you. He gave the original codicil draft back to his attorney; and then he left. It was a clever fraud, Bob. That's all it was.

"Look, Bob, Marty thought she was special as well. David let her get away with whoring all over the country as long as she was useful

to him. She also had her mother's protection while she was here. But where is Marty now?"

"*Who the hell knows?*" Bob still had lingering emotional pain over losing Marty. He was not ready to believe theories or innuendos.

"*Bob, you need to be smart here,*" directed Barbara. Her head was clear. She knew they were dealing with a monster mass murderer. Bob was still trying to come to grips with what she was telling him. "*Chief has theories about what happened to Marty and one of them is the worst case. I saw skulls; insects. She may be dead, Bob.*"

"*Come on, Barb. Stop this,*" pleaded Bob, not wanting to believe the worst happened to the woman for whom he still harbored feelings. "*I know you didn't like her, but you're saying she's dead?*"

"*Think, Bob.*" Barbara appealed to his reasoning ability. "*Who decided to hold off on filing a missing person report?*"

"*Susan and David both did.*"

"*Yes,*" replied Barbara, "*but did you consider that Susan wanted to save her daughter from embarrassment? That explains her decision, but what about David's? Why was he so nonchalant about one of his marketing stars going missing?*" Barb raised her eyebrow.

Bob had an answer. "*By then I was doing sales nationally. We'd changed our marketing strategy.*"

"*Sure, but suppose you failed; and what about continuing sales from the locals? That was Marty's area. Why wouldn't David want her lying on her back, fucking for local sales?*"

"*But Barb, I was succeeding. Our sales were going up faster than ever before.*"

"*You're right!*" admitted Barbara. "*That's what I could be missing, but that would give David even more reason to….*"

"*You're not suggesting what I think you are*" Bob cut her off.

"It's one of Chief's theories, an active theory," her voice grew intense. "It fits everything so far, except Marty's body. David might have figured if the two of you got married that could result in a marital blow up. David would believe you'd figure out that Marty was a whore. A fight might follow. Sales would suffer. So, David decided to get rid of her. It's possible. I saw human skulls in David's green room. They were partially decomposed with insects crawling all over them. He uses insects to dispose of his victims' bodies. Listen to me. One of those heads had its scalp cut where Marty's red birthmark would be. That skull could have been Marty's. I think it was. And that's not all, Big Horse. Chief and I did a little tracking work. David started a subsidiary under the firm's holding company to do real estate investing. But it's just a front for money laundering.

"He has an exclusive deal with a Mexican drug gang. They arrange contract murders through David. David keeps the hit men separate from the contractors who order the kills. Marks are killed by long-distance sniper fire from high-velocity target rifles with silencers. A separate unit immediately picks up the dead bodies and takes them to the barnyard for processing. There's no body; no evidence of any crime; just people disappearing. Sound familiar, Big Horse? David is paid cash for the hits. The remains are fed to the barnyard animals and the insects. Insects that need disposal are fed to his guinea hens. It's an ingenious cycle. The real estate subsidiary also runs a string of whorehouses. Cash from prostitution and drugs is put in a lawyer's escrow account and used to buy dilapidated houses in dodgy neighborhoods. Man Child goes along with the lawyer to the closings dressed as a simple carpenter who's going to rehabilitate them.

"The houses get fixed up and the tops are popped to add bedrooms. Then David buys underage girls and boys from Cambodia, Thailand, and south of the border who are trafficked to the United States to do prostitution in the houses. They also sell drugs there, the hard, nasty stuff; and the house managers get the girls addicted to cocaine and heroin, making them dependent on drugs and willing to prostitute for their fixes. Debbie keeps a secret set of books for the operation.

"Bob, Chief has taught me how to track animals and how to understand their behaviors. I have tracked David as I would track any animal, by the trail he left, his paper trail; and by his behaviors. I got all of the records of his criminal activity; all the details; and all the involvement of Marty in the murders they did. I sent a copy of all these records to Chief. They run seven houses in the metro area and two houses in Springs. The houses each make five million a year, tax free. There are pages in the murder file with each girl's name, all Asian and Latino names with ages and house numbers next to each. It's a complete record of each girl's production, sex specialty, and drug costs. There's also a record of girls that went bad, were disposed of, and needed replacement.

"Girls who rebel or get out of line are murdered and processed at David's murder factory, then fed to the animals and the insects. These girls are just parts in a machine that get replaced when they outlive their usefulness. Men that get cross wise with David's drug cartel friends also get murdered. There's no inventory paperwork on those hits. But David maintains a list of men's names who were 'disappeared.' Chief checked the names. Some were high up in the drug business, so they'd have protection.

"How David murdered those guys had to be ingenious. We haven't figured that out yet, but Chief is working on it. He's made some phone calls. He has a theory that David and Marty are somehow involved in those high-end murders. He believes there may be some sort of codependent evil relationship between the two of them where they both know some dirt about each other. That's what binds them together, like a pair of binary stars that orbit each other. Neither star can break away from the other."

"So, David may have felt threatened his secrets could get out if Marty broke away? You think he killed Marty because he was afraid that I'd pull her out of her orbit and we'd leave the Firm?"

"Something like that, possibly. Chief isn't sure. You must understand that David doesn't see people as you and I see people. He sees them as enemies and competitors, like an insect sees another insect. He's completely disassociated from human feelings. He's like an insect himself, trapped inside a human body. He has no empathy for those he murders and disposes of. His murder operation gives a whole new meaning to the word 'insecticide.'

"Some of the money taken in by the operation goes to bribe politicians and police to look the other way. David has fifteen thousand Johns on his lists of regular customers. Through each house he credits the regulars' accounts up to fifty thousand Dollars each. Then, if they don't pay up in cash, the Mexican drug guys do enforcement work. Many Johns are prominent Plaintown politicians and businessmen. The houses pay their expenses in cash wherever possible. Payments that must be paid by check, like real estate taxes, are paid by the Firm's subsidiary. It's a big operation, and it's growing fast. It's much bigger than the Firm's legitimate businesses.

"And the other operations are not only about making money. There's also a subsidiary of the real estate subsidiary. It sells junky consumer products. The come-on is that if the customer doesn't like the product, they can get their money refunded by sending it back. So, people buy all sorts of things made in China and Vietnam. Then they decide they don't want them. They try to send back their mechanical exercise machines and espresso machines and mail-order motor scooters. None of these items work.

"The hitch is they must call the company to get an authorization number to send the crap back. When they call, they must give up a lot of personal information. David puts the information into a data base to use later, possibly to sell, we can't be sure. Then customers are put on hold for an hour; and then the call disconnects. For David, this is all a big Yuk. He loves screwing people. That's what juices his life." Barbara's eyes bored into Bob's. She was pleased with herself and her sleuthing. She smiled like a cat that just ate a canary.

"I can't believe I'm hearing this." Bob was dumbfounded. "It's hard to accept that there are people who think in terms of screwing other people."

"Trust me, Big Horse, such people are out there. I'm sorry this is hard for you. Think of it this way. David loves to pit people against each other. The firm is like his personal amusement park. He has girls in the office fighting minor turf wars over stupid stuff all the time. He has different ones order different amounts of pencils and then he sets them up to blame each other for which one of them made a ten-dollar mistake while he's making millions every month. He puts two different people in charge of the same thing and then makes sure the project fails so he can watch them blame each other and fight about it. He loves instigating fights. He loves watching people fights.

"And Bob, as I told you, his sociopathy extends to insects too. He loves to watch tarantulas and scorpions fighting to the death. He loves watching spiders eating grasshoppers and crickets. He loves seeing a scorpion paralyze a roach and eat it. I'm telling you, Bob, David is sick. He loves destroying young girls' lives with his whorehouse businesses. He destroys children in the schools through his drug distribution business. He destroys employees' homes and marriages by loaning them money and then cutting their pay for some idiotic reason or another, so they can't pay him back.

"He does the same sorts of dirty tricks to people whom he loans monies to, outside the companies. He loves to destroy. He is a classic sociopath; a monster. He just hides it well behind this image of a benevolent man who runs the business. It's all bullshit, Big Horse. It's a disguise for what he really is. He's a destroyer of everything and everybody. He drains the work, the careers, and the lives out of everyone he comes into contact with. Unsuspecting people trust their money to this monster.

"Now Bob, what makes you believe a man like this wouldn't pit you and Marty against each other to see who would defeat the other? Can't you see it? Weren't the two of you fighting initially, before you started screwing her?"

"Yes. We were at odds," admitted Bob. "She tried to block everything I tried to do, at first; but she failed. I leapfrogged her blocking moves by going nationwide."

"Yes, and that worked. That showed David you were smarter than she. Can't you see it? He tested you both. He probably instructed her to give you a hard time to see what you were made of. She failed. You succeeded. He looked at the two of you as corporate gladiators. She lost. So, she had to die. Don't you get it?"

"That's pretty crazy, Barb."

"Is it? What if the two of you got married? What if that kept you here in Plaintown and not on the road selling? Can't you see what a threat your marriage would be to sales growth? David whips you constantly for more sales. I see it. He's squeezing the life out of you. He even persuaded you to become a Jew because he believed that would help you get more sales. He's got you on the road; working you to near death. You're out there in the rain and the snow. He's here in his warm toasty office, playing with his homosexual boyfriends and laughing at you.

Bob, listen to me. Chief and I talked about this. Chief is wise. He believes the father-son business David did with you was a con job to take advantage of you. It's do for me now; and I'll do for you later deal. It has caused you to make decisions to work like a dog, for David; not out of logic about what's best for you, but out of your emotional need for a father figure. Chief believes David has turned you into an emotional cripple."

"I'm an emotional cripple?" Bob's head canted and he scratched his cheek in thought.

"Yes, you are, Horse. And, Marty was emotionally crippled also. He used emotions to cripple both of you, like he cripples insects by taking some of their legs off. Then you, like the insects, are at his mercy and dependent upon him for your survival. He uses you as he pleases; then he gets rid of you. But you are not to worry, Big Horse. Sparrow loves you, truly loves you. Sparrow and Chief and the People will heal you. We will, Big Mighty Wounded Horse, whom I so much love. But you must see what has happened for yourself before you can begin to heal."

Barb finally had Bob's attention. He *was* being worked to near death by David. That was true. He remembered his mother's comments about how Gordy Goodman worked his father, Nevin, to death and then treated Estella no better than a stranger.

"Have you noticed, Big Horse, that when you now fly between cities you are routed to take as many flights as possible? Did you ever think that maybe David changed Judith's instructions to try to wear you out; get you sick; or possibly, get you killed during one of your many takeoffs and landings? If you go to fifty cities in a year, you could normally do it on a hundred or a hundred and thirty flights, right? But Big Horse, you are taking four hundred to five hundred flights. Doesn't that make you stop and think? David is destroying you!"

"Look, I admit it's hard, but I sleep all right on planes. I try to keep costs down." Bob defended his torturer.

"But, does anybody else keep costs down?" asked Barbara. *"The firm and its subsidiaries are gushing millions of monies every month. David and his boyfriends are always off partying in some hotel or bathhouse. They go to Las Vegas to see all the shows. They spare no expense. Do you?"*

"Well, David's worked all his life and he deserves a—" Bob started to voice his rebuttal.

"Bullshit. You need to stop being Stupid Big Horse. You are being played. It's time to stop." Barbara's anger cut him off. "David has fucked off his entire pathetic sick life. He's never worked a day in his life. You're allowing yourself to be manipulated by this creep because you lost your real father and you have a blind spot, Horse. I feel sorry for you about that but you must break free from it. You can do this.

"David is excellent at spotting human weaknesses, and he found your number. You believe you are special to him. He's conned you into thinking that. He spotted your weakness right off. He's good at conning people. He conned people out of cookies as a child. He's a con. That's all he's good at.

"You are not special to him, Big Horse. No one is. He keeps a file for you also. He has you set up with phony invoices and even has a photograph of you kissing some woman named Rita in a seedy bar. Did you like holding Rita's bare ass, Horse? You are like tissue paper to David. He intends to blow his snot mess onto you and throw you away. You need to understand that you cannot take the words and behaviors of a sociopath and juxtapose them into explainable terms as if they were merely quirky oddities emanating from a normal person.

"A sociopath like David is far removed from normal. He is vile. He is evil. He is, at his core being, a hateful inhumane monster. He believes he is better than everyone else. He believes he was chosen by God to fuck over everyone he meets. He is the devil who walks among us. If you don't come to grips with the true character you are dealing with, he will find a way to destroy you; because all he knows and understands is destruction. He has no capability for empathy or love or kindness or any other sort of normal human feelings toward others."

Bob recoiled with alarm at Barbara's description of David. But she was right about the invoices and Rita's bare ass. He felt frightened and threatened. He was ready to believe her. *"Okay, so you think he killed Marty. You think he's going to kill me next. You think I should break my deal. Are you going to the police with this? What else?"*

"No. Not the police. That would be too good for David. There's are better ways to deal with this," she said coldly.

"How?" Bob couldn't think of any way to deal with crime, other than going to the police.

"You leave that to me and Chief. We have our ways. Our ways are the best ways. They are not the white man's ways. They bring finality and closure. You must know nothing and you must say nothing. Mark Sparrow's words. You just play along with David. But always be careful and always remember: David is an extremely dangerous man. You are dealing with a very clever mass murderer who happens to run a major financial institution. He's extremely clever. Never assume anything when you are with him."

Bob was in midair, like when he was a boy tempting fate at the dam breast. He needed to put his trust in the unknown. Would his skates come down and bite hard into the ice and save his life? Barbara was likely right. Yes, she was always right. Her logic was impeccable, as usual. David had gone to Old Mac and tasked him to draft a codicil giving Bob the operating companies of UGGA, free of tax, upon David's death. The question now was, did Mac keep a copy of the codicil that he drafted for David? Bob would close his eyes; hope he'd land on the ice and not go over the dam breast. He was no longer a boy with his trusted ice skates; he was a man. But now, he had to again close his eyes and pray. He looked at Barbara without the slightest hint of concern. He needed to measure up to his role. He needed to be Big Horse; fearless and brave.

"I'm not worried, Barb. I throw a very hard punch and I don't go down easily. Don't you worry about me." Bob gave her a reassuring smile.

"There's nothing more to say about this subject now, Horse; except, be careful." Barbara said in her most officious tone. *"Remember, you are simply being used like a piece of tissue paper. Be very careful!"* She spoke emphatically. Bob knew she was serious. She cared about him. She was taking a risk by talking to him this way.

"This is just one of Chief's theories," she continued. *"Chief says we must both wait. If David has a card, he will play it because he must play it. He must change the situation. It cannot go on as it is. Be ready for it and do not be stupid, Big Horse. Know that Chief and Sparrow are with you all the way on this. Chief's theory is that David is unlikely to kill you. Marty disappeared. If something happens to you or you also go missing, that would be too suspicious. Chief says you must just be careful and wait. David will act like a rat that must come out of hiding. He will make his move. When he does, we will get him."*

Bob looked out the window of the coffee shop. The white snow and cold outside contrasted sharply with the dark coffee and warmth inside. The world always offered choices. He reckoned he'd need to make one, soon.

Sleep was restless for Bob that night. He tossed and turned and wondered. Was it the coffee? Was it the full moon sending its beams through his half-opened window? Was it the things Barbara told him? Did he need to be afraid of David? Finally, he settled down and fell into a deep sleep.

But as the moon rose high in the night sky, he awakened with a start. He shivered with fright. The hair on the back of his neck stood on end. He felt an unnatural presence in the room; another person. He opened his eyes in the dim from the street light outside. Suddenly, he was alarmed. His life was in danger. Something lunged at him. Reflexively, he raised his arm to block his attacker. His arm burned from the cut of a knife blade. Someone was there, standing over his bed, holding him down and with a knife poised to stab him, again. Quickly, he rolled over to the other side of the bed and focused his eyes. It was Marty!

She stood there with her blade poised. It was dripping blood. His blood. She was trying to kill him. Why? How did she get in his room? He hadn't heard his apartment door or his bedroom door open. Why was she here? Barbara had just told him that she had been murdered by David. Yet, there she was, standing opposite him on the other side of the bed. Now, she rushed around the bed to face him directly; her knife poised to strike his chest. She lunged for him and attempted to stab him a second time. But now his senses were engaged. He caught her arm with his hand and held her away from him.

He took a close look at her. Her eyes were wild with desperation. Her lips quivered. And her body was glowing beneath a shimmering nightgown.

"Marty, it's me, Bob. What are you doing? Why are you trying to hurt me?" He stared at her, dumbfounded. She lunged for him a third time. This time he caught her body in his arms and blocked her lunge; held her; looked into her tortured eyes. *"Answer me. Talk to me."*

"I need to murder you. Stop fighting me. I must do this. Please, do not try to prevent me from what I must do." Her voice was haunting; pleading.

"Why would you say that? Why are you dressed this way? Why would you hurt me? We are lovers, Marty. Don't you remember?" Bob shook his head and gazed into her eyes, hoping there was something logical about what was happening; hoping there was some mistake or that he was having a bad dream.

"I need to murder you for us, Bob. I've got permission from Death to come for your soul and take it back to Death with me. I only have twenty-four hours; then I must return to Death because my father is waiting for me. His soul is taking my soul with him to

my new life where I will be reborn in life. But I want you to come with me. I need you, Bob. I need your love. I must murder you so we can be together again. I'm doing this for us. Can't you see?"

"No, Marty. You're not making sense. Murder is bad. It's hurtful. Why would you do that to me?"

"Because I need your soul, Bob. I want to take your soul with me, back to Death. Here, make love with me. Remember how good it was? Remember what a bad girl I can be? I'm even better in Death. You'll see. I promise. We'll make love in Death; then we'll be reborn again, together."

Marty wrapped Bob in her arms and kissed him. As her lips plied his, she reached her hand to his penis and stroked it. When it became hard, she lifted her nightgown and guided it into her vagina.

"See, darling? I'm already soaking wet from just thinking about fucking you. I'm even slipperier; and warmer; and more wonderful than I ever was before. You want me, don't you? Don't you want us to have this, forever? Don't make me beg you for your penis, darling. You know you want me. You love me, Bob, don't you?"

"Yes, I do want you. You are wonderful. You are even more wonderful than I remembered from before. Of course, I want you. Yes, I love you. I will always love you. You know that's true."

"Yes, I know it's true. We have something wonderful together. Ohhh, I feel you. You are coming inside me now. Oh, how I've missed this; how badly I've missed your wonderful penis. Yes, you're doing it just right, like you always do. Oh, yes. Keep it there. Yes, now, rub it over me slowly. Yes, that's it! It's always so special when you do that. When you come with me to Death, we'll do this every night; many times, every night."

"Wait, Marty. I don't understand. Why do you need to murder me? Why can't you just come to me, like this? Why can't we do this whenever we need each other?"

"I can't just come to you like this every night, Bob. Death holds me close. He only gave me this one chance to come see you. I had to give him a lot of favors to come to you. Death owns my soul now. But if I can murder you; separate your body from your soul, I can then take your soul with me to Death. I know the way. Don't be afraid. You'll love it in Death. I promise. The black horse of Death will come for us. We will fly away on him as he takes us to Death. It's beautiful in Death. You'll see. Once your soul is in Death with my soul, our souls can be together like this, forever."

"But Marty, I can't go with you. I can't let you murder me. Your spirit came to me a few weeks ago and told me that I needed to make a life with Barbara. You know that all spirits meet with the council of spirits. The council decided that your soul needed to go into Death and remain with Death; and that my soul needed to continue living in life, with Barbara's soul. Your spirit assured me that we would be together again, someday; and that our spirit souls would find each other in new bodies. I remember that your spirit said something about you and I becoming Sheila and Danny. But it did not say anything about you coming for me to murder me and separate my body from my soul. Are you sure that your spirit wants you to murder me?"

"I don't know, my love. Sometimes I act impulsively. I can't help myself. I just start thinking about your huge, wonderful penis; and then I must be with you. I must have it inside me. All I know is that my heart loves you so much that I needed to follow my heart and disobey my spirit and come to you; to be with you. I need that closeness with you; that wonderful intimacy. I only know that I need you and I truly love only you, because you are the only man who ever truly loved me, for me.

"All I know is that my heart tells me that wherever you go, I must go; wherever you are, I must be. My vagina begs to have your penis inside me. Can you understand how strong that urge is; how *it overpowers everything? I do not care what the spirits do to me for my disobedience. I only know that I must be with you, always. What I do does not matter to anyone else; so, I don't care about that. I only care about being with you. You are all that matters to me. Am I making sense, my love? Sometimes I get so fuck crazed that I can't think straight. It's my nymphomania. You understand my nymphomania, remember?"*

"Yes, I remember. It's your curse; but it's a lovely curse. It's why you are so loving and honest and irresistible. I think it's what made me fall in love with you; made me obsess over you. I love you for your honest self and for your disease, Marty.

"But more importantly, I love you, for you. Ever since we lay together at Assateague's shores and we saw the mare and her foal, I have always loved you, for you. That's when I knew that I loved you, for you; for all your hopes and dreams; all your ways of being you; all the ways you looked when you did things; all the ways you thought about things; all of you; everything about you. You are the love of my life. You know you are."

"Then be my love, Bob. Let me remind you of the love that our souls have for each other: Marty then lifted above the bedroom floor and positioned her honey pot over Bob's mouth. *"Can you taste me? Do you remember how I tasted when our souls first met?"*

"Yes," answered Bob. His tongue had found Marty's clitoris. *"How could I ever forget? My soul remembers all the past times when it was together with your soul. Your female essence is as soft and delicious tasting as it always is; and it is so inviting for love making. You taste and feel the same way you did when you were the glorious high priestess of Baal; before the time of Sumaria, the first Mesopotamians, or the twelve tribes of the Hebrews. Remember?*

"We were at Baalbek. You saw me and singled me out to come to you. It was twenty thousand years ago. You had scented yourself with aphrodisiacs; cinnamon spice and your blended perfumed oils

of jasmine and gardenia. As you are now, you were then; delicious and tasty; delightful beyond words to describe you. You commanded me to taste you and then enter you. I loved consorting with you then, as I am loving it now."

"Do you remember what else we did that day?"

"Yes. Our tribesmen had captured and enslaved the tribes from Gobekli Tepe. You murdered their warrior men in a grand, festive ceremony. You eviscerated them with your obsidian knife. You removed their hearts, livers and testicles and had your assistants prepare them for our feast so that their strengths and procreation forces would leave their souls and come into our souls; and we ate of their life essences at that feast. Then, after the feast, you and I consorted together that entire night. You were ravenous. Our love making was heavenly. Our endurance and passions were without limits."

"Yes, Bob. And that is when our souls bonded together for eternity and why we have eternal strength. Please, honor our eternal bond now and come away with me."

"I cannot. If I disobey the spirits, we would then both disobey. They would then forbid us from ever being together again. We must not assume to know better than the spirits, my love. We must be patient and we must trust that our souls will be together again in our lives in the future; in our many lives together in the future."

"But it is so hard to leave you. I want you so badly."

"I understand. But the spirits have their reasons and their ways. Your father waits for you in Death to join his soul to your soul and, with you, to leave Death together. He wishes to atone for his mistake of leaving his life with you before it was his natural time to die. He has repented to the spirits; and now he needs you to be with him; to bind your soul to his soul, so that you will know good, wholesome parental love in your next life.

"Then, after the spirits are satisfied that you are secure in matters of love, your soul will have other lives and other loves. And my *soul will be one of those souls that your soul rediscovers in life again. Try to remember the names of Danny and Sheila. Your spirit visited me with those names. Their lives will hold our souls, Marty. We will be together again. We will have our love in life, again."*

"I understand. But, before I go back to Death, I must make love with you one last time. I must feel your penis on my lips and my tongue. And I must know the joys of your penis entering me and thrusting inside me one final time. Please, Bob. I must have you."

"Yes. I also want that. I want to remember you this way, always."

Marty then kissed the head of Bob's penis and sucked him until he was hard. And then Bob entered Marty; and he knew her glory and her sweet hot wetness. And together, they thrusted while they kissed. And semen from the giver of life united with the glorious holy receiver and birther of life; and Bob and Marty became one soul, blessed by both their spirits; and honored by their spirits for their true and enduring love; their love and rejoicing in their freedom to love; and their renewed vows of Pagan love's eternal truths of soul mating; and the sacred, unapologetic fornications needed between like souls, as they had honored their same eternal vows many times over many millenniums before.

After they renewed their eternal love making, Bob held Marty apart from him to behold her wonders. He noticed something: *"Marty. You have changed! Your butterfly has disappeared. It's gone from your upper thighs!"*

"No, Bob, I have not changed. I am the same woman who made love with you in life. I had the tattoo placed much later, during our recent lives together, in that life which I have just finished. I wore the butterfly again tonight, when I came to you; so, you would hold it in your mind as a remembrance of me. Here, enter me, again." And Bob did reenter her.

"See, you now know I am my same soul. I am the true me who will always love you. I am the same woman. You now know that I

am who I am, my love. So, reconsider. Please come away with me into Death. Permit me to murder your body so that I may free your soul from it. Then, let your soul come away with my soul. Then we'll be together, always, continuously, and forever."

"I cannot come with you, Marty. Your spirit spoke to me and told me to live out my life with Barbara. It told me to find my love in life with her. You know that our souls must obey the spirits. Your spirit promised me that we'd be together again; but that our togetherness would happen sometime in the future, in our new bodies; and our souls would discover those new bodies and go into them. And then we would know our love in life again. And we would be reunited in love again. I must and I will respect the will of the spirits. Understand that it is not my will. It is their will. Understand that my soul loves your soul and that it will patiently wait until the spirits free my soul to again join with your soul in life."

"But that might take a long time, my love. My nymphomania craves you now and always."

"I don't think our souls can know time, my love. I think, once one's soul is in Death, even with nymphomania, time becomes irrelevant. I think one dies; then one wakes up in one's new live, as if one's soul is coming into life for its first and only time. This process of joining the undying soul to new life happens within the mystery of Higgs-Boson particles and cosmological energy waves to mass conversions.

"Regardless of how it happens, we know that it does happen. We know it happens because people have reincarnation memories from events of times before they lived their present lives; and because many people have realistic dreams and flashbacks into their soul's past lives. So, sweet love of my life and my eternal soulmate, we must accept these things, although we do not fully understand them."

"What are you telling me, Bob?" Marty's doe eyes looked into Bob's eyes with a look that said what she was about to hear would be hurtful.

"I'm telling you the truth, my love. You must leave me now and you must return to Death."

"But I don't want to leave you. Ever! I love you. I don't want to go back to Death. I want to be with you, forever."

"I know. I also want us to be together, forever. But that cannot be. You are a soul that needs to be reborn into a new life body. You cannot defy the will of the spirits and take my soul with you into Death and thereby join our souls together in that way. I know it is hard to say goodbye, my love. But we must say goodbye. We must respect the wishes of the spirits. We must have faith that this parting is the will of the spirits and that our souls will discover our love again in our new bodies. So, let me kiss you this one last time. And then you must return to Death and your soul must wait for me in our new lives."

"Yes. I understand. I am only my soul's simple apparition. I know my soul must obey the will of the spirits and I must return to Death. And I accept that your soul must go on living in this life and it must live with Barbara. And I wish you happiness and wellbeing.

"Go to her; love her; have children with her. And leave your thoughts of me until you know another life. And when you are with her and when you make love with her, think only of her. I understand it must be this way. But parting from you is so hard, my love.

"So, I will leave you with an eternal memory of me. I separated my butterfly tattoo from my soul, which once lived in the present. The last willful act of my soul will be to leave my spirit's messenger to make you joyful and happy. See? My butterfly tattoo has come to life. It flutters and dances for you and brings you joy and happiness. I will leave behind my beautiful Monarch Butterfly to continue its

life of fluttering; to always remind you of my eternal love, until our souls are joined together in life, again.

"So, let's kiss now, for one last time, my love. Let's kiss our final kiss in honor and remembrance of our love. Let's hold each other tightly. Let's feel our souls clinging to our eternal love. Let's now kiss our last kiss." With those last words, Marty embraced Bob. They kissed a long, French kiss. After their final kiss, they held each other at arms' length and stared longingly into each other's eyes for a long, lingering moment. Marty's apparition then said good-bye. It turned its back to Bob and walked away. It walked through the wall of the room without looking back and disappeared into Death. For a while, Bob stood there, wondering:

'What just happened? Was that a dream? It seemed so real! But it could not have been real, could it? Souls can't return to real flesh and blood life, can they? But this cut on my arm is real! And, there, on the floor, lies a knife! It, too, is real! Marty left it for me. She left it to let me know that her soul was here, with me. What just happened between us was real!' Bob picked up the knife and studied it:

'This knife is special. It has a bone handle made from the antler bone of a Stag deer. It is wrapped tightly in a leather strap, fashioned from the hide of a deer. It secures the handle firmly to the blade. The blade is not a steel blade. It is not some ordinary kitchen knife. It is razor sharp, shaped from flaked obsidian stone. It's a prehistoric blade! Marty's soul came to me from across the millenniums! She once used this very same blade to sacrificially murder those who did not accept her tribe's prostitution rituals. She killed those who refused to worship her fornications!

'What happened here, tonight, was real! My true love knows me. She knows my soul. Her soul tracked me and followed me. She was here! She lives! Marty lives! She lives forever in the spirit of the Monarch Butterflies and in the spiritual consciousness that surrounds

me every day. And she truly loves me. Yes, Marty loves me! She is the very essence of love. I know that I will always be loved.'

Bob then looked at the window of his bedroom. There, on the sill of his window, appeared a Monarch Butterfly. She was a very large Monarch. She noticed Bob looking at her. She faced Bob and opened her wings; then she turned away from him to face the closed window pane.

"You need to be free to flutter and make love, don't you? You are creation's spirit of love, aren't you?" Bob spoke to the butterfly. The Monarch Butterfly again opened her wings, as if to say: *'Yes.'*

Morning had just broken. The pearly onion full moon had set and Marty's soul had departed. The sun was ascending, inch by blazing, glorious inch; radiating new warmth through the freshly-born azure sky. Dawn of a beautiful Spring Day had arrived. *'I have to let you go now,'* said Bob. He opened the window to let the Monarch have her freedom. He stood and watched as the butterfly fluttered away.

CHAPTER TEN

What stately vision mocks my waking sense? Hence, dear delusion, sweet enchantment, hence (Horace Smith: An Address without a Phoenix)

MENTORING

David decided it was time to develop a new protégé. Bob's rebuke and rebuffs had crushed his hopes and sobered him. He understood now that he was never going to have a male romance with Bob. Acceptance of that truth followed years of denial; but acceptance now came, slowly and angrily. David experienced self-loathing. Despairing exasperation followed:

'How did I go so terribly wrong? Have I not given Bob everything? I gave him a career path with security. I showered him with gifts and perks. I gave him a fully paid-for arrangement with the world's most famous sexpot porn star. I paid for his romantic trips. I gave him executive prestige; cars; a lavish compensation; an extravagantly appointed office and secretarial help. I freely gave him all these things. Have I asked much in return? Perhaps a blow job now and then; maybe a hug or two; or, possibly some soft words of love for an older man who adored him? Were those things too much to ask? Why did Bob humiliate me so badly? Did he enjoy seeing me cry, begging for his love?'

David wallowed in self-pity; crushed by his thoughts of inadequacy and rejection; unwilling to face the truths which his questions asked. Self-loathing and despair slowly gave way to wrath. Whenever he noticed Bob and Barbara looking at each other, he recognized hope and love in their eyes; his bitterness intensified.

He began finding petty faults in everything Bob did. A sales call forgotten, a stock analysis that seemed hurried, indecisive, or inconsequential. David took all incidences as indicating that there was something besides the firm that was vying for Bob's attention. David upped his pressure on Bob. He demanded that Bob make more sales calls per day and per week; insisted that he take more flights; pushed him to run faster, ever faster.

David's prima donna sales executive fell from his grace. David now saw Bob as a mere mortal; no longer a god. Bob's faults revealed themselves under David's increased pressure. He changed Bob's environment. He made Bob feel like a quarterback feels when he's down three scores; hindered by an injured offensive line; without wide receivers who could remember their routes or playbook; and who had only two minutes left to play. The more pressure David applied; the more mistakes Bob made. And deliberately, David produced poor investment results.

Predictably, bad news came. A rival firm stole a salesman away; a brokerage branch office stopped selling the Firm's products. If this were football and David were coach, he would be finding fault with everything his quarterback did. A hurried throw; an interception; an incomplete pass; every fumble; every play that fell short of the line to gain became Bob's fault. Coach David accepted no blame for bad play calls or idiotic sales ideas. If Bob's offense hadn't even been on the field and the team's defense gave up a touchdown; somehow that, too, would become Bob's fault. Money manager David blamed his own poor results on poor financial analysis; not his own, Bob's.

David decided it was time to groom a new successor. He knew that wouldn't be easy. In his heart of hearts, David understood that his own poor investment performance was causing money to walk out the door, making new sales more difficult to come by and more expensive to buy with side deals from thieving brokers. Also, there was that troublesome deal which he had made with Bob. He no longer intended to leave the companies to Bob. He wanted out of the deal he made.

David's frustrations boiled. He turned to an inner self, seeking new direction and purpose. He recognized that it would be hard to get rid of Bob. Bob's sales network trusted him and liked him. If he broke his deal with Bob and canned him outright, business would surely suffer and backslide. *'But there has to be some way to get out of the deal. There's always a way,'* thought David. *'Perhaps there's a trick?'*

'I must first mentor a new protégé. But where will I find one? Who will he be? I have so many things on my mind; so many things to keep track of! There's the business and then there's also all my secret businesses. Whom can I trust? Can I find another man whom I can also fall in love with? This is maddening!'

David slipped into dementia. "Dolly," said David to his black sheep, *"I'm going to watch a big fight tonight. My new blue scorpion will take on my number-two-ranked tarantula to see who gets a shot at the title. I won't be with you tonight, sweetheart. I'll be watching the big fight with Andy, my new best friend."*

Dolly just stood there chewing her grass.

That night, in the green room, David took down the fetus jar and placed it on the chair next to his. He took a swig of whisky from a trusty bottle. Then he opened the dividers between the tarantula and the blue scorpion. David and Andy had ringside seats. The scorpion and the tarantula were mortal enemies. And they were both famished. They faced off in the glass arena. Each gladiator knew what it needed to do. Both recognized that only one combatant would survive this encounter.

"Andy, it's time you and I had some serious discussions about your future," David began, taking another swig of whisky while addressing the fetus in the formaldehyde jar. *"You see, you and I actually have a great deal in common. Nobody loves either of us. My mom and dad didn't love me; and your mom and dad didn't love you."* David lied to his imaginary protégé. He knew there was love between Marty and Bob. But his sick mind brooked no difference between truths and lies. He said whatever best served the moment, even to the fetus.

Of course, the fetus in the formaldehyde jar said nothing. It was dead and forever preserved. But in David's addlepated mind, the fetus had a lot going for it. For starters, it didn't give David any back talk. David liked that. Silent obedience was the single quality he valued most in a protégé. David demanded loyalty. He understood that loyalty was everything. As David saw things, Andy was the ideal successor to manage David's Firm.

"No. Trust me. Bob and Marty did not love you." David argued with the disagreement he imagined hearing from the fetus. *"Don't try to tell me that they loved you. That insults my intelligence. I know they didn't love you. Your dad only loved your mom's vagina. He did not love you. He didn't even know you were conceived. So, he couldn't possibly have loved you. I'm never even going to tell him about you, either. Why? You're asking me why I won't tell him about you?*

"Because, you're too good for him, Andy. He will never even know you were alive. So, he will never love you. And you will never look up to him. You'll always look up to me! And you will always respect me! I deserve respect, Andy! And, about your mother, Andy. Your mother was more interested in fucking than she was about caring for you. Her lifestyle might have hurt you, Andy. You might have been born with a

disease; or some man's penis might have dented your brain. You poor thing. You needed love but you had a mother that could not possibly give you love. You might have been born mentally disabled. But I have saved you by killing your mother and taking you away from her.

"Now you belong to me, Andy. Now we can share our innermost feelings. We have each other, Andy. We'll always have each other. I'll tell you how the world works; how to live and how to think about things. I want you to pay close attention to everything I say. Remember, Andy: Always do as I say. Never do as I do. Why, you ask? Because I'm a bad boy, Andy."

Of course, Andy said nothing. The silence from the fetus troubled David. His deranged mind felt he had to address it:

"Well, I'll explain why I say that, Andy. Sometimes I can be a very bad boy and I do terrible things to people. I don't want you to grow up to be like me. Not that way. I want you to grow up to be a wonderful man. You'll be a very wealthy man. Possibly, you'll even become a senator or our governor. I know you'll go far, if you'll just listen to my wisdom, Andy. Now, listen to your first lesson:

*"People are the most important factor to be managed in busi-*ness," David began his pontification: *"Most executives look at people and categorize them by their talent areas, like mathematical aptitude for analysis, conversational abilities for salesmanship training, attention to details for bookkeeping, neatness for secretarial work, things like that. But that's the wrong way for an executive to think about people, Andy. The correct way is to categorize them into only two categories. There are smart people and there are stupid people.*

"Smart people should never be hired in the first place because they try to take advantage of you and squeeze you for money. They ask too many questions. They want to know what's going on all the time. They are a nuisance. What you really want working at the Firm are stupid people. You can make promises to stupid people. They will work for a promise. They assume that you'll keep your

word. You can promise them anything. And then, you can screw them after you've gotten the work out of them.

"Your mother and father come from the stupid crowd. Marty believed I'd give her the moon. She screwed her ass off for the Firm. Now she's gone. The beauty of her deal was that we've kept the assets she brought in; and we have no residual costs. The men she fucked can't come to us and blackmail us or turn us in to the regulators, because she's dead. See, like me, you need to think ahead, Andy. Only pick dummies to work for you. Promise them whatever they need to hear. Then, get the work out of them, before you screw them. And be thinking about how you'll screw them in the end, before you even hire them in the first place.

"Your dad still works for us, Andy, but it won't be for long. I have a plan to screw him. I've had this plan for a long time. I'm going to screw the shit out of him. All I need to do is get him to sign a simple piece of paper and we'll be rid of him. Don't get upset with me, Andy. Remember, he never loved you. He only wanted Marty's vagina.

"I'll be honest with you, Andy. There's one employee that's an enigma to me. It's that Indian woman, Barbara. I'm not sure I figured her out correctly when I hired her. I thought she was a dull person who would do as she was told. I researched her background before I hired her. It was sketchy. She lived on an Indian reservation, and then she went to college. There was no information about her parents. I asked myself how much could a couple of dumb fuck Indians possibly know about business? I researched Indian women who were beautiful, because she is very beautiful. And guess what? I found this article about beautiful Indian women. It had pictures of about twenty of the most beautiful ones in the country. They were scantily clad in bikinis and very sexy outfits. And there she was!

"She posed for her photo in that article. So, I thought, naturally enough, that someday she could work as a beautiful company whore. I figured I'd have her fucking her brains out for sales and making great money doing it, right alongside your mother. But that *didn't interest her, Andy. In her job interviews she surprised me. She said she wanted to start working, not in sales; but in the clerical staff. Can you imagine that?*

"She said she wanted to do every menial job that no one else wanted do. It didn't make sense to me. Here was this knockout, beautiful sex symbol; wanting to work in the most inconspicuous jobs possible. I figured she was trying to hide from a boyfriend or maybe she felt guilty about being beautiful. I figured she'd lie low for a while; then move into sales where she could get out of the office and fuck her brains out. So, I told Susan I voted to hire her. All women are nuts anyway, Andy. I decided it wasn't worth my time to figure her out. Hiring her was Susan's call. But if I had objected Susan might not have hired her.

"Now I'm not sure hiring her was smart. See, Andy, the Barbara woman studies the business. She reads regulations; learns everything about how the firm works. She knows more about the minutia of the business than anybody. She even knows more than Susan. She also studies investing. Why she does that, I'll never know? She doesn't make enough money to invest in anything. We barely pay her enough to live on. I think she knows more about everything; all the firm's businesses, even our illegal ones, than she lets on. But she keeps quiet about it. And she never asks for a pay raise. It's almost like she doesn't want money! Maybe she's afraid if she doesn't know everything, she'll get fired?

"I don't understand her. I felt her tits one day, not too long ago. I gave them some nice hand squeezes. I thought I'd try her out and see if she'd want to become a company whore. I thought she'd like getting her tits squeezed.

"But she gave me this mean look. It felt like her eyes were telling me she was going to kill me. That really felt weird, Andy. Most women giggle when I feel them up. They all secretly love it when a man squeezes their tits. They love the attention. They just don't like to admit it.

"But Barbara was angry with me; like hostile Indian angry! That's too bad. She's got terrific tits. I'd gladly feel her up lots of times; even suck her nipples, if she liked me feeling her. But she didn't. Anyway, her tit issues are only one concern that I have about her.

"She's also sweet on Bob. I see how they look at each other. It's like they have a secret code or something. I don't like it when I don't know what's going on. Watch how I handle this situation, Andy. There will be a lesson in it for you. I'm going to make you into the best executive the Firm ever had. You're learning from the master. Just trust me and believe in me. Remember that I always have your best interests at heart. You have a brilliant future at the Firm.

"Now, play close attention, Andy. This is important. You must understand Israel. Israel is the Mouth of the World. The Mouth seeks to swallow up the soul of every Jew; and it wants to devour the world's wealth. It's a hungry, ravenous mouth and every rabbi works to feed it. You need to be careful with the rabbis. Do not let them talk you into giving everything you have to Israel. Money can do a lot for you. Learn to hang onto it. Mother's soul got eaten by the Mouth. She even dragged Father's soul into the Mouth with her.

"But there's something that the Mouth did not swallow, Andy. It did not swallow the jewels that Father kept for brokering Jews out of the holocaust and for running the Nazi rat lines to Argentina after the Second World War. Susan used her love tricks to dupe Father into leaving the jewels to her. She buried them under the ponds to taunt me; keep me here where she could watch me and drive me insane. She is a common thief. She will not get away with it. I can't murder her; not just yet. It is still too close to Marty's death. The police might suspect something. We must wait. When the time comes, you'll pay her a visit. You'll distract her while I ambush her. Then we'll do away with her. We have some time to work out the details, Andy. I'm just giving you a heads up.

"The jewels are in huge metal storage trunks, buried deep under the duck ponds. We have a small problem, Andy. It's only a detail. Susan owns the mineral rights to the land under the duck ponds. After she's out of the way, I'll get the county commissioners to condemn the land. Then we'll build a huge hotel on this property. We'll excavate the ponds for the hotel's foundation; and we'll take the jewels.

"We'll use them to finance a huge Savings and Loan Company. We'll make loans to poor Blacks and Hispanics. We'll also buy a deserted gold mine that has a mine shaft. We'll make sure our borrowers can't repay. We'll have our gangster friends kill the deadbeats and throw their bodies down the mineshaft. We'll seize their properties; and then rent them out. We'll make a killing, Andy. Ha, ha, ha! Did you get that, Andy? A killing!"

"Andy, look! The arachnid just parried that direct thrust from the scorpion. Now the tarantula has two legs pinning the scorpion's stinger. This is getting exciting. The scorpion can't use his stinger. If the scorpion can't pivot around, the spider will soon find a chink in his armor and put its bite beak into the soft flesh."

The delicate dance of death between archrivals got David excited. He had an erection. He unzipped his trousers and began masturbating. The heightened sensory pleasures of his childhood returned. He felt joy. He was reliving his boyhood happiness; when he was tearing wings from flies.

Thus, began mentoring conversations between David and his formaldehyde fetus protégée. Spider and scorpion continued their ancient rivalry, mindlessly tearing each other, limb from limb; winner killing and devouring loser. The shared experience; the goodness of healthy male fellowship; the kindheartedness that builds by helping a troubled soul; and the shared camaraderie of watching gladiatorial thrills from ringside sated David's need for love.

CHAPTER ELEVEN

When the wind is in the south it blows the bait in the fishes' mouth (J. O. Halliwell: Popular rhymes)

Thinking solves problems. But thinking is hard work; most people resist thinking. But you can think if you decide to do it. Television jangles the mind and prevents thinking. Start thinking by turning the television off. (Rosemary Ness Bitner, author)

REYNARD THE RED

When Bob was a young child in Milltown, he spent a lot of time at his uncle's farm. Uncle Eddie, Florence's husband, understood people from his years of running a pool hall. Eddie loved animals. He acquired a learned understanding of them. Most animals found Eddie's favor. He even loved skunks and raccoons, regarded by most people as pests. The only animals Eddie didn't care for were crows, ravens, and starlings. Eddie, thinking nature somehow erred by having blackbirds, nurtured a deep hatred toward them. Blackbirds killed young songbirds and the babies of squirrels and rabbits, creatures that pleased him, even though they ate his produce. Not a man content to allow nature to take her course, Eddie did some deep thinking. Then he devised a trap for the pesky blackbirds.

His trap first required that he capture a red fox. To catch his fox, Eddie built a chicken coup. It was a magnificent chicken coup, with a trap door between the upper floor and the lower floor. In the coup, Eddie placed some chickens. Then he waited. Sure enough, in a few days a fox showed up. He was a handsome red fox with beautiful full fur. Eddie called him Reynard the Red.

Reynard enjoyed his evening chicken feasts so much that he became bold about raiding Eddie's unprotected chicken coup. One day, Eddie kept the upper floor's access door propped open for the fox. His prop was a wooden clothesline stick. That evening, Reynard entered the coup for his customary meal of chicken. Eddie's prop was attached to a long clothesline. Eddie waited patiently on the other end. While Reynard was inside, seizing a chicken, Eddie pulled the clothesline, yanking away the door's prop. The door swung shut. Reynard was caught.

Eddie made Reynard into his pet, as much as anyone can make a fox a pet. Eddie was proud of Reynard. He took pride in showing Reynard to his friends and to his nephew, Bob. Eddie fed Reynard; brought him fresh water; talked with him daily. Reynard was fed so well, it's doubtful he would have left the coup, even if offered the choice. Reynard had comfortable private quarters on the warm, wooden, lower floor; with dry straw bedding. Eddie and the fox developed a friendship and an understanding. One day, Eddie explained to Reynard that he was going to change his diet from chickens to blackbirds. Eddie assured Reynard that the blackbirds would taste much like the chickens and promised the fox that he would supply him with many blackbirds.

Each day, Eddie set out a trail of corn near the coup. Like he had done to capture Reynard, Eddie held the upstairs access door open with a wooden clothesline prop. The blackbirds followed the corn trail. They ate their corn all the way up and into Eddie's chicken coup, where Eddie offered them a corn bonanza. When the coup became filled with blackbirds, Eddie yanked the prop away. The door to the main floor closed, capturing dozens of blackbirds inside the coup.

The birds never suspected that Eddie had devised a between the floors trap-door inside the coup. The blackbirds met their fate when Eddie pulled on a second clothesline. That opened the coup's trap door and gave Reynard access to the upper floor. Each day Reynard ate a meal of between ten and twenty blackbirds. When he finished dining, Reynard returned to his quarters on the lower floor. The next morning, Eddie reset the trap door and laid out his bait line of corn. As days passed, Reynard became a very fat, happy fox. All the other animals and songbirds approved of Eddie's arrangement with Reynard. Melodious songbirds proliferated. Squirrels, and rabbits multiplied profusely. Eddie's farm became the happy, blackbird-free paradise that Eddie envisioned.

It so happened that Bob was selling Firm product in Roanoke, Virginia one day. That's when he saw a beautiful print of a red fox. The print reminded him of Uncle Eddie's farm and Eddie's pet fox, Reynard. Bob bought the print and took it with him to Plaintown. On the day he took it to a picture framer, he remembered the little plug of reddish hair that he had found in David's barn:

'*That would add a nice touch to the picture,*' thought Bob. He had the gallery place the plug of reddish hair into the picture's lower left corner, opposite the artist's signature. Bob liked his framed print and the way the hair inside the frame appeared that it might have come from the fox in the picture.

Bob hung his framed print in his office. As many times as David was in the office, he never once looked closely at the fox print. But Judith, Bob's secretary, was drawn to the picture. She had an eye for symmetry and detail. If something was out of place in a picture, she noticed it immediately.

She admired the fox portrait, and studied it closely. She surmised, incorrectly, that the plug of reddish hair had come from the same fox that was in the picture frame. Slowly, the story behind the picture filtered out to the other women in the office.

The picture on Bob's wall was different office decor from David's animal heads and portraits of dead people. When Bob was away, office staffers came into his office to admire his fox picture. All agreed it was a great picture of a very handsome fox. The office staffers all believed Judith's erroneous conclusion. She took the liberty of telling them that an actual plug of the animal's hair was in the frame. The office grapevine story of Bob's fox became even more convoluted. Everyone believed that Bob shot the fox; then placed the plug of hair, as a memento of his hunt. Bob, of course, never hunted. He just fancied the picture and bought it.

Barbara was different from the other employees. She dealt in certainties; knowing truths, and demanding facts. She inspected Bob's picture with the keen eyes of a huntress. She studied it closely, for a long time. And, she deciphered that the picture contained a telling clue. She had seen many fox pelts on the Lakota Indian Reservation where her father had raised her. She noted that the plug of hair in the picture looked *different* from a fox's coarser hair:

'Hair as silky as that could not have come from a fox or coyote! It is much too fine. That plug of hair was more like human hair; hair from a young adult human; not hair from any fox hair I've seen!'

She later learned that Bob had picked up the plug of hair in David's barn. Her tracking skills clued her that David had something to do with Marty's disappearance. She believed that the skin she had seen on David's altar grille was a likely remnant from Marty's rendering. She also surmised that the skull being cleaned by the ant and silverfish in their plastic compartment was likely Marty's.

Likely, she reasoned, David murdered Marty; but somehow that reddish-streaked portion of Marty's hair must have escaped from the murder scene. She remembered what she had observed when she looked at the skull. Dark hair was visible; but there was no streak of reddish hair. That had left Barbara believing she may have seen the skull of a different woman; and that uncertainty had thrown her theory of Marty's disappearance into question. She considered that her visit from the apparition was possibly her mind playing tricks with her.

But now, the red hair streak was here, looking back at her from inside the fox picture frame!

'Is Marty's spirit ghost telling me something? Is the red hair plug evidence of a gruesome murder? It likely took place at David's farm! And Marty's red hair plug is no longer in David's possession Is that it? Is it in the picture frame?'

Her mind whirred through possibilities. The red hair plug was in Bob's fox picture! Did Bob have something to do with Marty's murder? That seemed too incredulous. Bob loved Marty. Bob's personality was very opposite David's. Bob was a kind, considerate, loving man; very unlike David. From her tracking skills and understandings of behaviors, Barbara ruled Bob out of complicity in committing Marty's murder. He was, after all, Stupid Big Horse. He must have been somehow duped into picking up the hair plug after the murder, not realizing it was Marty's hair. Barbara reminded herself that her Big Horse needed instructions about understanding people. She reminded herself to address that blind side in Bob's skill set, later; after she married him.

Barbara, ever wise and crafty, kept her thought schemes to herself. She knew if there were ever to be true retribution against David, it would not be her rightful place to settle things. Her sister-like love for Marty did not extend to Marty's bloodline. By Barbara's tribal traditions, she had no blood rights to avenge Marty's murder. David could *not* be her rightful kill. Someone who had Marty's bloodline had the natural right to make that kill. Barbara decided that David should properly be Susan's kill, by virtue of a mother's blood rights:

'Yes, I will put Susan onto David's trail. I do not wish to reveal all that I suspect by turning the matter of Marty's murder over to the police. David would merely lawyer up and prolong matters. Even if he were convicted and imprisoned, retribution justice for Marty likely would never be served. There is a much better way; the painful way; the ancient Lakota Sioux way.'

Barbara did not trust White Man's justice in such matters as murder of a family member. It did not provide for retribution and closure. Instead, she told Susan about the wonderful picture in Bob's office. She made the point of emphatically telling Susan to look very carefully at the beautiful hair plug:

"When you see that hair plug, be sure to look closely at it. Be sure to study it. Then think about it. Ask yourself: Have you ever seen hair anywhere as beautiful as the red hair that is attached to that hair plug?"

Barbara thusly set into motion her plan to avenge Marty's murderer. Then, Barbara patiently waited. She would observe the movements of the human animals in the Firm's offices and let nature take its course. Barbara prayed that Susan's blood would stir when it saw her daughter's plug of hair. She trusted that a mother's blood would cry out for vengeance. She knew Susan could be vicious; and capable of delivering murderous retribution to David. She trusted that Susan would deal with David in her own way.

Eventually, Susan made a point of visiting with Bob while he was in his office. She admired his fox picture.

"That's beautiful artwork," Susan opined. She carefully inspected the hair plug, staring at it for a long time. "Why did you keep that patch of hair from your uncle's fox?"

"Oh, that's not from my Uncle Eddie's fox," Bob told her. "That was something I happened to pick up in David's barn. Apparently, a fox got in there. Somehow, that plug must have gotten ripped from the fox's fur."

"It must've been a fox with pretty long hair," Susan said. *"It's a very lovely picture,"* she again complemented Bob's artwork and left his office. But it occurred to Susan that there was something very odd about that picture. There was an unsettling truth standing behind a closed door in Susan's mind. But she was not yet able to open it.

Human senses constantly acquire data inputs. Acquired data miraculously finds a location to repose itself somewhere in the human brain. There it quietly waits, asleep in safekeeping, as if it has no importance. Sometimes the mind represses what it sees for good reason.

It was easier for Susan's conscious mind to believe that her daughter Marty was still alive somewhere than to objectively evaluate evidence to the contrary. Yet, her subconscious mind knew that the plug of hair did not belong in that picture. It fit into some different picture that was being concealed from her. Bob had just confirmed to her that the plug had not come from the fox in the picture. He thought it must have come from a fox that was in David's barn. But Susan intuited that Bob's reasoning made no sense; yet she could not explain why not; at least not yet. She left Bob's office with a vague feeling of uneasiness.

Months, even years, might pass while a brain's sleeping data point lies undisturbed. But then, during one future day, a second data point also may find lodging in that same brain. The two data points may slumber, isolated and unaware of each other. But then a small miracle can happen. Somehow, usually, when the mind is in its relaxed, unhurried state, a spark of neural electricity generates. It leaps through synaptic nodes and neural pathways from one data point to the other. Miraculously, these two sleeping dots awaken and become dancing partners, much like former high school sweethearts meet unexpectedly and go tripping down memory lane together.

That fateful spark fired in Susan's mind about a week after she saw the fox picture. It happened during a late Thursday afternoon as she leaned back in her office recliner; reminiscent and remorseful over her missing daughter. She was recalling the time she'd traveled to the East Coast to visit Marty during Marty's junior year. That was the time Susan was shocked to learn the true nature of her daughter's heart. Marty was going to be the queen of the senior prom at the neighboring high school. All the schools' boys voted for her, and she was trying to decide which one should drive her back to her dorm after the evening's parties. Susan tried to alter her daughter's life course during that weekend, suggesting that Marty join the Peace Corps.

"There are so many children in Africa who are starving to death. You could be a big help to humanity if you went there and worked with them in one of their villages. Help them learn how to raise crops and animals so their children won't starve." That was the gist of Susan's parental suggestion. And that's when she heard Marty's truth.

"Mother, don't be ridiculous," was Marty's rebuff. *"After you spent your whole life pushing me away from you, so you could have your precious career, now you want me to join the Peace Corps? Puh-lease!"* Marty rolled her eyes and laughed at her mother. *"There's no way I'd ever do that. Look at it this way, mother. If we help them, they'll just reproduce more of themselves until the world is filled with starving children. They'll overrun the rest of us. It's never going to be possible to save all of them. By saving a few of them, you won't make them stronger. You'll only make them more dependent and weaken all of them. It's better to just let them starve and hope the survivors figure it out."*

"You sound so heartless," replied saddened Susan. *"I don't like hearing you talk that way. It's sad."*

"I'm just a realist, Mother, and I know who I am and where I want my life to go. Frankly, I care far more about this one cute boy that I'm scheduled to fuck next, than I could ever care about African kids dying of starvation. I keep my priorities straight, Mother. I'm a whore, like you, mother; and I have no time for distractions."

Susan had gulped and swallowed hard when she'd heard Marty talk that way. She gulped and swallowed again now, recalling that afternoon. It was not possible for Susan to ever stop loving her daughter. She'd been missing for almost a year, but the lumps in Susan's throat, her feelings of guilt from not being closer to Marty, would not leave her. She remembered her daughter as the beautiful child she was, how curious and happy and full of life she had been, and how Susan sometimes braided her hair into pigtails. There, in Marty's dormitory room Susan had sat staring at her daughter, marveling at how beautiful she was, standing there preening and brushing her hair. While staring at her red hair streak shining so beautifully next to her stunning angelic face it was hard for Susan to accept that Marty was proudly fixated on having a career as a whore. That remembrance sent a dormant data point in Susan's mind on its way to join another data point.

The plug of fox hair in Bob's picture frame suddenly played upon Susan's mind. Something about it didn't make sense. Hadn't she heard from David at one of the company parties that coyotes were getting after his geese and had even killed off all the foxes around his farm? If that were true, then how could a fox end up in David's barn? A chill went straight down Susan's spine. That was the fateful moment when she suddenly realized nothing could ever be the same.

No one stayed late at the Firm during the quiet times between regulatory report deadlines. Susan lingered that clandestine night, waiting until all the at-will employee hires left. She walked the halls to be doubly sure she was alone; then she made a super sleuth corporate secretary move. It was the kind of move that set her apart from the worker-bee time clock punchers. She slipped into Bob's office with her night tools, a paring knife, a screwdriver, and a small pair of cuticle scissors. In a few minutes, she'd lifted the fox picture from its place on Bob's wall, removed its backing, and snipped a small sample of hair from the underside of the plug of hair. She reassembled the picture and hanged it in its original position. Inspecting her work, she satisfied herself that no one would notice the missing hair sample.

Then she left.

More to come.

PREVIEWS FROM
BUTTERFLY LOVE

"*I haven't lost my mind*," David sought to reassure Bob. "*The lawyers just want uniformity for the regulators. We still have our deal. Nothing changes that. Just sign this damn thing and let's get this over with.*"

Bob leveled a skeptical gaze at David. "*NO.*" he said firmly . . . . Chapter One.

"*I hereby order you to produce that document to me forthwith. Bring it to me in my chambers here no later than one o'clock today. Let no one else see it or touch it before presentment to this court.*"

"*Yes, your Honor,*" Old Mac replied. . . . . Chapter Two.

Two law school students who clerked for the judge sat in the back row of his chambers office. One whispered to the other, "*The plaintiff now has a copy of the codicil! Can you believe what we just saw? This case has legs!*". . . . . .Chapter Two.

"*Are you a devoted Jew, David?*'

"*Yes.*" David answered.

"*Was your father also a devoted Jew?*"

"*Yes.*" David answered. . . . . .Chapter Three.

"*The question is, when you were showing Bob the codicil, were you still intending to honor your pledge to your father and the State of Israel? It's a yes or no answer, David. Did you intend to honor your pledge to your father while you were showing Bob the codicil?*"

*"Yes. I have always tried to be a good son, and I intended to leave the companies to Israel when I died when I showed Bob the codicil. . . . .*Chapter Four.

"Verify the work order, please." commanded Susan.

"It's from Lab Termanspeil, Neumuehlequai, Zurich, 8006. Order 3PLR34." responded the caller.

"Take it to the UPS box in the basement of the Western Bank building," ordered Susan. *"At exactly six o'clock, drop the envelope with the report inside it on the floor in front of the box and leave without looking back."*

"Understood." said the caller . . . . Chapter Five.

"Good heavens! How did you do that?" Susan feigned disbelief. *"I've heard they're pretty strong animals. How did you hold them down while you cut them up? How did you get them to stand still for that?"* Susan was wily. She projected honest curiosity about Muscle Boy's talents.

"Oh no, Ms. Mallory, I strung them up and killed them kosher style," he beamed. *"David showed me how the rabbis kill kosher. He uses me to do it because he doesn't like paying a rabbi to do it. I didn't do any blessings on them though. I just cut their throats and let them bleed out before I cut the guts out of them . . .* Chapter Six.

Susan gazed at her blazer hanging on the back of her door. Marty's beautiful butterfly pin over its right pocket seemed to come alive and flutter. It symbolized so many things now. And it connected her to many memories . . . . Chapter Six.

"I am a man! Damn you, old chair!" Marvin confronted the chair and shouted at it. *"I will not feel one shred of guilt while I make the sweetest love with the only woman I can love. Have you ever been*

in love, old chair? Have you ever tasted its wonders? Has your heart ever opened with joy at the sight of your lover? No, of course it hasn't!

and

"And, so, dear chair, I thank you for your service. I have decided it is time for me to pass our family's custody of you to David, my son. Perhaps you can work your guilt on him.... . . . . .Chapter Seven.

"He's not a Jew!" exploded David in mock rage, "He's just a Reformed, a wannabe Jew. Reformed Jews aren't real Jews! They are just idiotic fuckups! I offered to help him get an Orthodox rabbi and he didn't want to take me up on it. He didn't want to become a real Jew!"

"He testified he's a Jew! He isn't stupid," David elevated his voice for effect. "He knows when God and Abraham made their berit, their covenant between the cut-up animals, that God told Abraham that Abraham's own issue shall be his heir."

and

"That was about Ishmael and Isaac. They were both Abraham's issue." corrected Ben. "Abraham and Sarah had Isaac. Sarah and Isaac pushed out Hagar and Ishmael because their blood wasn't Hebrew. Stop trying to rationalize what you did to my client by playing the Jew card. That's never going to fly, David. You made a secular deal. You made a covenant deal, one man to another man; and you made it under secular law; and you broke your deal, David! It's clear. You live in the United States of America, not in the land of Ur or the land of Canan . . . . Chapter Eight.

"The legal system is a farce, Andy. It's a device to make the little people believe there is justice and a way to make things right. But when you understand it like I do, Andy, the legal system is just made up of people; and since they are morally weak as all humans are, we can bribe the legal system's judges and the lawyers to get whatever *we want. You must see money as a weapon for use in combat, Andy. It's kind of like hitting a little guy, by dropping a big bomb on him, from ten miles above his head, when all he's got is a knife* . . . . .Chapter Nine.

'What kept me there? Was it love? The security? The sex? The jewels? If only I had kept Marty in Plaintown and not blocked my child out of my life. What was my own role in all of what brought me to this? Yes, I am committing a murder, of a sort. But it is well planned. I will not be caught . . . . Chapter Ten.

Barbara looked at Bob and smiled: "*Those dragonflies are telling us something.*" She leaned against him, then placed a soft, loving kiss on his lips.

and

"*There's an arrow mark pointed up and there's the mark of the 'V' beside it.*"

"*Yeah, I saw those when I was a kid. I wondered what they meant, and I'd forgotten about them. They look very old. Do you know what they mean?*"

"*I do,*" said Barbara. "*Follow me!*" . . . . .Chapter Eleven.

Did you forget your pledge to Meyer? I was there with you at the Flamingo when you promised him that you would return every jewel so he could trade them for arms for Israel. I was so proud of you then, Marvin. Did you forget that, Marvin? You held back, didn't you, Marvin? You turned your back on our people to seek the favors of your gentile whore's cunt, didn't you, Marvin . . . . .Chapter Twelve.

"*No, I's ain't nuts! Dere's somepin goin' on about dat butterfly. Watch. It will go to dat one headstone, the one of dat guy dat had the Injun wife. Watch it.*"

"Oh, yeah, I sees it," remarked Wayne. *"You're right. Dere, it sits on dat headstone, like you sez. It's like putting on a show for all to see. How'd you know it'd do dat?"*

"It always does dat," declared Buzzy . . . . Chapter Thirteen.

"I will have to try again next time," Marvin's soul said to Susan's soul. *"When will you be back for me?"*

"Soon," said Susan's soul to Marvin's soul. *"You must try very hard, Marvin. Untangle yourself and be ready to come away with me."*

"I will. Soon then, Come again, soon," replied Marvin's soul. Then it fell back into its grave to suffer in torment next to Eloweiss . . . . .Chapter Fourteen.

"What's a Lobo," asked John, the second ranch hand.

"He's part wolf; but much bigger than a wolf. And he's part coyote; but much smarter than a coyote," said Jim.

"Well then, which is he, wolf or coyote?" asked John.

"He ain't neither," said Jack, the third hand.

"Then, if he ain't neither, what is he?" asked John, again.

"He's hatred," said Jack. *"He's meanness. He's all the evil around you for a hundred miles, all packaged up into a canine animal that's bigger than an English Mastiff; maybe almost twice as big as one of those. He weighs a good two hundred fifty pounds. His bite force is twice as strong as a wolf's. He can bite through a buffalo's leg like it's a toothpick.*

"And, the special thing about Lobos is they are always angry. Not ordinarily angry like a dog gets when it snarls at you. No, not like that kind of angry. A Lobo anger is different. It's anger that wants to tear your body apart and rip your guts out of you and snap all your bones in half, because it wants to make sure you'll never walk again, even after it has killed you. It's a demon, packed up tightly inside a

canine body. And it's a demon so God-awful fierce that it can't help itself for being so hateful mean. And it's got canine teeth that are like daggers; twice as long as a Timberwolf's canines, for biting chunks out of you. It's got paws with claws that are longer and sharper than a cougar's claws, for ripping and shredding. And it loves to shed your flesh while it eats on your body because it knows that shredding you like it does causes you the most pain. So, you asked me what a Lobo is. I tell you. A Lobo is pain. He's God-awful, horrible pain. It's all the pain from hell, all packaged into one animal. And it's got those Satan eyes that glow in the faintest light. It sees better than a lynx in the dark. It hears better than an owl. And it likes to kill because killing gives it pleasure."

"Jesus Christ, God help us," said John . . . . Chapter Fifteen.

"And how will I find a good woman to marry, Big Chief? The only women I know are whores."

"You are not to concern yourself with that. We have met the spirit of your future woman. The Great Spirit of All Living Things brought all of us together for a meeting. The Spirit is in her now. Her spirit is that of a very fine and good woman. Make yourself ready for her. When you are ready, she will know. You need not search for her. She will find you. That is the way with women . . Chapter Sixteen.

Well, employees are fighting over a logo, animal heads are coming to life, an outdated computer that's screwing investors and making David good money while destroying the building; that's life at the Firm! But it looks like David's attempts to woo Bob and seduce him have fallen flat. Bob is a red-blooded male, a woman lover. Even worse news for David is brewing. Barbara has given Susan the clue she needs to discover what happened to her daughter. LOVE AND MADNESS has prepared us for what comes next in the twists and turns of our saga.

In our next segment Susan plots revenge. The ghost of David's father appears and tells David what he can expect for what he's done; the United States Supreme Court makes an unprecedented ruling that upends David's world view. Is there still one desperate way for David to keep faith with his Father?

Questions of death and love swirl around David, Bob, Barbara and Susan as our drama reaches a major inflection point. A Lobo coyote, drunken gravediggers and spirits that carry reincarnated life on the wings of Monarch butterflies join us in our most shocking segment yet. Expect a symphony of emotions with all instruments playing forte!

Flutter along with me, Minna Morinette, as I narrate our next thrilling segment: BUTTERFLY LOVE, the fourteenth book of THE SECRET BUTTERFLY SERIES.